Advance praise for Rayo Casablanca and *Very Mercenary*!

"Mad as a bag of artistic squirrels. With guns. Very brilliant and very original."
—Allan Guthrie, author of *Savage Night*

"Anarchy as art, rampaging hitmen, and some serious Daddy Issues fuel Rayo Casablanca's violent, savvy, and propulsive *Very Mercenary*. Think Andy Warhol meets The Monkey Wrench Gang and you're getting the picture. Casablanca's writing cuts hard, fast, and deep as a buzzsaw. Reader beware: you're going to bleed."
—Craig Davidson, author of *The Fighter*

And outstanding praise for
Rayo Casablanca and *6 Sick Hipsters*!

"Casablanca nails the cheesiness of the neighborhood and its residents . . . there's a good time to be had watching the skinny jean set suffer, and that may be enough to hook a chunk of readers."
—*Publishers Weekly*

"*6 Sick Hipsters* is a wild, poignant, twisted, bitterly funny page turner with dead-on dialogue and a wonderful ensemble cast. Rayo Casablanca has written the big novel the hipster generation has been waiting for."
—Jason Starr, author of *The Follower*

Turn the page for more praise
for *6 Sick Hipsters*. . . .

D1023894

"You're not bound to read anything else this year quite like it. An engaging, knowing and purposely fucking nuts of a satiric novel."
—*Bookgasm.com*

"Rayo Casablanca's first novel is thoroughly amusing and utterly demented. It features a killer baboon, sewer diving, men in silly jumpsuits, hipster assassins that will stop at nothing to get what they want, and interesting information about paleontology and knitting. What else do you need to know?"
—Owen King, author of *We're All in This Together*

"*6 Sick Hipsters* is a wild ride of a novel. Something of a magical realist noir that brings a whole new meaning to the fashionable idea of the death of the hipster. It's enough to make one nervous about leaving the house in a Pavement T-shirt."
—Jeff Parker, author of *Ovenman* and *The Back of the Line*

"Offers chills, laughter and a healthy grimace or two. Its social commentary is razor sharp and it wields satire like a blunt weapon."
—*Pressconnects.com*

"*6 Sick Hipsters* is a wild ride into the underworld of hip that takes more daring, shocking, bloody turns than *Pulp Fiction*. Rayo Casablanca pulls no punches. Oh, but you'll take 'em . . . and love every jolt."
—Kemble Scott, author of *SoMa*

VERY MERCENARY

rayo casablanca

KENSINGTON BOOKS
http://www.kensingtonbooks.com

KENSINGTON BOOKS are published by

Kensington Publishing Corp.
850 Third Avenue
New York, NY 10022

All Kensington titles, imprints, and distributed lines are available at special quantity discounts for bulk purchases for sales promotion, premiums, fund-raising, educational, or institutional use.

Special book excerpts or customized printings can also be created to fit specific needs. For details, write or phone the office of the Kensington Special Sales Manager: Kensington Publishing Corp., 850 Third Avenue, New York, NY 10022. Attn.: Special Sales Department. Phone: 1-800-221-2647.

ISBN-13: 978-0-7582-2284-8
ISBN-10: 0-7582-2284-X

First printing: April 2009
10 9 8 7 6 5 4 3 2 1

Printed in the United States of America

The insane are people who push creativity further than professional artists, who believe in it totally.

—John MacGregor
Intuit (1998)

CHAPTER ZERO

Nine days out

1.

The lights have been on for maybe five minutes and Lester King's apartment is already boiling.

Leigh Tiller's sweating in her Elie Saab evening dress and wishing she had just bailed on this whole thing. She heads to the upstairs bathroom where Marie from Senegal has all her makeup set up. On the stairs, she passes someone in a ratty monkey costume. The kind you see on people waving signs on corners. The kind you see on public-access kiddie shows. Leigh says, "Nice suit."

The monkey doesn't reply.

When she gets to the makeup room, Marie seems stressed. "Have a seat." Her African patois is as thick as butter. Leigh has to repeat the sounds of it in her head several times to make sure she's got the meaning.

Leigh sits and Marie loads up the mascara. Leigh complains, "Like a raccoon?"

"Hank wants it super thick."

Leigh pulls out her iPod and settles into the makeup chair.

She's zoned out on something Bollywood when Marie nudges her. "Huh?"

"I said I saw that interview with Larry King you did with your dad two weeks ago. Really interesting. He seems like quite a character. You guys close?"

"No. Not at all."

Leigh is so sick of talking about her dad. She wonders if there is a full moon out or maybe a comet passing close to the Earth. Something, anything, to explain why lately everyone is asking about her dad.

Marie frowns. "That's a shame."

Leigh shrugs. She doesn't say anything, but the fact is she's broken up over her dad. That their fucked-up relationship is eating a hole in her stomach. That the physical pain of it is so bad she saw a gastroenterologist and got scoped. And even though the doc suggested it might be emotional, he under-scored that stress can wreck a gut just the same as too much digestive acid can.

Therapy hasn't helped either. Like any good heiress, Leigh has been in therapy since she was old enough to remember her dreams. At eight, the psychoanalysis centered on her mother. When Leigh was twelve and Mom had been in the ground for two months, it was all about grieving. In high school it was about boys and friends and the fact that Leigh was sure she should be depressed but wasn't. That was really concerning. At twenty it was panic disorders and Xanax. At twenty-two it was her ex, Lane, and biofeedback. Twenty-three was a mix of Dad, Mom's death and Lane and lots of X. And now, at twenty-six, it's just Dad. Dad, Dad, and more Dad. Dad not appreciating her. Dad not noticing her. Dad not loving her. Whenever anyone asks her about Kip Tiller, Leigh always replies the same, "He's the world's biggest prick." Leigh didn't invent that either. Her dad gets all sorts of hate mail and a good two out of ten times it's addressed to "The

World's Biggest Prick." Leigh suspects most of this mail comes from her aunt but she's never actually read any of the letters.

Marie says, "You're done."

The scene they're setting up, Leigh knows it's going to be a nightmare. This is her favorite part in Morrissey's original. The way it plays out in the 1970 version is Joe Dallesandro goes to this LSD freak's pad and has a really fucked experience. Then, the LSD freak was Andrea Feldman and she was bonkers in front of the camera. It was Feldman's shtick, her self-expression, both heartbreakingly brilliant and bizarre. She called her spiel "Showtime" and Feldman would commandeer tables at Max's Kansas City and dance on top of them while whipping her top off. Just straight-up craziness. Blame amphetamines. Feldman jumped off the fourteenth floor of her apartment building in 1972. She died holding a rosary in one hand and a Coke can in the other. This movie, Hank's remake, the LSD character is played by someone who goes by the name Liu. No last name, just Liu. She's short and has a shaved head and smells like ozone.

Liu's been hanging out in Lester's kitchen the whole night eating fried chicken skin and talking to the director of photography, Srdjan Juerging (fresh from Yugoslavia), about Tantric sex. Liu has this skinny bald Yugoslavian cornered and she's spent the whole evening prepping for her performance by doing squats and going on and on about Tantric sex. Srdjan is Yugo pale but he's been turning paler.

Liu rubs her buttocks and talks about "Yab-yum" and says things like "my clitoris is totally controlled with Pranayama" and "my throat chakra was blocked until I had his penis balls deep in it."

The way Hank envisions the scene, Leigh's there too. It's not just standing in the corner and watching Hank make it with Liu, but actually participating. Not sex but dialogue. Though Hank makes it clear pretty quickly he wouldn't mind if things get a bit more "intense."

"Seriously," he says. "There are no limits to what we can do. It's our film. We're remaking something that was totally taboo-busting in the seventies. If we make this chaste it will mean nothing. We'll be soiling Warhol's name."

Leigh looks to Marchesa, her personal assistant.

Marchesa wags a finger at Hank and says, "We're not doing porn."

Hank looks appalled. "I wasn't suggesting . . ."

Marchesa repeats, "No porn."

"Let's just get this done," Leigh says.

It takes another fifteen minutes to get everyone in place and then the cameras are rolling and Hank is doing his best strung-out drifter. Liu truly is manic. She has no scripted lines and is totally channeling Andrea Feldman. She's even got the nasal New York grotto accent down pat. And Leigh, after two or three takes, is back into character and feeling pretty good about her performance. There is another person in an animal suit, this one a shabby-ass cat. The cat is lounging on a divan by the punch bowl and pretending to lick its ragged paws.

Leigh asks Marchesa what the deal is with the animals.

Marchesa, face illuminated BlackBerry blue, says, "Probably just Hank being arty. You know how he likes to slum it up with the performance crowd."

"They're freaking me out."

"You need something for that?" This is the first time Marchesa has looked up from her phone in hours. Her face reads sincere and concerned.

"No. I'm ready to shoot."

The scene calls for Liu to talk Hank into bed and she's good. Hank looks genuinely intrigued. The cameras follow them to the floor of the apartment where he's taking off her shirt and sliding his hands into her spandex pants as she's moaning and slipping her tongue in and out and in and out of his left ear. Ten people, all under the brightest lights imaginable, crowded around and staring at Hank getting it on. And Leigh's still in frame; she's standing over them. At first she's doing her scripted dialogue. Talking about acid and money and finding a "hole to crawl into" but after a few minutes she abandons the script and just stands there mute.

There are two cameras running. One is trained on Hank and Liu, and the cameraman is getting in close. The other is in Leigh's face, close enough that she can practically smell the sweat of the kid manning it.

The lens picks up the smallest pores on Leigh's nose.

The quiver in her cheek.

She closes her eyes. Seems to swell with emotion. The cameraman doesn't breathe; he wants there to be no skips. No beats in the film. He wants this moment to be captured perfectly. There is a tension in the air. A small saliva bubble hangs precariously on the cameraman's lower lip. The hairs on the back of his neck stand rigid.

There is moaning coming from the floor.

Leigh's eyes are trained offscreen. Staring at the threadbare cat and fucked-up monkey sipping mai tais on the divan. Framed in the harsh light, her features are flattened and softened. She looks angelic. Unspoiled. The cameraman, his brain whirling from lack of oxygen, imagines that this shot, this single take, will earn him an Oscar.

The cameraman is about to pass out when Leigh turns to the camera, her eyes cold, distant, and she says, "I can't do this."

She walks out of frame and the cameraman chokes on his first breath.

The moaning continues, the rest of the crew huddled in even closer, and no one but the panting second cameraman seems to notice that Leigh has left. She stands outside the huddled mass and lights a cigarette. The cameraman walks over befuddled, holding the camera limp at his side.

"Why are you out of the shot?" he asks.

"I'm just not into it," Leigh says. "Sorry."

The cameraman gives a half smile. "Hank's gonna be pissed."

"So?"

"Just telling you."

The cameraman walks back over to the huddle. The moans are increasing in frequency and tempo. Leigh heads to the kitchen to get something to drink. Marchesa and Marie, the Sengalese makeup artist, are snorting coke off a mirror on the stove and gabbing.

"You want any?" Marchesa asks Leigh.

Leigh shakes her head.

"Sounds pretty crazy in there," Marie says.

Marchesa is texting. "I thought you were in this scene," she says, not looking up from her phone. "If not, there's an art opening at Otto's in like thirty minutes."

Leigh says, "I'm beat."

Marie snorts another line and then rubs some coke on her gums. She smiles at Leigh and asks, "Everything okay?"

Leigh shrugs. She opens the fridge and dips her head inside. "Is there any wine? Never mind, I found it."

She settles down at the black kitchen table with an opened bottle of dolcetto. She swigs from the bottle and some of the dark wine spills down her chin and onto her dress. "Fuck it."

Marchesa pipes up. "You hear about Anise Miller's dinner Friday?"

"Of course."

"I can't believe she had the gall to show up with Brooke Marshall. With all those things the *Post's* been saying about her grandmother and the way they've got her doped up, feeding off her. Disgusting. They say it was Anise's statement of support or something."

"Brooke Marshall's always been a bitch, Marchesa. That's why Phillip Englehard was brought in. He's basically overseeing her life."

"And her poon."

"You said it, I didn't. Do either of you know what the deal was with those animal suits?"

Marie says, "You know Hank, probably just extras for something later."

"I have to say I'm disappointed," Leigh says. She's sketching Marchesa and Marie on a napkin, the pen cutting through the cheap paper. The ink bleeding.

"Why?" Marchesa asks. "Want me to say anything?"

"No. This just isn't the outlet I was looking for."

"It's indie."

"It's not enough freedom. I thought it'd be a chance for me to get more involved, maybe have a say in how things went. You know, be involved in the creative end."

"I'm sure they'd be open to your input."

"I know. But I don't want it to be just input."

Marchesa brings the conversation back around to talking about her boyfriend, Carsten, and Leigh decides to head out. "Tell Hank, sorry," she says.

Marie asks, "Can we see that sketch?"

Leigh hands it to her. "Not very good."

Marie looks it over and then hands it to Marchesa. She grimaces and says, "I'm not really that bony, right?"

Leigh shakes her head. "See you."

Marie and Marchesa wave, but neither sees her to the door. The valet brings around Leigh's Range Rover and she hands him a ten. He nods and says, "Have a great night."

Leigh, wine bottle tucked under her arm, says, "It's nearly three in the morning."

Her place on Ninth Avenue is all lit up just the way she left it. Bossanova plays. The second half of *The Wiz* runs silently on the sixty-inch plasma in the den. After Mother died and things with Dad reached fever pitch, she didn't want to feel alone. To feel her life was empty. Even if it was just filled with noise.

She pauses at her desk to leaf through some sketches she has piled there. The ones on top are of her father. All of them show him from afar. His hair a helmet with a tail. His face vague with jittery lines. His shoulders broad and hard. In the topmost sketch, he is standing in a conference room talking to several seated men, his back a thick shadow. In another he is only partially glimpsed through a series of windows. In yet another only half his face is visible. Leigh pauses on a sketch of her father stepping out of a car, waving. He has sunglasses on and is waving to someone across the street. It looks like an illustration you'd find in an airplane safety guide, the figures of her father and the man across the street mirror images of each other. Bland everymen. Leigh sometimes has dreams where the sketches are animated, these robotic figures of her dad in featureless seventies polyester suits slipping around corners and into elevators and under desks and behind books. These dreams are dialogue free. Leigh doesn't shout for her dad. His addresses in the boardroom are charades. And yet overlaying it all is really irritating lounge music. Early sixties schmaltz. The stuff Kip Tiller adores. She hasn't told anyone about the dreams, and doubts she ever will.

The other sketches are of Marchesa. Unlike those of her father these are precise and clear. No vagaries in the lines. Marchesa is ugly here. Flat and falling over. Her features stretched out in sharp lines that cut clear across the page. The eyes huge and pupils spirals. In these drawings Marchesa is a supernova of knife strokes. Leigh looks at them and shakes her head. After long nights out, this is how she sees all of her friends. These diamond people cutting through her life. All of them surface, all of them compact lines of fashion and eyes big with longing.

Leigh flips the drawings over, then heads to the bathroom and washes her face, paying special attention to the thick mascara Marie coated her with. She runs the hot water and relaxes in the steam for a few minutes and then brushes her teeth. Loves the crisp, clean feeling of freshly brushed teeth and the dreamy feeling of running her tongue over the smooth surface of her incisors. She opens the medicine cabinet and digs out some homeopathic sleep aid Marchesa got her in Montreal and shakes two of the lima-bean-colored horse pills into her hand. When she closes the mirrored medicine cabinet door she notices the bear in a top hat standing just behind her.

The person in the tatty bear costume says, "Boo."

Leigh gasps and holds her chest while this cheap bear with his wrinkled and dusty top hat, his missing eye and missing ear, sways back and forth like a boxer. Her being drunk helps take the edge off her fright.

"You scared the shit out of me. What the fuck are you doing here?" Leigh backs up against the sink. "This is my apartment. You need to leave."

She realizes how ridiculous she sounds and part of her wants to laugh. Part of her wants to scream. The bear says nothing, just rocks like an imbecile. Leigh jabs a finger into its rough and patchy fur. "You need to leave right now or I'm going to alert security."

The bear sways faster, giggles.

"Did Hank set this up? He send you over here?"

Snicker.

"Look, you need to get the fuck out of here right now. It's not fucking funny."

Leigh pushes the bear back against the wall and the bear's oversized plush head just wobbles and the snickering inside continues.

"Get the fuck out!"

The chuckling stops and the bear pulls a knife. It's a small knife, maybe it's a switchblade, but it flickers and fades in the sterile light of the bathroom and Leigh's eyes go wide. Her buzz gone, she leans back against the sink and kicks the bear into the tub. He topples over just the way funny bears do in cartoons or in children's shows. Then Leigh runs for the front door.

But the monkey from the film shoot blocks her way.

This dilapidated monkey, it's the same one on the stairs at the shoot, the same one that had been lounging with the cat. The monkey costume jumps up and down and the person inside makes monkey noises and Leigh's first thought is that maybe she's imagining this. That maybe she's going nuts.

The monkey isn't armed so Leigh bowls it over, smashing its threadbare head with her fists. The monkey goes down easy, with a curse and a sigh. Leigh makes it to the front door and is struggling with the lock when the door suddenly opens and two more animals arrive. A penguin and a cat.

"What is this!?" Leigh's screaming now.

The penguin speaks, a woman's voice. "This is the mouth of capitalism."

Leigh is able to knock the cat down before the penguin jumps on her. The feeling, like being smothered under mildewed grandma blankets, is suffocating. The penguin doesn't move, just lies on her face. The person inside the costume whispers, "We'll inoculate you, don't worry. Don't fight it." Leigh isn't sure if it's her imagination but she smells anchovies. It's enough to make her heave and she panics, gets her legs up under the penguin and kicks. Penguin huffs like she's got the wind knocked out of her and goes limp. Leigh rolls out. Jumps up.

She is surrounded.

The bear with the top hat is there, giggling again, knife in hand. The cat lifts the penguin up off the carpet and pats her on the back. The penguin, breathing heavy, says, "You'll regret that, electro bitch." Leigh can't see how, but the penguin pulls a cattle prod out from somewhere in her costume. Flicked on, the black tube hisses with current.

Leigh backs up from the penguin toward the bear.

"Commence Artichoke two, baby," the penguin says.

"If you want money . . ." Leigh motions toward her bedroom. "All my jewelry. Even a safe that I can open for you. Car keys, I have three cars."

The bear laughs. "Exactly."

The penguin jabs the cattle prod out and an arc of electricity grazes Leigh's forearm. She thinks getting shocked by someone who's just scooted their rubber soles across a carpet, only ten times worse. Only really painful. "Please," Leigh begs, lump already in her throat. "Please, just go."

"Sorry," the monkey says. "But this is where it all begins."

The tattered animals move in. They paw at Leigh. Get closer and closer, almost on top of her. Leigh punches the monkey in the face. Her fist bounces off. All it does is produce little clouds of dust.

Leigh screams. Screams as loud as she possibly can.

Until the monkey pulls a metal spray can from somewhere under the costume. He says nothing. Doesn't even make a fake monkey noise when he presses the button on the top of the can and mists Leigh's face.

She fights it. The stuff burns her eyes and her throat.

Before Leigh knows it she's on the floor. Eyes flooded with tears and six shabby paws and two faded wings on her. The animals are hooting and hollering. The ruckus they're making is like something you hear at a zoo when all the tourists have gone home. Whatever was in the can starts to work. Leigh is suddenly so tired she can't open her eyes. And her limbs are deadweight. She's sinking into the carpet as the frayed beasts are getting farther and farther and farther away like in a tunnel.

They're laughing. Not animal noises but human voices. Laughing.

Then it all just fades out.

CHAPTER ONE

Five days out

1.

Midday and a man in a cheap navy business suit sips soda and takes small bites of a bologna sandwich in the bland cafeteria of Omni ConsumerTronics in Passaic, New Jersey.

The man is young and wears a fake moustache and thick-rimmed glasses. He sits alone. The cafeteria, however, is large and packed with similarly dressed businessmen and businesswomen.

Somewhere Muzak plays.

The man in the navy suit nods at passersby and when he finishes his sandwich he wipes the crumbs from his lips with a handkerchief. This he folds carefully and places in the right breast pocket of his suit.

An older man in a tight sweater asks if he can share the navy-suited man's table.

Navy nods.

Sweater says, "I'm Ron Gomez. Receiving."

"Hi." Navy half smiles.

Ron says, "These burritos are terrible but I just can't help myself."

"I've been warned about them."

Ron laughs. "Mexican and New Jersey go together like bagels and shrimp."

Navy coughs. "Excuse me." He pulls an albuterol inhaler from his jacket and takes two puffs.

"I like your 'stash." Ron smiles and points at his own upper lip.

"Enjoy your lunch," Navy says and stands.

Ron gives a thumbs-up. "Needs some green chili."

The navy-suited man walks over to the soda fountain where he refills his drink and looks out over the cafeteria. That's when a cell phone rings in the left breast pocket of his jacket. He answers, "Where are we?"

A voice cloaked in static says, "T minus five."

"What's taken so long?" Navy asks.

"Usual."

"Fucker. Give me a countdown, I'm moving to the east side."

Navy makes his way leisurely to the opposite side of the cafeteria, where the walls are mostly glass. Outside it's raining. A golf cart with two men in baseball caps maneuvers between a copse of elms beside a small pond. Navy says, "Where are the cameras?"

"South by the fire extinguisher, east by the deli counter. T minus three."

"Picture good?"

"Yes."

"Feed?"

"Good."

Navy stands at the windows and nods to the men in the golf cart. One of them waves. Navy says, into the phone, "Tell that moron to keep his hands down."

"T minus two. You ready?"

"Course."

"Wouldn't it be funny if the explosive charges we used were too big? I mean, if the place just goes down like when they do demo on skyscrapers. Just poof."

"Hilarious."

"T minus one. Do your thing, maestro."

The navy-suited man with the fake moustache puts the cell back in his jacket and turns to face the cafeteria. He clears his throat and cups his hands around his mouth. "Excuse me! Excuse me! Good employees of Omni ConsumerTronics, I am the chief operations officer for Strategic Art Defense and your corporate mess hall is about to be remodeled. Just sit tight. No one move and this shouldn't hurt a bit."

The good employees sit at their tables, look to each other, shrug, screw up their faces. The ones standing sit. Several make for the exit. But before any of them can speak there is a crackling sound and then a rush like a passing car and the walls begin to fall inward; all of them come billowing in like tossed sheets. Someone screams. Plates crash. But the walls don't thud to the floor and send bits of plaster flying like shrapnel; there is no cloud of dust and particulates. No, it's not the walls that have fallen but the floral-patterned wallpaper. Within seconds, the walls are bare of flowers and the floors and tables are draped. A number of people struggle out from under the sheaves of paper looking furious, looking confused. Navy suit, still at the window, shouts, "Remain calm! The operation's almost complete."

There is silence as the last wallpaper strips curl down. All of the Omni ConsumerTronics employees gaze in wonder at what's been revealed, at the wall beneath the wall.

Photo collages.

Each wall, all sixteen feet up and eighty-odd feet back, covered in three by fives like tiles. Each wall, the photos are aligned to produce large pictures from a distance. On the north wall the photos all come together in a woman, smiling and smoking a joint. Someone near the espresso machine says, "Isn't that Allison in human resources?" The south wall, it's a man holding aloft an inflatable sheep. Someone over by the cash register shouts, "That's Karl Asaro!" Last wall, west wall, the image is another man, this one in drag. Everyone sees it but no one shouts. Eyes, widened, avert. This is because the man in drag is Omni ConsumerTronic's CEO Andrew Godwin looking as cheerfully proper in a wig and makeup as he does in the portrait hanging by the clock above the entrance to the cafeteria.

The employees wander to the collages. They look, point, mumbling all the while. Each photo is a photo of an employee. And even though the faces are blacked out, they still recognize their coworkers. Some of them are just smiling and waving. Others are sleeping with their heads on their desks or smoking in the break room or making photocopies of their cleavage. The good employees of Omni ConsumerTronics see themselves in the collages. They see their coworkers going to the bathroom, their bosses fucking trannies on desktops. They turn away from the walls blushing or giggling or screaming or, in the case of one blond man, fainting.

The chief operations officer for Strategic Art Defense surveys the crowd and then bows his head and says, "Gentle employees of this multinational monstrosity, I bid you good evening. Enjoy the art!" And with a running leap he crashes through the large east wall windows, rolls on the rain-slicked lawn, and dashes out into the settling fog.

There is a loud crowd at Motor Town in the East Village and tables are scarce.

The jukebox is down again but one of the bar backs has set up a ghetto blaster, cranked up all the way, and while the sound is terrible and tinny the music competes amiably with the raucousness of the drinkers. Sitting on wobbly stools at the front near the Jesus icons that cover the walls, the chief operations officer for Strategic Art Defense, still wearing his navy suit, sips a Little King with the two men from the golf cart. One of them, black with smooth features, a menacing goatee, and a cowboy hat, says, "Any word from Uncle Al?"

"Yeah. All clear." The chief operations officer for Strategic Art Defense nods. He says, "Cops moved in half an hour later but not before the Net was blowing up with reviews, critiques. All brilliant, of course."

"And?"

"And the bids came rolling in about twenty minutes ago. Omni ConsumerTronics said they're willing to split any proceeds down the middle. Love to support the arts, they say."

"Naturally."

The third man, narrow eyed and gangly, asks, "We moving on the apartment cull?"

Navy suit says, "Tonight. Recon. The tour is wrapping up better than expected and I'm feeling good about the prospects in Newark."

"The stars are aligned." Gangly nods sagely.

Goatee asks, "When's Richter coming in?"

"The twenty-third. I'll give him love but bet he'll be drooling to help. I get why it's me who has to be the face of this thing and interact with Richter but I'm dying inside because of it. Cody, I'd love to see you try and suck up to him."

Goateed Cody says, "That's not my bag, boss. You're the one with the superhuman abilities." He looks over to the gangly guy and says, "Let's put Rufus on Richter detail."

"Hell no," Rufus says. "Supremely bad karma."

Cody scoffs.

"How do you see all this going down, Laser?" asks Rufus.

"We need experts," Laser, the chief operations officer for Strategic Art Defense, says. "Botanists. Engineers. People with solar backgrounds. We need entomologists too."

Laser says, "We start scouting here, one, maybe two jobs, and then, when we've honed it, we hit the big fish."

Rufus asks, "Send out the memo?"

"Sure. So who's coming with me?"

Cody says, "I'll drive."

From: Strategic Art Defense
To: All media outlets

We are your coworkers.

Your lovers. Your children. We are the people you sit next to on the bus. On the plane. The people you manage and think you know. The people behind you in line at the supermarket. The people bagging the groceries. The people ringing up your purchases.

We're here to tell you that your life is no longer safe from art.

You push it away. You enclose it in museums. Trap it in books.

But art is alive and it is real.

And you are not safe from it.

We, the multitudinous members of the Strategic Art Defense, have operatives throughout the United States ready and waiting for the clarion call of art. Our operatives are working dead-end jobs. They are sipping coffee and writing in notebooks. They are pushing baby strollers and buying socks. They are laughing out loud in movie theatres at terrible jokes and singing along with the latest recycled pop music. They are waiting.

Waiting for the call.

And, ladies and gentlemen of the unsuspecting

world, the call will come sooner than you think. When it does, your neighbors, the kid who cuts your lawn, the woman who does your nails, the man who drives the bus you ride to work on, all of us will rise up and re-create America in the name of art.

God took six days.

We'll do it in five.

Your humble servants,

The members of Strategic Art Defense

Cody and Laser are sitting in Laser's 1989 Chevy Caprice on Seventh in Newark eating burgers from a fast-food joint. Cody is laughing, saying, "Because that's how I *roll*."

Laser shakes his head like a parent after his son has just told him something embarrassing, something crude. Cody looks down at his burger and says, "Bet there's cancer all over this thing."

"There's cancer all over life, Cody."

"You are one morose motherfucker," Cody scoffs. "I'm hoping we can bust out the uniforms sometime soon. Itching to try those out."

"I'm not sure how they'd fit in exactly."

"Liven it up a bit. I don't know, give us some flare."

"Flare?"

"Uh-huh."

"Do you think we really need flare?"

"Couldn't hurt."

"Did Anton Nilson or Huey Newton or Benny Levy need flare?"

"Okay. Okay. It's just that we're also artists, that this is a revolution for art."

"And those uniforms help make that clearer?"

Cody huffs, "At least it makes it a bit more interesting. Hell,

Laser, you should just quit now and start your own militia in Bolivia or Uganda. You want it all dour and disciplined like we're in the army. Revolutions don't have to look boring, you know."

"I just want us taken seriously."

Cody shrugs. "I need coffee. I'm heading over to the shop on Sixth. Want anything?"

"Hostess fruit pie."

"You're kidding, right?"

"No. I eat one maybe twice a year."

"Shit, Laser, what flavor?"

"Lemon. If they don't have that, then cherry."

"I let you subject yourself to that and you promise me we'll bust out the uniforms at one of these apartment jobs. I don't need an audience like in Detroit, just let me wear the damned thing."

"Fine."

Cody shoots Laser a quick smile and then hops out of the car. Before he closes the door he leans in and says, "I won't tell the other guys about this. It'll be our little secret, okay?"

With Cody gone, Laser flips through a tattered copy of *Fighting Stars Ninja* before scanning the Abako Apartments building across the street. It's maybe midcentury and in serious decline. He's noticing the way the sodium light from a high-rise a block down reflects off the penthouse windows when he sees her. She's naked. He can't see her face, but he can make out the shape of her naked body and he can see her palms against the glass.

She's there long enough for Laser to get out his night vision binoculars. Takes him twenty-six seconds to realize he's looking at Leigh Tiller, kidnapped heiress. But it takes him thirty to breathe again. Laser stares at her face. She looks asleep. Her eyes are half closed. He notices her eyelashes, how long and dark they are. For a second he thinks back to the women he's dated and realizes that he's never noticed anyone's eyelashes like this before. Until now it was like eyelashes didn't exist.

He notices her body as well. He doesn't linger on her breasts or the tight curls of pubic hair. He feels dirty just passing his gaze over them. It's like she's modeling. Like she's on display. He wishes he had a camera. He thinks of taking a snapshot with his cell phone but knows that it wouldn't turn out right. For the first time in a very long time he wishes he had a sketchpad. There is something ethereal about Leigh in the window. She's as remote as ever but stripped bare and only Laser can see her. Though she's naked for the entire city to see, this show is Laser's alone. Her there in the window, it's art. The finest art Laser's seen.

She is a mirage there.

And yet her beauty only steels Laser's nerves. Seeing the way her hair ripples over the surface of her features, he stifles the urge to sigh. To sit back, mouth agape, and ogle her. He does this because he knows that she is more than just a kidnapped heiress, more than an attractive woman. He does this because he knows she's the ultimate commodity. If he plays his cards right he can use Leigh to bring Strategic Art Defense to the masses. She can be the winning hand.

He's startled when Cody gets back into the car. "Only had chocolate, my friend. I've never had one of these tasty treats but the guy at the register informed me that most people prefer the fruit fillings. Sorry."

Laser says nothing. He hands Cody the bulky binoculars and points to the apartment building. Cody takes a few bites of his beef jerky before raising the binoculars to his eyes. "What? You like that building?"

Laser says, "Penthouse windows."

Cody moves the binoculars up and then chokes. "Is that . . . ?"

"Yup."

"Are you fucking kidding me?"

"You're looking at her."

Cody turns to Laser. "You called the cops?"

"No."

"Good. You thinking what I'm thinking?"

"This is going to be very tricky. We need surveillance night and day. We can't be seen. We need everything documented. All I've seen is her. No clue how many kidnappers."

"How much you think we can get?"

"Not about money."

"Taking it higher, huh?"

"As high as it goes."

CHAPTER TWO

Two days out

1.

The Serologist's face has a strange geometry.

Like it was shattered, the way good china shatters, and glued back into place. Thing is, the pieces just don't fit quite right. There's something off about the nose. Something unsettling about the way the eyes don't line up, the way the right one droops like it's fallen asleep on the cheek below. It's the scars, white spiderwebs and red rivulets, running across his skin like the drag marks on freshly tilled farmland.

And the Serologist, hidden beneath the gristle and scar tissue, uses his face like a weapon. He leers and he mugs. Giving each and every broken angle its share of the spotlight. It's a performance, what this man does. It's a Kabuki dance from hell.

"The thing you need to know about me is that I don't know when to stop," he says to Olivier Geome, who is tied to a bed frame. "Nothing new, really. Problem I had since I was just a kid. Back then it was schoolwork. I'd do my share and more. Read ahead in the textbooks, go to the library on weekends and research this and that. It's basically an addiction. Simple Psych 101 stuff."

Olivier is hardly listening. This is because he's missing his ears. They are sitting in a teacup on a desk beside the bed. This is all happening around eight in the morning in Olivier's small apartment, a place on West 8th that he's had for about fifteen years. It's in a quiet building, the neighbors are all elderly and the place is rent controlled. He never expected to be in this position, in this much pain, in his own place. Sure, it's small and it's dusty and the furniture is cheap. But it's Olivier's retreat, his own private slice of peace and quiet. Here he can get away, shower and pray. This is his place and the thought that he's being brutalized here, that thought alone makes him so very sick.

"You know, it's funny how this always goes the same way. Time and time again. Sad, really. You boil my life down and it's just repetition. You ever see that movie *Groundhog Day*?" the Serologist asks.

Right now, Olivier's head is throbbing, drowning out everything, and he's really no good at reading lips. So he nods.

"Clever movie but it cuts a bit close to the bone for me. I'm stuck in this repeating pattern. Just me catching people unawares and then torturing them until I get the information I want and then it's the same old 'body disposal' story."

This terrible-faced man in a shabby suit is crouched next to Olivier's bed. He's sitting there beside the night table, his face all craters and mountains from the angle of the desk lamp, and he's holding a long, serrated knife. The knife glints like something far beneath the surface of the water.

Olivier asks, "What did I do? What do you want?"

The Serologist closes his eyes, swallows. After a moment, maybe a heartbeat, he says, "To be honest, I worry that if I don't work every day, then I'll get rusty. I think that's a very legit concern. Don't you?"

Olivier groans. He stares out at the Serologist with his blood-shot right eye. The left is swollen shut.

Olivier asks, "Why me?"

"I couldn't find anyone else," the Serologist chuckles. "Like I said before, this thing is a compulsion with me. You know what I tell all our clients, I tell them that once they hire me, once I'm on the scent, so to speak, I can't be shut off. I'm in 'til the end."

"But I'm your partner."

"And you're an even guy, Olivier. I've worked with all sorts. I can't even begin to tell you how many times I've been disappointed. You know, they complain a lot about customer service in these post-9/11 days. There's the woman at the grocery store that doesn't bother looking you in the eye. The punk at the gas station who can't break a twenty because he can't figure out the change. Irritating stuff, really. I think I've actually been blessed with good help. You are one of the best. Most devoted for sure."

Olivier only catches some of that. He whispers, "Why are you doing this, then?"

"It doesn't make any sense, does it?" The Serologist nods, pats Olivier's shoulder.

"No," Olivier mumbles. His lips are numb and his teeth are shrapnel.

The Serologist pauses for a second. That one second of silence is like an eye of a hurricane. For the first time in what seems like a lifetime, Olivier's muscles relax. He sighs and a long shiver runs up his spine. He thinks about crying but worries that it will just make the wounds on his eyes sting. So he closes his eyes and waits. He prays.

The Serologist leans over and whispers in what's left of Olivier's left ear. Really, it's just a clotted hole. He says, "How long have we worked together?"

"Seven years," Olivier says. "In one capacity or another."

The Serologist sits back up. He sighs and pulls a switchblade from his breast pocket and cuts the ties on Olivier's hands. Cuts the ties on Olivier's legs. Smiles and says, "Sorry about that, Olivier. I think I tied these pretty tight."

Olivier says nothing. He rubs his wrists where the ties were. The skin there is cut and bruised; it's mottled purple and gray. Olivier wonders if he'll ever regain feeling in his fingers and toes. At least the few toes he has remaining.

The Serologist stands up, stretches and says, "Well, I guess I'll dispose of these." He picks up the teacup with Olivier's ears and he reaches under the bed and pulls out a bedpan that has, as far as Olivier can tell, a toe, a finger, and some ruddy congealed mass that has a clump of curly hair smack on the top of it. Olivier has no idea where on his body it's from but he's worried. The Serologist walks over to the kitchen. He stands in front of the sink and pours the contents of the bedpan and the teacup in. He turns on the water and runs the disposal for a few seconds. Then walks back over to the bed.

"How long have I been here?" the Serologist asks.

Olivier leans over and checks the alarm clock on the floor. The pain in his lower back is immediate and unrelenting but he pushes through it, worried that the Serologist could always get crazy again. He'd rather worry about the physical therapy later. The clock says ten PM. Olivier lies back and sighs and says, "Two and a half hours."

"My, how the time flies," the Serologist replies. He walks to the bathroom and returns with a damp towel. He sits next to Olivier on the blood-drenched bed and wraps the towel around Olivier's head. There is a buzzing sound in the Serologist's pants. He pulls a cell phone out. "I thought you might call me."

The Serologist leaves the apartment and steps out into the hall. He leaves the door open and watches Olivier as he nods and paces, the phone glued to his ear.

Olivier pulls himself up from his bed. He stumbles over to the couch. It's only about ten feet away but the brief walk is so agonizing that when he reaches the couch he promptly passes out. He regains consciousness thirty seconds later and the pain has subsided. He looks out at the hallway and doesn't see the Serologist.

He waits a few breaths and then Olivier digs his hands under the pillows of the couch and pulls out a half-filled bottle of Percocet. It takes him over two minutes to open the bottle. His fingers are blue and rigid. When he does, he throws about five tablets into his mouth and chews them gingerly. Careful not to break any of his remaining teeth.

Then he digs back under the cushions on the couch and finds the remote.

He turns on ESPN and closes his eyes and falls asleep.

He is awakened a few minutes later.

"Olivier, we've got a gig." The Serologist shakes Olivier's shoulders. "Come on, out of your stupor. We're needed."

"Just leave me here," Olivier moans.

"No, no. I need you to drive. You can wait in the car if you like."

"Am I still bleeding?"

The towel wrapped around Olivier's head is red. Red and wet. The Serologist looks at it and shakes his head. "You'll be just fine," he says. "This won't take long at all."

Half an hour later and Olivier pulls his '85 Sentra up in front of an apartment building on East 71st.

The doorman looks at Olivier sitting in the car, his face bloodied and bruised, and narrows his brow. "He's okay," the Serologist says and hands the doorman a fifty. The doorman shrugs and opens the door for the Serologist.

When the elevator doors open on the twelfth floor the Serologist sees there is only one apartment. The front door is open and he walks in. A butler, wearing a name tag that reads Marcus, takes his coat and leads him to an expansive and underlit kitchen. There are three pit bulls lounging on the floor, two of them breathing heavily through strings of drool.

"You like dogs?" Kip Tiller asks when the Serologist walks in. He's sitting on a stool at the kitchen table, smoking a joint and rolling the smoke around in his mouth and then letting it slip out slowly. Letting it curl in the air like cream in coffee. He's old, old enough to be the Serologist's father, but he's got a young mouth and a gray ponytail. It fits with his pin-striped suit and reeks of money.

The Serologist nods. "Sure."

"You like pit bulls?"

"Haven't known many. Shot a few."

Kip shakes his head dramatically. "See, that's a fucking shame. These are beautiful dogs and ill-treated by society. I can't tell you how many of these pups I've personally rescued. I have a shelter, you know, out on Long Island. Rehabilitate mistreated pit bulls. They are the most misunderstood of all animals. Hell, sharks have a better reputation."

"The ones I've met, ones I've shot, were pretty nasty."

"'Cause someone made 'em that way. Dogs are not inherently bad. They are loving creatures and pit bulls have massive hearts. Love families. Love children. Honestly, they are the best dogs you can own. It is disgusting the way they've been smeared. All these breeders, these baiters . . . Don't get me started."

"Okay."

"You've seen the ransom video, right?"

The Serologist takes a seat and shakes his head. The machine hum of two silver refrigerators is white noise. And the kitchen is white, all white. They look odd, these men like two crows, perched on stools in that shadowed room.

"How could you miss that?" Kip asks, stunned. "It's been on every fucking news station for the past forty-eight hours. They took her Saturday and the video's all over the news by Tuesday morning. Unbefuckinglievable."

"I don't have a television set. I like to go to the movies."

"Well, let me be the first to describe it to you. It's about three minutes long and looks for all the world like a God damned Islamic beheading tape. These faggots in animal costumes holding my daughter between them. It's only at the end of this atrocity that they mention, in voice-over no less, that they want fifty million dollars."

The Serologist groans. He asks, "Do they identify themselves?"

"They call themselves the RPA. Revolutionary Patients' Army."

"Interesting."

"I have it on good authority that these people are a bunch of whack jobs who were busted out of a mental asylum ten months ago. Police won't say that. Not yet. But my sources tell me it's true."

"Busted out by whom?"

Kip Tiller smiles. He says, "Their therapist."

"That's something new."

"Tell me about it." Kip takes another long drag of his joint.

"It won't be hard to find these people. These guys, more than others, are bound to slip up. That's what crazy is."

"The pay will be as expected."

The Serologist leans in. "We've worked together for a while now, but not in this capacity. Do you know who I am?"

"The man who gets things done."

"Right. It's like a Pandora's box, calling me. Once I'm here, there's no going back."

Kip rolls another joint. "You can do this? This is a bit different than usual."

"Of course."

"Right." Kip lights the new joint and drags on it. "And when you find her? The people that took her?"

"What do you want to happen?" The eyes shrouded in the Serologist's cracked-pudding face sparkle with some electric current.

"Just that they suffer. Suffer unbearably and that you film it. I want to see it."

The Serologist chuckles. "I'm open to anything, Mr. Tiller. And I'd be lying if I told you that I didn't have my own little 'film' collection."

"Good. That they suffer, that's the most important piece."

"No worries. This won't come out perfect. What I mean to say is that a situation like this one, it never ends nicely. Things like this, well, they don't come out in the wash."

"You think I don't know that?"

"No. Of course you know that. I just want to make sure it's clear. Crystal. Because when I come back here for the rest of my money I want to get it. No excuses."

Kip is annoyed. He says, "You just get her. Get her and you get your money."

The Serologist nods. He stands to leave and Kip says, "I've got to be honest with you, these people scare me. Scare me something good. Who knows what they are capable of or what they want? What they've already done to her?"

The Serologist smiles. "Do you think I scare easy?"

Kip laughs and laughs and laughs at that.

The Serologist leaves the table and goes out the way he came in. Kip Tiller does not stand. He says nothing as he cashes his joint and closes his eyes. One of the pit bulls farts and Kip chuckles.

2.

It's near nine and Laser Mechanic is lying awake pissed off at Lulu's heavy breathing.

It is clear that Lulu is not a ninja.

She doesn't have the breathing down at all. She's huffing and puffing in the bed beside him like a tractor engine. He's sure people across the street can hear her. Let alone the neighbors in apartment 5D.

Laser's lying on his back, wide awake and controlling his breathing. Slowly letting the air pass through his nostrils without a hint of whisper or vibration. If Lulu were conscious she'd have to put a hand on his chest or her ear to his nose to even tell he was alive. He is that ninja.

It started out as a commando thing. When he was ten and lived in Elizabeth, Laser loved imagining himself as an undercover, household commando. Probably it was related to him first seeing Arnold Schwarzenegger's *Commando*. He saw it at Andy Clifton's place during a sleepover and even though he was appalled by the brutality of it, he loved the control Schwarzenegger had. The muscles didn't impress him as much as the stoicism. The cold exterior. Those narrowed eyes. Schwarzenegger was a finely tuned machine. The one-liners—"Don't disturb my friend, he's dead tired"—weren't funny to Laser; they were just calculated, perfected. Like math. He convinced his parents to take him to the Army Surplus store and get him some camouflage pants and war paint. He didn't want a gun. The thrill of being a commando wasn't about violence; it was about control.

Laser started lifting weights. Ten years old, eighty pounds, and he's bench-pressing one hundred fifty pounds in the mildewed basement with a single lightbulb swaying overhead. That's when the asthma first became pronounced. It had been there during bouts of flu and even with mild colds. Been there when it rained for days on end. When he went over to Todd Brixton's house and lay on the comforter where the cats slept. Between lifts Laser would tug on his albuterol inhaler like it was a nipple. If anything the disease only made him push harder. If anything it was a sign that there was weakness in him, another hurdle to overcome.

Warriors don't have asthma, he would tell himself.

Laser overheard his parents talking about him at night. Mom, Rochelle, the librarian at the local elementary school, who had been a peace activist in college though she never actually marched on anything anywhere, and Dad, Geoff, a chemical engineer at a pesticide company, avoided any and all confrontation. Individually they were sweet, inspiring. Together they were meek, parsimonious. In Laser's mind the human equivalent of broccoli. This was before the divorce. Back when his dad thought of his mother as a partner. A mate. This was before Shira.

His dad: "Just don't get it. What's the appeal of all that? No one military in the family. We've never talked about war outside of damning it."

Mom, whispering: "He's a boy. Isn't this what boys do?"

"Sure. But he doesn't do anything. He doesn't patrol the house. He doesn't even want a gun. I can't think of any kid I've ever known who wanted to play soldier without a gun."

"He doesn't like guns."

"I know. I know. That's what worries me."

Mom, scoffing: "If he *was* into guns that would worry me more."

"Do you think he's too sensitive?"

"What's that mean?"

"I don't know."

"Why say it, then? Sensitive is good. Women like sensitive men."

"He's ten. He's not looking for women."

Mom, shifting: "Do you think the boys at school are teasing him? Bullies? Maybe he's getting into fights. He wants to bulk up."

"No. He would have said something."

"Maybe this is just something an only child does."

"Maybe."

"He never seems bored, though. I think this is coming from outside."

"I never worried it was us."

"You never would."

And neither of them did get it. It wasn't about bullies or look-ing tough. It wasn't about war or violence. It was about power. It was about control. Laser, when he talked to himself about it, de-cided it was akin to meditation. It was training his body for per-fection, prepping it for the rigors of the outside world. He wasn't sure why he felt this was important. There were, to be honest, no imminent threats. For Laser Mechanic steeling himself was, at its basest, all about expression.

It was his first true stab at art.

Laser would control his breathing over dinner with annoying relatives. At sleepovers with friends. At Grandma's. He would camp out behind the large potted fern in his mother's living room and use his cheap telescope to spy on his babysitter while she yapped on the kitchen phone with Hilda, the cute Austrian exchange student.

Then ninjas came into vogue. At least in Laser's mind.

It was an ad in the back of some ratty old comic book that got him tuned in. Ninjas. Throwing stars. Nunchucks. The whole deal was white hot. But he never sent away for any of the ninja training manuals advertised. Laser decided to train himself.

It began with itches.

Whenever he'd get an itch he'd hold as still as possible and not scratch. And not scratching made them come alive. He'd let the itch burrow under his skin. Rustle every sensitive hair and nerve fiber as it moved. After a few minutes he'd be sweat-ing but kept his breathing calm. Relaxed. Laser'd think about other things, maybe sex, maybe smoking a bowl with Jeffrey Cancer out behind the school shed. Eventually his skin would turn numb. Cold. And the itch would retreat and his mind would be focused. That was more than commando style. That was ninja.

Then came the breathing.

Laser could stand behind the other potted fern in his mother's bedroom for hours ignoring and conquering an itch but if he was breathing like a cow it wasn't going to matter. Mastering breathing control was a necessity. It was critical. But the training was hard. Laser had to really develop his lungs. Swimming was the best for that. Laser learned to hold his breath for longer and longer periods of time. He'd even hang upside down in the deep end of the pool, legs over the tiled edge, arms crossed. Laser would close his eyes in this position, letting the water noises fill his ears, drifting up and down with the swimming pool tide and making like a nautical bat.

Then began land-based training, which was all about regimen. Land-based training was relatively easy. Laser'd find a secure and quiet spot, maybe behind the couch in the basement, maybe under his bed, and he'd just lie back and breathe. Focus on something, like water damage on the ceiling or the fine fur that hung from the bottom of the bed. Lose himself in the water damage or the fur. Memorize the lines, the shapes, the shadows, even the mildewy scent if he could pick it up. Once he was focused, reining in the breathing was a snap. He could make it so shallow, so subtle, that you couldn't hear a thing. Almost ninja perfection.

Who knew what it would lead to? Laser's parents certainly didn't.

They were actually surprised when he dropped out of high school and went to Japan. There, he taught English in Osaka and trained with Masaaki Nishina, forty-second linear grandmaster of the Yon-po Hiden Ryu, "The School of the Four Secrets." The headmaster had only opened the school to Westerners a few years before he arrived and Laser was the last student accepted that year. Master Nishina liked Laser's conditioning. Training was not like it's portrayed in kung fu films. Laser was not trained to catch flies with chopsticks or break bricks with his big toe or fast for two weeks. Mostly it was meditation. It was spiritual refinement. Laser spent six months at the school before picking up a sword. They didn't believe he had asthma. Actually, they didn't believe the disease existed. Master Nishina said, "It's your American constitution." While Laser nodded in agreement his chest ached every night and later, when he wasn't supervised as closely, he snuck albuterol into his room and would puff on it in secret. He told himself this was okay because changing his constitution was nearly impossible and he was satisfied with that one sliver of inbred failure. Didn't Master Nishina also say "the perfect man is like an urn with a hairline crack"?

Eventually Laser mastered the eighteen disciplines of ninjutsu. He was a seventh dan shidoshi in Yon-po Hiden Bujinkan Ninpo. When someone would ask him what the hell that meant, exactly, he'd respond: "It means I have complete control over my senses. That I can kill with my mind. It pretty much means there are maybe fifteen people in the entire world who can sneak up on me."

But Lulu?

No way she could get away with a sneak attack. She could never hide from a team of marauding assassins either. She'd be dead meat. Laser isn't exactly sure why but it pisses him off enough that he decides to get up.

Laser stands in front of his bedroom mirror naked and posing.

He's disappointed in what he sees. Long gone are the fatless days of muscular perfection. Now, Laser's had to assimilate to American norms. He's lost some of his edge. He's gone flabby at the boundaries. Laser studies his muscles like he can measure them with his eyes. The mirror is full length so his whole body is there and there are parts he's ignoring. Mainly it's his gut. The immature beer belly that's just made an appearance in the last two months. He sucks it in and sticks it out. Neither makes him happy. He groans and gets dressed. Pulls open the curtains and lets in the diffuse Newark light.

All for a good cause, he tells himself. *Practically undercover.*

Lulu moans.

"Sorry." Laser shuts the curtains again. He goes out to the kitchen and has a spoonful of peanut butter and a tall glass of milk.

When he returns to the bedroom, Lulu is awake. Her bleached blond flattop sparkles in the morning light. She isn't wearing a shirt and she's smoking. "What day is it?" she asks. "Feels like I've been in here forever."

"Tuesday," Laser says. He sits on the end of the bed and clips his nails over a small wastebasket. Nearly every nail clipping misses the basket and spins off into the shag carpet. "Didn't you tell me you had some ninjutsu training?"

"Huh?"

"Martial arts. You said you were a black belt."

"Oh, right. Just said that for you."

Laser sighs hard. Cuts another nail and shakes his head. "You have a show tomorrow?"

"Fuck yes. Big show."

"How big?"

"I'm hoping for a hundred."

"That is big. Any reps?"

"Haven't heard."

"Were there reps last show?"

"I think so."

"That guy with the mullet and the tie?"

"I think so."

"That's cool."

Lulu drops her half-smoked cigarette into a beer can by the side of the bed and gets up. She walks into the bathroom, pulling her thong down and leaving it on the floor. She leaves the bathroom door open and Laser can hear her piss splashing. He closes his eyes and groans for a second time. Tries to remember if sex with Lulu last night was enjoyable. He's not sure but he doubts it was great.

"You have a last name?" Laser shouts.

Lulu laughs. "I didn't tell you?"

"No."

"Seriously?"

"Yes."

"How many days have I been here?"

"Two. But sleeping mostly. I think you've been awake maybe six hours. You ate a burger yesterday. Watched that one movie about Klaus Nomi."

"That was fucked up."

"What's your last name?" Laser shouts.

"I like being anonymous."

"Seriously?"

Lulu comes out of the bathroom, grabs her underwear and sits down on the bed next to Laser and kisses him on the cheek. She says, "It's been fun. Fun for you?"

"Sure," he says, not looking up at her. He's using the nail-file end of the clippers to pick something out from under his thumb. Maybe it's a poppy seed. Maybe just a bit of fuzz.

Lulu stands up and pulls her underwear on. She digs around in Laser's closet and grabs a T-shirt and some shorts. "I can't remember if I came here wearing anything," she says. "You mind if I borrow this?"

She holds up the T-shirt. It's black and says Shinobi.

Laser looks up. "Actually, I'd rather—"

"Thanks," Lulu says. She throws the shirt on braless and pulls on the shorts. She walks over to Laser and kisses him again, this time on the lips, and then she licks the tip of his nose. "I'll see you tomorrow night," she says and then she leaves.

Laser gives up on fishing the black thing out from under his nail. Decides it's just paint or ink. He gets up and opens the shades again and lets in the light. There is light traffic outside but it's enough for him to decide that he'll wait to drive over to the electronics store. He grabs a manila envelope from on top of his dresser and catches himself in the mirror across the room.

He is not lean enough. He stretches and poses and is self-conscious the whole time. Turning twenty-five was something of a cold shower. Laser's metabolism downshifted when he turned twenty and now he has to work out to stay fit, not just to remain toned. Looking in the mirror, he doesn't see the new weight so much as he sees the stress grinding away at him. He looks haggard and sleep deprived and not nearly as energized as he thinks he needs to be. For the first time in forever he reminds himself that he has a way out. That he could chuck the manila envelope in the trash and go back to bed. Even more he could disappear. The thoughts pass quickly, sharply. He shakes his head and pinches his eyes closed. Laser is sure of this. Butterflies will not dissuade him. Stress will not sideline him. *I can sleep when I'm dead,* he tells himself. Laser smiles and says, whispering, "This is going to work."

Laser meets Gustav Richter in the lobby of a hotel in Chelsea and already the bile is coming up in his throat.

It's always this way. Laser abhors these meetings but sees them as a necessary evil. Part of him, a very large part, wants to just fast-forward to when he doesn't need money like this. Money from someone like Gustav. Laser swallows his pride and rage and just smiles. Gustav, older than he looks in clear plastic-framed glasses and a gray goatee, gives Laser a big, long hug. "You look fantastic. I can't wait for you to tell me all about this latest endeavor of yours." His Austrian accent thick as the lenses of his glasses.

Gustav escorts Laser to a table in the back of the lobby adjacent to the café. A waitress appears almost immediately. Gustav orders coffee and Laser a Bloody Mary. When the waitress leaves,

Gustav, grinning wildly, rubs his hands together and says, "Tell me. I've already heard some rumors."

"Really?"

"Yes. These building remodels, if they're anything like the one you did in Passaic, are going to be massive. I'm estimating, and this is just based on stuff we've done together in the past, that we'll come in about twice what you needed for the Consumer-Tronics murals. Rumor has it you've got your eyes set on something really big. An apartment complex perhaps?"

"At least twice, Gustav."

"Oh, you do have something good for me."

"Better, actually. The rumors are true. We've been toying with an apartment building, someplace here in Newark. The vision is taking something slated for demolition or just fallen into total disrepair and creating a green living space out of it. Cody sees a hollowed-out center with a garden and spiral staircase. Rufus sees solar panels and interactive water features. I've been partial to seeding the place, letting nature run riot and then bombing over the overgrowth."

Gustav nods along to every word.

"But the plan has changed. We're doing something spectacular."

"Yes."

"Your first two down payments have allowed us to set up not one building but three. Cross-country. We've already got months put into this and over three hundred operatives. A small group of us will head West and organize, do overnights like we did in Bangor and Silver Springs. In and out and the community is transformed within hours. Take a look." Laser pulls a sheet of paper from the manila envelope and hands it to Gustav.

Gustav reads, shakes his head. "This is incredible. This second one . . ."

"Boulder?"

"Yes. I can't imagine how this will look. You said three. There are two here."

"Last one's a surprise."

"Do tell."

"The Tiller Casino in Vegas."

"It's certainly a nice target—bastion of everything wrong with America. I heard it was originally going to be a replica of the Taj Mahal but that got too pricey. Regardless, it's officially the most wasteful and hideous construction site in the United States. But to get in there you'd need hundreds of people and months of preparation. Please tell me you're kidding."

"We'll do the Tiller Casino. Already have several hundred people lined up to help. Uniforms have shipped."

Gustav laughs. It's an uncomfortable cackle. "Don't be ridiculous, Laser. There are over fifty floors, several hundred rooms. Not to mention the fact that the building will be open by the end of the summer, mid-August at the earliest. How would that even be imaginable?"

"I've got a secret weapon is how."

The drinks arrive. Laser sees himself kicking the table up and pouring his drink over Gustav's head. He takes a deep breath instead. For his part, Gustav takes a long sip and eyes Laser over the brim of his cup.

"Secret weapon? Do tell."

"I trust you, Gustav. You trust me with your money. I am one of the few artists working today in this arena that has as generous and understanding a benefactor. You have never questioned my methods or my art. That being said, I really need you to trust me on what I'm about to tell you."

Gustav licks his lips in anticipation. He leans in close, eyes narrowed.

"We're going on a rescue mission."

Gustav nods. "Yes. And?"

"I know where Leigh Tiller is being held, and me and my crew, we're going to rescue her tomorrow night."

Gustav leans back, hands out, shaking. "You're kidding, right."

"No."

"No, really. This is crazy."

"It's brilliant."

Gustav shrugs. "Tell me how."

"We've been looking at these burnt-out apartment buildings over on Seventh Avenue. Recon missions, usual stuff for us. Last week I found her. There's this one near where the old Christopher Columbus Homes were, it's actually a nice 1925 building, and she's there, in the penthouse, being kept in an empty pool. When I first found her it was around dusk. She was standing by a window and I could see her face with my binoculars. Never really thought she was that attractive, you know, from the things I've seen, but standing there, she was like a mirage."

"Why not tell the police, Laser? You're an artist, not a cowboy. To think that you could just run in there and take her is ludicrous. You have seen the television reports, these people, this RPA, they are all insane and they are armed. Why don't you let the police handle this? You will still get some press."

"Because there is no art in that, Gustav."

"Where is the art in what you propose?"

"The danger. The overhauls, these remodels we've been doing, they're great at making a statement and there is a certain illicit quality to the actions that makes them risky. But being arrested is the worst that can happen, and every time we're bailed out and the press has a field day. It's preschool. This, this is something else entirely."

"Suicide?"

"Maybe. But it's a calculated risk."

"And after the rescue?"

"We do the tour. We hit the other targets and move in on the

Tiller Casino. Leigh is our ticket in. With her, the red carpet will be out. Once her daddy has her back, we'll be celebrities. And that's when the real art begins."

"Sounds a bit corporate, my friend."

"Not what I've got up my sleeve."

Gustav laughs. Chokes. "This is impossible, Laser. So many uncertainties."

"Take a look at the folder."

Gustav skims the short stack of papers inside. "Talk me through these."

Laser reaches over the table. "Blueprints for the building and the apartment complex next door. Here, these are sketches of the people holding her. There are three of them. Two down, one upstairs with her. Essentially unarmed. And here, the times. Every move they've made for six days. Like clockwork. We've already done two practice runs. Way we've got this planned, we'll be out of there with her in a matter of minutes."

"You said they were essentially unarmed. How's that?"

"One of them has what looks like a harpoon."

"Odd choice."

"These appear to be very odd people. Psychiatric patients. Schizophrenics. Rumor has it they're doing this to spark some sort of revolution. Cops have some leads. It isn't who they are but where."

"This isn't a turf war, is it?" Gustav laughs. "Revolution? I detect a theme."

Laser shakes his head. "These people aren't artists."

"And the girl? How is she?"

"Drugged up. I'm guessing they've got her on tranqs. That'll be the easiest part."

"And after?"

"We go public, bring her home with cameras and fireworks."

"Why don't we set up another meeting, have some of my colleagues look this over? I know many people that I trust very dearly who could look over it and give you honest opinions."

"No, Gustav. We need to move now. I saw some detectives going door to door a block over only yesterday. No, this needs to be swift. Trust me. I can do this."

Gustav closes his eyes, takes a deep breath. "What's in this for me?"

Laser smiles. "Gustav Richter presents *The Rescue of Leigh Tiller,* an interactive performance by Strategic Art Defense. I can't even begin to imagine how good that will look on the ticker at Times Square. Best of all, we film it all and we keep the rights. Video feeds, website downloads, DVDs. Frankly, it will be the most spectacular event in the last fifty years."

"And if you fail? What then?"

"We won't."

"This is crazy."

"It's what I do, Gustav. This is everything I stand for. Come on, you've taken so many risks over the past four years. So many. Let's kick this up to the next level."

"What will you need the money for?"

"Production costs. Traveling."

Gustav cracks his knuckles and then stands. "You're a genius, Laser."

Laser stands and they hug, Gustav smiling and patting Laser on the shoulder. Laser cringes the whole while. He reminds himself that it's almost over. That this act is only another weapon in his arsenal.

"When will I hear from you?"

Laser says, "By Wednesday."

"Excellent. I'll have the money in your account by the end of the day. Good luck, my little savant. Be careful. Be safe. But most of all . . . have fun. " Gustav winks.

"No worries. These guys are so well trained they're practically SWAT."

CHAPTER THREE

Set up

1.

Leigh dips her feet in the water to touch the cool, slick surface of the weeds.

The purple, fleshy vine bobs slightly beneath the weight of her feet, sinking a few inches into the ocean water. Three bright red crabs scuttle down into the knots of weed and a scattering of sea lice skip across the placid surface like thrown scallop shells. The water is as cold as Leigh remembers it. So cold, in fact, that for a second she holds her breath. The feeling is actually exhilarating. Like chewing mint gum and sucking an ice cube, and Leigh is struck by it. But she doesn't dare slip her feet back in again. Already, she can see the bulge of the larger things moving stealthily toward the ship. The darker things a few feet beneath the mats of seaweed creeping forward encased in shadow.

She stands up and stretches in the noon sun. The heat has been oppressive the past three days and she's spent the afternoons tucked under the fore galley scribbling in her journal. Mostly doodles of spirals and swirls. A few deliberate illustrations of the Sargasso Sea stretching out beyond the ship—large swaths of curlicues and a bank of low clouds on the horizon, the mast of the nearest derelict like a cross jutting from the weed. Many of her journal entries involve vivid fantasies about the ancient derelict foundering just south of her ship, the *Lucinda*. Leigh imagines that the great-grandchildren of the survivors still live there, pacing the decks and looking over at the *Lucinda* and wondering if Leigh can see them. Feeble children with long, pale hair and bright, uncluttered eyes. At night, when the moon is full, she stands out on the deck and stares as hard as she can into her binoculars, scanning the deck of the wreck for any trace of life. She never sees any.

Sometimes she photographs a crab before she eats it. Day before last she'd gotten a particularly large one with an opalescent shell that cracked into a hundred tiny slivers when she hit it with a rock. Leigh sketched the remains of the crab, the busted shell and the pile of mirror pieces lying around it. The image was striking but she was unable to capture it on film.

The days whir by trapped in the desolation of the weed. One bleeds into the next the way the pale underside of the crab bleeds into the bright red top. The line between them is very nearly indistinguishable and Leigh spends many hours staring at that most subtle demarcation hoping to find a thin line, a boundary. She does that merely for the sport of it. And she is so fucking bored.

Besides the derelict ship that hulks over toward the setting sun, there is very little in Leigh's world outside of her own body and the body of the *Lucinda*. Both are young and the product of good breeding. Leigh has an athlete's legs and a whore's chest. The *Lucinda* has a similar build, the bow rising up out of the water at an almost obscene angle. She was built for long voyages. Pleasure cruises from Eastern cities to South American beaches, and Leigh's dad had captained the ship nearly clear around the world. Leigh got it for her twenty-first birthday, a seventeen-million-dollar gift that now rusts in a net of seaweed somewhere in the South Atlantic. A testament to something.

Leigh stares hard into the clear water and down into the weed.

The large shapes are there. Huddled like children just beneath the waterline but deep enough that Leigh still can't discern their shape.

"Dirty fuckers," she sneers. "You only wish."

Looking at them, these shadows taunting her, Leigh thinks about her father. About how he sits beneath the surface of her life, of everything she's ever done, taking toll. It's him and his elegant ponytail behind everything she's ever accomplished. Any success in her life, no matter how far from the family, it's his face she sees reflected in the prize. His smile, his hands clapping, his eyes taking stock.

When she had her first modeling gig he rated it, her performance, with a scorecard. Sitting in the front row, his sunglasses on, he held up a white stock card as she walked by and it said 5.4. Everyone laughed when they saw it. Even he was laughing. It would have been something of a funny joke if it hadn't been her dad. Anyone else's dad would have put up that card to poke fun, punch holes in the sanctimonious atmosphere around the catwalk. Anyone else's dad and the card would have meant "Don't take it all so seriously." But not Leigh's father. He meant it. He wanted Leigh to know she wasn't performing to par, that she was somehow letting him down. That his investment, his daughter, was compromised.

He came backstage after the show and grabbed Leigh's friend Trisha's ass. He smiled and told her that she was "fabulous." Then he walked over to Leigh, kissed her on the cheek and shook his head. He said, "That wasn't exactly what I'd expected."

"What did you expect?"

"Just a bit more life. You didn't think you looked wooden?"

"No, Dad. I felt beautiful," Leigh said, feeling the tears well up. She was sixteen and she'd been breaking into sobbing fits every other afternoon. Mostly it was for reasons she didn't really understand. It was something said at school. Mostly it was just being sixteen and struggling to find herself.

Dad sighed. "Of course, honey. But the point wasn't for you to feel beautiful. In fact, maybe that was the whole problem. You're up there the whole time enjoying your own beauty and it got lost somewhere inside you. Hasn't anyone ever told you that modeling isn't really about you?"

"Of course," Leigh choked. "You have."

"Right. And a lot of good that's done, huh?"

She smacked him then. That was the first and the last time. She walked over, mascara trails down her cheeks and under her chin, wobbly in the heels, and smacked his tanned face as hard as she could. When her hand touched his face, the feeling of her weight and her anger and all her misery crashing against his jaw and nose and lips was monumental. It was the best crying jag she'd never had. The sound was wonderful. Maybe it was his skin and some extra coating of lotion or maybe it was her hands, covered as they were with sweat. The sound was a triumphant slap, a crescendo. It felt so good Leigh almost said, "Take that." She didn't.

And then he smacked her back.

She'd never seen his eyes so hard. Not the time she crashed the Jag or the time he'd caught her with acid. The look was pure murder, it was beyond reason, and his smack came so strong and so fast that she just cringed and didn't bother dodging it. She couldn't have. His hand sent her spinning to the floor. Leigh felt it in slow motion. She imagined it was like a clip of a boxer getting beaten down, spittle flying and her lips all rubbery and distorted. It even felt as though a few teeth were knocked out. She landed on her bony ass and the pain of hitting the tile with her tailbone was almost more painful than the smack and the emotional devastation that went along with it.

Dad stood over her and rubbed his smacking hand and said, "You need to learn to take criticism. I appreciate your desire to fight back, to not take any lip, but you can't smack everyone who tells you you suck."

Leigh sat there, her left cheek as red as her lipstick, her pupils dilated and ass bone aching, and she gave her dad a middle finger. "I hope you rot in hell," she said.

He laughed, rubbing his cheek. Then he smiled and said, "Bravo. You are a Tiller. One day, you'll look back at this fondly." And then he left. The other girls in the dressing room with mouths hanging open, Leigh stunned and silent. The tears no longer slipping down her made-up face.

Truth is, ten years later, when Leigh thinks back to that slap she feels nothing but hope. The worst over, two years of near silence, and eager to be back in her father's favor. She almost chokes when she thinks why: Leigh is lonely. With Mom gone and the whole city only looking at her for her next appearance, her friends only hanging on because they know they'll be blogged about if they do, she feels utterly, entirely alone. It gnaws at her. Drains the color from her features. She needs someone to love her. Needs someone to remind her of why she's alive. Even her asshole father should be able to provide that. Leigh hates to admit it but being mistreated is better than being ignored.

At sea, the night falls fast and hard. The *Lucinda*'s auxiliary generator comes on quickly and that lone speck of humanity in a sea of vegetation is soon flooded with fluorescent light and the throbbing bass line of one of Leigh's favorite DJ mixes. The silver fishes flit in and around the ship, almost in time with the cacophonous break beat. The crabs bask in the artificial light. The darker, larger shapes sink deeper into the weed and are soon gone.

2.

"Diego Rivera."

"The Mexican muralist?"

"Yeah," Cody Letts answers, picking at his goatee. Cody is sitting behind the wheel of an idling El Dorado and staring hard at the Abako Apartments building across the street. The windshield is steamed up. It's pouring outside and the rain is warm.

Rufus, next to him, asks, "A cannibal?"

"Uh-huh."

"How's that?"

"In art school, cadavers. He and a couple other students snacked on the corpses. He said it was throwing off the shackles of superstition and irrationalism."

Rufus gags. It's a fake gag, more show than anything. "I always liked those murals," he says. "Would you do that? I mean, for your art."

"No."

"Seriously?" Rufus seems shocked. "I would. I mean, if it's a question of inspiration. I'm all about trying something new to get the creative juices flowing."

Cody picks at a poppy seed wedged between his two front teeth. He says, "The greatest taboo, eating people. That's something universal, Rufus. You just don't fuck around with taboos that are universal. Sure, some indigenous peoples in the jungles of wherever ate a few of their enemies' hearts. And yeah, maybe an aborigine or two tried to consume the spirit of his dead ancestor. But every known culture frowns on eating human flesh just for the sake of eating human flesh. Inspiration isn't a good enough reason to go breaking a moral chain going back fifty thousand years, Rufus."

Cody is officially the chief technical officer of Strategic Art Defense. It is a role he relishes. Cody is something of a whiz kid. Not only did he graduate from Swarthmore with a degree in biochemistry but he was recently pursuing a painting/print-making MFA from Pickens School of Art and Design in Newark. His sophomore project was a piece—a crucified piglet atop a woman in a burka done in oil on planks—entitled *Lickety Spit,* praised for it's blunt politicism though Cody claimed it had nothing to do with politics. While Cody excelled in school, he never took his studies as seriously as his parents (an Angolan immigrant mother and an asshole Texan father) assumed he should. Cody was never a lab rat. He lifted weights. He picked fights. Drank too much. Once, in college, after a particularly loud discussion about valence electrons during which Cody threatened physical violence, his professor pulled Cody aside and asked him who he thought he was. Cody said, "I'm a contradiction. I am both a brute and a beacon of intelligence. I am cocky. Cocksure. I will rule the world." The professor wanted to fail him, was itching to fail him, but couldn't. When Cody graduated it was assumed he'd go to medical school. His advisor, who also hated him, assured him that getting in would be easy. "It's what's expected. You've got the GPA, the MCAT scores. And you're black," she said. Cody bristled. It wasn't the race comment but the "expected" one. Cody said, "I don't do 'expected.'" He enrolled in Pickens and went three semesters. It was the least expected thing he could possibly do. And it was the first time in his life that he actually felt challenged. That he had to study. Organic chemistry had been difficult, so much to memorize, so many different variations. But it was elegant. It was mathematical, arranged. Art was a whole other place. Cody first approached it with his analytical style and while that worked in art history it didn't work in life drawing. It didn't work in painting. Or in sculpture. Or mixed media. When he let go of his rational take, when he just let emotion do the work, things started to click.

Cody met Laser in Hoboken. Laser was an instructor with a Budo master named Fletch Morris. Cody was a promising student of ninjutsu but what he and Laser found themselves talking about after class most was art. Laser was intrigued by Cody's outré take on modern painting but he loved Cody's fuck-it-all attitude toward popular culture. Over some pitchers of Bitburger organic lager at the Oasis they devised some performance-art pieces that utilized Cody's painterly acuity and Laser's stealthy abilities. Their first action as Strategic Art Defense was three years back, Cody's painting *Void Dance* smuggled into the Hunterdon Museum of Art. Things spiraled from there into performance-art pieces (like the one in Union Square Park involving fake tourist guides and trained baboons) and interactive sculptures (the business park in Delaware City where they erected a twenty-foot cast of Cody's left butt cheek). Prospective members flocked to their enigmatic website and soon they had a burgeoning number of collaborators and followers across the country dubbed Strategic Art Defense Irregulars. More than that, money started pouring in. Richter emerged from the shadows last year. Laser left Morris's school and gave himself over wholly to the art of S.A.D. The assault was launched.

"Look," Rufus interrupts. "Just like clockwork."

There is movement at the entrance to the apartment.

A man and a woman are leaving. They light cigarettes and talk in the entranceway. Rufus leans forward. Rufus is wearing a fisherman's vest and it's bristling with artist's pencils. He pulls a thin blue pencil from his right breast pocket. Looks it over and then puts it back and pulls a thicker pencil with a tip worn down to a dark nub. From his left breast pocket he pulls a small sketchpad the size of a paperback book. Rufus angles it in the midmorning sunlight, the motes spinning around it, and he begins to sketch.

Rufus recently dropped out of high school. He's drifted in and around the New York art scene for the past few years on the heels of his famous older brother, the renowned sculptor Axel Feldman. Axel's work is a bit highbrow for Rufus. He doesn't see what is so freaking compelling about bronze casts of horses' hooves. And he doesn't like all the parties where people sit around and sip wine and eat Brie and talk about form and method. It's all too sterile and procedural for Rufus. He wants to make work that's down and dirty, work born of suffering and rolling in the streets. And he doesn't let the fact that he's quite untalented hinder him. He sketches religiously. Everywhere he goes. That's how he met Cody. Another Axel art opening. Another night of Brie and wine and another night sketching guests. Cody noticed, said he saw something in the sketches. He wasn't too clear on what it was but his praise was certainly welcomed. Axel never even bothered looking at Rufus's shit.

Cody showed Rufus a few tricks. How to crosshatch responsibly. Use edges and erasers. Wasn't long before Cody was dragging Rufus along with him everywhere. He had him sketching out ideas. Cody would sit back and dream out loud and Rufus became—having nothing better to do, really—his artistic stenographer. Got so that Rufus could do a quick sketch that would be nearly incomprehensible to anyone else, almost an artistic shorthand, and Cody could read it. These would be gathered together in little books that Rufus would tote around and, as they talked, when Cody wanted a reminder of something he'd thought of, Rufus could just whip it out. For his services, Cody gave Rufus a stipend. It didn't amount to much but it was enough for Rufus to keep on doing nothing.

Cody didn't bother involving Rufus with Strategic Art Defense right away. Rufus was off balance and weak. He was shy around girls and avoided conflict. Cody pushed and prodded him, provoked and angered him, and Rufus's reaction was always the same: retreat. Cody was surprised that it didn't annoy him. If anything, it made Rufus more likable. He needed Cody; he needed guidance and protection.

The only thing that really bothered Cody about Rufus was his superstitious nature. Rufus was driven by invisible signs and portents. For him, the world was merely a mask upon a hidden

topography of mystical energy. The landscape around him buzzed
with geomancy—ley lines and megalithic nodes—the sky above
him spun with celestial warnings and chaos magic. These were
the laws that dictated Rufus's life. He once chose an apartment
because it was on the same block as O'Brien's Pub, a Shamrock
gas station, and Duffy Supplies. He said, "That's as clear a sign
of ley energy as I've ever seen." Cody argued with Rufus at first.
He told him to cut the shit and stop with the New Age claptrap
but it was a no go: Rufus was hooked. Cody let it go. He understood that a protégé needs his own quirks. It's healthy.

Rufus's sketch of the man standing in the apartment doorway is coming along nicely. "Make sure you get Osama's shad-
ing right," Cody instructs, looking over at the quickly manifesting
drawing.

Rufus nods. "Yeah. He's got tone like a Moroccan."

"I'm guessing Egyptian."

Cody looks over at the woman standing beside the man.
"And get her hair right this time. It's practically white."

Rufus's right hand moves quickly, scattering dark pencil across
the rough surface of his notepad. The pencil tip breaks. Rufus
looks up at the dark-skinned man and curses under his breath.
Cody sighs long and hard.

"What are you using? Is that a fucking 2B, you dumb ass?"

Rufus looks up at Cody, shrugs. He goes to pull another pencil from his coat.

Cody stops him. "That's not soft enough, Rufus. Seriously,
dog. Were you paying no attention? Look, you need at least a
4B—maybe a 6B—to catch this."

A walkie-talkie suddenly buzzes at Rufus's feet. He picks it
up. "Go ahead."

"The captain is back," a voice says through a wall of static.

Cody takes the walkie-talkie and asks, "And? What's he got?"

The voice says, "Looks like a speargun."

Cody says, "Sure. Whatever. We don't really care who they are, Tyrell. In fact, it's probably better that we don't know."

"Wait," Tyrell says. "It's not a speargun, it's a harpoon. Like whaling."

"Seriously, Tyrell?" Cody turns to Rufus and screws up his face.

"Seriously," Tyrell says.

"How do you even know what a harpoon looks like?"

"Discovery Channel."

"Fine," Cody says. "Get your ass down here and let's powwow."

Tyrell asks something but the static is too loud.

"Repeat!" Cody shouts into his walkie-talkie.

"Where's Osama and The Former Mrs. Stallone?" Tyrell asks. It comes in clear.

"They've left," Cody says.

"Cool," Tyrell sighs. "I'm coming down, then. Over and out."

Cody clenches and unclenches his jaw, tips his hat back, straightens up in his seat and asks, "How's that sketch coming along?"

"Just the perfect bit of chiaroscuro. It's totally Rembrandt stuff. I'm just grooving on these lines. Catching them just as they fade into nothing. It's like I'm remixing shadows here."

"Sounds good, Rufus," Cody says, cracking his neck. He leans forward to look at the building but by now its shape is largely lost in the long shadows. He looks over at Rufus's sketch and picks at his teeth. Says nothing.

"What do you think?" Rufus says, smearing charcoal.

"Not bad."

"Yeah. That's good coming from you. My harshest critic."

"I provide structure in your young life, Rufus. If you think that's criticism, well, fine. You'll look back at what we're doing here. . . ." Cody spreads his hands as wide as the interior of the car will allow. He says, "This is art, my friend. We're creating something here that will never be forgotten. Something like the Sistine Chapel but better. It'll be in 3-D. We are shaping life and history itself. That's the purest art."

Rufus, still sketching, mutters, "Amen."

The sun slinks behind the building. The streets are quiet, save for a few kids hanging out in an alleyway throwing a basketball around. Their cussing breaks the hum of distant machinery and car honks. The pinging cadence of their "fucks" and "mutherfuckahs" like birdsong.

The sun is gone and the shadows engulf the car. Rufus is finishing his sketch. Cody looks asleep, hat over his face, and there's a rap at the driver's side window. Cody, not removing the hat, reaches over and rolls the window down.

"Report," he says, his voice like he's in a movie.

"Can I get in or what?"

The man at the window is young, young like Cody and Rufus, and he's got a sweatshirt hood pulled over his face. He's like a monk in the dark standing outside the car. Cody unlocks the car doors and the monk slips into the backseat. He sits with a sigh.

"So, when's this going down exactly?" he asks.

Cody sits forward, pushes the cowboy hat back on his head and turns around to look at the guy in the hooded sweatshirt. Rufus turns around as well and lights a cigarette.

Cody speaks first. "Tyrell, we already told you how this is going to go down exactly. You remember?"

Rufus blows smoke into Tyrell's face. Long and slow.

Tyrell waves his hand, annoyed, like he's shooing away a bothersome insect. But he says nothing.

Cody says, "You remember, Tyrell?"

"Yeah, something about bios first." Tyrell crosses his arms.

"Right," Rufus snarls. "We haven't seen yours yet."

"Still working on it."

"And when are you gonna turn it over?" Cody asks.

"I said I'm still working on it. Figuring it out, you know."

Tyrell slumps down into the faux leather of the backseat and pouts. He's got a boxer's face. Nose is crooked, to the left, and he's got those thick, lazy eyelids that you see on people who've spent most of their life being pummeled. That and he's got a smile that's jagged. Snaggly. Tyrell is really Colin "Tyrell" Mullins from Utica. He is old enough to have been in and out of art school for five years. At Burchette College of the Arts he wound up getting heavy into installation projects (his most memorable was titled *No Visible Means* and involved twin propellers, a garland, and a rubber glove). At Ashman School of Visual Arts and Communication, Tyrell was into textiles (*Grimoire* was a ten-by-ten tapestry of "found" elk-hunting tableaus). He bounced out of both schools within a year, bored by what he claimed was an "adherence to the mainstream" by the professors and running low on cash. He spent two years failing to teach himself tracking at a Ute reservation in New Mexico before returning to New York. Ten months ago he enrolled at Allstrom College, started going to openings and that's how he met Cody and, by association, Rufus.

"Better get that shit together," Rufus says. "We can't do this until all the pieces are in place. You know how methodical Cody here is."

"Methodical is just another way of saying disciplined. And we need to be disciplined to carry this off." Cody snatches Rufus's cigarette and drags on it hard and fast. Smokes the whole thing down to a crimson stub. He leans in and motions for the others to lean into a huddle. "Boys, we'll be infamous. This is really our one and only act. The one that will make us money, get us notoriety, women, prestige. It's like the KLF when they burned a million pound banknotes. That cost them a million but it earned them the respect of the world's artists and they have gone down in history, unequaled. People will study us in coming years. Forty years from now this will be considered genius— matchless in scope and artistic fervor—it is the ne plus ultra."

Tyrell smiles. Rufus is smiling too. They both nod at each other smugly.

Cody points to Tyrell. "Get that fucking bio together."

Tyrell dodges. "Nice ride, Ru. Why's Cody in the driver's seat?"

"I named it Quartz," Rufus clarifies. "Nothing stops this car. Seriously. Been in at least ten accidents. Three rollovers and not a scratch. As for Cody, he just likes to drive. I don't mind."

"Has anyone talked to our fearless leader?" Cody changes gears.

Tyrell looks confused. "Cody, I thought you were the leader."

3.

The Serologist is sitting at a table in his tattered suit and he's spattered with blood. Olivier sits behind him reading a paperback book. On the table is a hacksaw, a band saw, a screwdriver, a drill, two syringes (one empty), a hammer, and a vodka cocktail. There is a video camera set up and running on a short tripod on the tabletop.

Across from the Serologist and Olivier sits a man with the face of a child. His eyes are red. Cheeks are puffy and he's got sweat escaping down his face.

"Where is she?" the Serologist asks.

The man who looks too young swallows hard and then says, "I already told you I don't know."

The Serologist says, "Mojo gave me your name, Ben. I'm fairly confident he wouldn't lie to me. He's just not that bright."

Ben shakes his head.

The Serologist smiles, his dimples are off, and he asks, "How old are you exactly?"

"I'm thirty-eight." Ben rubs his face on his shoulder, wiping away the sweat. His cut-off left hand is on the floor beneath his chair. It looks like a dove sleeping in a dark puddle. His severed right foot, still in its gray sock, lies nearby. Ben says, "You did an excellent job. Weren't sure how you were going to make that cut around the talus. Something of an anatomy freak in med school. You're of course—"

"You're thirty-eight and yet you look like a kid," the Serologist interrupts. "Like a ten-year-old. I'm sure I'm not the first person to mention that to you. How do your patients react?"

"They don't seem to care."

"I'll bet you use that to your advantage, right?"

"Huh? What?"

"I mean with girls. You like to hit on the high-school girls, don't you? Or maybe the young attempted suicides that show up at your facility? The pretty ones."

"No." Ben shakes his head. He takes a deep gulping breath and then exhales very, very slowly. He has been breathing like this since he came to.

The Serologist prods him and says, "It won't help."

Ben takes another breath, lets it out so slowly through his nose. "I've been practicing Kundalini yoga for ten years. You could cut off my other leg and I'd still be conscious. Still be talking."

"Come on." The Serologist walks over to Ben and leans down. He's got his twisted face in Ben's face, just a few inches from him, and he says, "I can chop you up into tiny pieces and then sew them back together all wrong. The pain will be divine. Let me tell you about this one guy I worked on. I think his name was Carl though everyone at the time called him Bull. This guy was a hulk. Two hundred pounds easy and not a lick of fat on him. Long military history, all sorts of Navy SEAL shenanigans. A real hero. I got started with a needle and after a few hours he was mewing like a newborn kitten. This guy had been trained to resist torture. That only made it worse."

Ben spits blood. "You are the lowest rung on this ladder."

"And what ladder would that be, Ben?"

"The social hierarchy that you are oblivious to. These people, the ones you're after, are trained to hunt down and destroy people just like you. The scum. What you do is the end result of uncontrolled capitalist propaganda. You are the pawn."

The Serologist walks over to the table and turns the video camera off. "Just tell me where she is and you can leave. Honestly." He walks back and puts a hand on Ben's shoulder. It's wet and he quickly takes his hand back, looks at it like it's been contaminated. "Honestly," he repeats.

"The money Tiller is paying you, do you think it will make your life better?"

The Serologist sighs. "No bullshit, Doc."

"Do you?"

"I enjoy the money but that isn't why I do this."

"Do you know the real cause of schizophrenia? The real one?"

"I don't really care, Ben. Who has the girl? Where is she?"

"Capitalism. Commerce. Our culture of want breeds insanity. We're treating these people for something inside them, something broken, an assumed chemical imbalance. . . . But the real problem, it's not in the blood. It's outside. It's us. You are a classic case. Textbook. Can we say antisocial personality disorder? Capitalism is the root of your illness. Tiller is feeding the virus in you. Probably been that way since you were a child, indoctrinated into the cult of the almighty dollar. You were a reckless, impulsive child? You were better than everyone else and you despised authority figures, right?"

The Serologist chuckles. "Nothing of the sort, Ben. I was a good person once. A common, normal person. This . . . this is about how none of your tests can tell you anything concrete about someone. It's all wishy-washy guesswork. Me, I'm the result of system catastrophe. Biological terror. I'm what happens when you strip away the analysis and the numbers, the charts and the textbooks, the hippy-shit theorizing. I'm what you deny. I'm proof that we are nothing but glorified machines."

Ben breathes deep. He closes his eyes, the lids pale as bone. "I can't tell you where they are. I just show them where the insanity really is. I just inspire them. Set them free, literally and figuratively. But you don't really want to hear about that, do you?"

"No. I don't care about your antipsychiatry bullshit."

Ben closes his eyes and says, "I don't know who set it up. I don't think they even know. Someone else outside. They were looking for a chance to make a statement. I know they talked first about an assassination. Then about a bombing, maybe a bank or a retail store. But then the kidnapping idea came up. They liked it. It allowed them to make a proclamation. Be . . . be artistic."

"Who set it up?"

"They didn't tell me. Really, they didn't know. Someone looking to do something. These guys, they don't take references. . . ." Ben goes limp. He shakes to consciousness in a quiver a few seconds later. Eyes snap open and teeth rattle. The Serologist steps back around to his side of the table, sips the cocktail and picks up a syringe. He asks, "Time for another dose?"

"I guess so." Ben drools deep red. He sees it and says, "That's a bad sign."

The Serologist asks, "What's in it for you since money is off the table?"

"Revolution." Ben's voice is fainter.

"Just tear it all down, huh?"

"Maybe."

"And what next? You've got me curious. I'm impressed by your commitment. Most people would be bowed over by now. Most people would be begging for a bullet between the eyes. Not you. You're on a mission."

"Just trying to prove my point to you. I'll fight with every breath. Maybe something I said will stick with you. Anything counts. How about that dose now?"

The Serologist walks over and sticks the syringe in Ben's neck, right where the artery beats against the surface of the skin. Ben flinches but not hard.

"Ben, I told you I'd let you live if you talk. You've not much left to chop. I want you to preach your message and to have at least something to catch the girls' eyes."

Ben nods and a crimson string of saliva hangs like a fishing line from his mouth. He says something but it comes out as mush. The Serologist leans in close. Close enough that his nose breaks Ben's string of spit. He whispers, "Go on. Tell me. What's going on?"

Ben's eyes close. He droops. The Serologist slaps him awake.

"Where is she!" he shouts when Ben's eyes snap back open.

Ben croaks, "She's in Jersey. There are three."

"Just three?"

Ben chuckles lightly. "Three from this year. More about two years ago. No one found them. Not yet at least."

"I don't give a fuck about them. Who are the three?"

"RPA members. An Indian guy, Charles. Cyclothymic. A woman, Jessa. Schizophrenic. They are lovers, paranoid, terrified. And Garfield. He's also psychotic. Last time I saw him he thought he was a whaler."

"Where?"

"Newark."

"Where in Newark?"

"A pool." Ben coughs.

"Where's this pool? You mean a pool hall?"

"No, a pool. A pool at the top. . . ."

"Of what? Top of what?" The Serologist puts a hand on Ben's shoulder and squeezes it. It's the oldest shoulder squeeze in the book, the one that says *It's okay, everything will be just fine, buddy.*

Ben is struggling. His breathing is slowing and his eyes are half closed.

"It's loss of blood. The stuff, painkillers, I've given you have made you drowsy. No worries, it will all be over soon enough." The Serologist squeezes Ben's shoulder again. "Tell me about where the pool is."

"Top . . . top . . . building."

"What kind?"

"Apart . . ."

"Apartment building?"

Ben nods. His eyes close.

The Serologist shakes him. His knuckles white on Ben's shoulder. He says, loudly, "Where is it, Ben? Tell me where this apartment is in Newark."

Ben's eyes flicker open briefly. He says, ". . . apartment."

"Where?"

". . . a . . . part . . ." And those are his last words.

The Serologist sighs and walks back over to the table. He sits down, sips the cocktail and smiles. He chuckles once and calls Kip.

"She's in an apartment in Newark. She's being kept in a penthouse pool. Shouldn't be too hard to find."

Kip Tiller says, "Who told you that?"

"An unwilling informant. Why?"

"The news. You watch the news?"

"I told you I don't watch the news."

"You should start. Cops have some good leads. They're narrowing this down. I just got a call from my lawyer, says for me to expect to hear something in the next eighteen hours. They are assembling a team. Do you know what that means?"

"I think I can figure it out."

"You can reach her first?"

"Sure."

"Good," Kip says. "There's been a change of plans. I'll need for you to do a little something more for me."

The Serologist pauses. "A change of plans costs money, Mr. Tiller."

"I'm good for it."

"What do you have in mind?"

"I think you might like it. I want you to kill my daughter."

4.

They're at Cody's pad.

A rent-controlled two-bedroom in the East Village and Tyrell, Cody, and Rufus are all lounging on a futon taking turns playing Xbox and watching CNN on a second television. They've had nothing to drink outside of decaf iced teas but the room is buzzing with nervous energy and sloppy small talk. Cody's just now gained a foothold in the conversation with his old art stories and he's about to get into the time he painted an old man and a goose when Laser walks in.

He sits down on the futon and sighs hard.

"You see the news tonight?" Cody asks.

Laser says, "What did you hear?"

"There's chatter about the police having some leads. They even put up a sketch of The Former Mrs. Stallone on the news. Not nearly as good as Rufus's—"

"Not nearly," Rufus interrupts, "but it's definitely her. Same eyes, same nose. Same hair like she had in *Beverly Hills Cop II* or even *Cobra*. If it isn't Brigitte Nielsen then this woman's her twin sister or a clone or something. Pre-boob job, of course."

"*Cobra* was pretty sweet," Tyrell chimes in. "Did she get naked in that?"

"Can we turn the fucking game off?" Laser asks.

Cody puts down his controller and turns off the television. Rufus leans back, annoyed. He mumbles something about "just getting to the fourth level."

"Fine," Laser says. "We're going to do this tonight, then. Met with Gustav and he's down. The cash was transferred into my account about two hours ago. We're good to go."

"Hey, check it out." Rufus points to the television.

Laser says, "Turn it up."

A reporter with gray hair standing in front of an apartment building says, ". . . *right, Melissa. What we're hearing from the police is that these people are former patients at the Tungsten Secure Treatment Center, a mental health facility in Syracuse. Apparently, and a lot of this is unconfirmed, three weeks ago a number of patients were released from Tungsten. All of them were in the care of a Dr. Ben Rollin. Anonymous sources at Tungsten tell CNN that Dr. Rollin has been reprimanded on numerous occasions by the administrators at Tungsten for what they called quote ethically unsound treatment unquote. There are also unsubstantiated rumors that he had released numerous patients over the past few years and some suggestion that these patients had been trained for what sources say are anticapitalist, terrorist activities. The bigger question remains just how many—*"

The TV goes black. Laser puts down the remote. "We need to focus."

"But?" Rufus squawks.

"But nothing, we need to run through the game plan again. Tyrell, you have that communiqué ready?"

Tyrell nods.

"Cody, you have people prepped to deliver it?"

Cody nods, says, "Yeah. Yeah." Then he disappears into his bedroom.

"Where's he going?" Laser asks.

Rufus says, "He said he has a surprise for you."

Cody returns twenty seconds later with two briefcases. He lays them down on the coffee table in front of the futon and opens them up and swivels them around for Laser to see. Each case holds two antique silver six-shooters.

"What the fuck are those?" Laser asks, eyes wide.

"They're pistols. Incredible, right?"

Laser says, "I'm fucking speechless. Are those antiques? Did you fucking buy antique guns?"

Cody pauses. It sinks in that Laser is pissed. "I wouldn't call them antiques," he says. "These are refurbished weapons and they cost a pretty penny, to be quite honest with you. A hell of a lot more than we had originally planned. I kicked in an extra two grand."

Laser just sits there. The look on his face tells Cody that Cody's life is in danger. Cody scrambles. He picks up one of the guns and hands it to Laser. Laser won't take it. He notices the mother-of-pearl inlay on the handles and grimaces.

"Look," Cody says. "These work great. I've been practicing with them this weekend and they fire great. Honestly, Laser, we can't just go blasting in there with retarded submachine guns or something. That would look so freaking corporate. It would be like a state-sanctioned attack. I'm just saying that we've got to do this up as much as possible. Everything. From the costumes to the gear to the guns. Right? I mean, right?"

He looks to Tyrell. Tyrell nods. He looks to Rufus. Rufus nods and says, "The guns are really cool."

Cody is bolstered by the encouragement. He continues, holding the gun up to the light. "These, my friends, are Colt ACE .22 LRs. Manufactured in 1936 and refurbished to working condition by a pal of mine in Houston named Randy Glahn. These guns are engraved. Very detailed work, eagles and flowers and whatnot. Even the barrel bushing has little hearts engraved on it. Not only can we take down the Captain with these but we'll look really good for the cameras as well."

Laser finally speaks. "I hope you're kidding."

Cody frowns. "No, Laser, these are the guns."

"I won't be using one of those," Laser says, shaking his head.

"No matter how good it looks. This is about life and death and I won't be caught with a seventy-year-old gun."

"Randy is a professional," Cody says, putting the gun back in its case. "He is world class and these are some of the finest weapons he's ever worked on. They will not misfire. It's insulting that you would even suggest that."

"Whatever."

"I like the guns," Rufus says. "I think they're going to be incredibly kick-ass. Good sign that they're Colts. You know, Colt was buried in an ancient—"

"Thanks, Ru," Cody interrupts. He sits down on the futon next to Tyrell and says, "I appreciate that."

Tyrell turns to Laser. "Why don't you just do what you did to that horse with these guys? I mean, shit, then you won't need a gun."

Cody shakes his head. Rufus and Laser say nothing.

Tyrell asks, "What?"

"Moving on," Laser says, reaching over and closing the open gun cases on the coffee table. "If the cops are sniffing around what we've found, then chances are they're going to be moving in soon. And I'm sure they're not the only ones who will move on this information. With what the Tiller family is offering, I wouldn't be surprised if every cowboy in a fifty-mile radius is going to be moving in on our catch. Let's get down to business. Move these fucking antiques and bring me all we got."

Cody reluctantly moves the gun cases while Rufus unfolds a large map and lays it down across the coffee table. It's a hand-drawn blueprint of the apartment building. Rufus then lays several sketches on top of the blueprint.

"Okay." Laser motions for everyone to lean in and look at the sketches Rufus has just laid out. "Leigh Tiller is being kept on the tenth floor. The whole floor is a single long room with a swimming pool. There is one entrance, a small foyer and access to an elevator and the stairs. From the tenth floor you can access the roof. Tyrell, fill in."

Tyrell clears his throat and leans forward, tracing a line along the southern outer wall of the tenth floor. "You all already know this, but we're going in this way, along the roof and then down the stairs and into the pool room. The Captain is fucking lazy. He sleeps most of the time in a leather chair near the elevators in the lobby. He smokes. He drinks. And he carries a speargun or maybe it's a harpoon. It's hard to tell."

"But he'll be easy to drop, right?" Rufus asks.

Tyrell nods. "Yeah. Should be cake."

"Good," Laser says. "Let's keep Cody's silly-ass pistols holstered. We all agreed not to spill any blood. Speaking of, what do you have for us on the other two, Cody?"

Cody ignores Laser's pistol dig and holds up two of Rufus's sketches. "We've got two on the ground floor. Osama, possibly Egyptian. Who knows? And The Former Mrs. Stallone, who, of course, looks exactly like Brigitte Nielsen. These two don't seem to do much other than talk on their cell phones and get coffee every now and then. They stand guard on the first floor most of the day. They go upstairs at ten, two, and eight. They talk with the Captain via walkie-talkies. I figure we cut the line to them and they'll be out of the loop super quick. Right, Rufus?"

Rufus nods.

Laser says, "Here's how it will go down. It's four now—at sunup we need to be in that pool. We go in via the adjacent building and walk across. Slowly. One at a time at two-minute intervals. Once we're all on the roof, we'll cut open the lock on the bunker to the stairs, make our way down and get the girl. We'll have about five minutes before we'll need to intercept the Captain. I want him dropped immediately. No questions. Tyrell, you're on Cap'n detail and I don't want you looking anywhere else but his tethered ass. Me and Cody will get Leigh and get her the shot—"

"What's the shot?" Tyrell interrupts.

"Tranquilizer. Anyway, Rufus will monitor the lines and the street. Once the Captain is immobilized and the socialite reclaimed we'll make our way down the stairs and bring down Osama and The Former Mrs. Stallone. Tyrell, you and Rufus have the Arab. Me and Cody will take the Amazon. Once they're trussed, Tyrell, I want you to call your friend and have him upload the video to our site. We will call the cops using the dirty cell that Rufus got and then head back to my place to watch the fireworks."

"You make it sound really easy," Tyrell says.

Cody says, "It will be."

"Look." Laser leans back and folds his arms behind his head. "The key to this thing is ensuring that we're all at the top of our game. This is the best performance you'll ever give and you'll need to give a thousand percent. We've been watching these goons for only two weeks but they operate like clockwork. These people are machines and if we don't tip them off, they won't change their routines. That's the key—we run silent and we run deep."

"I hate to bring this up now but Tyrell never did his bio and now there's no time," Cody says.

Laser rolls his eyes. He says, "Sorry, Tyrell, but that's your problem. It forces me to cut any and all mention of you from the video and the site."

"Can't I just be anonymous?" Tyrell asks.

"Like a crony?" Rufus chimes in.

Laser rubs his chin. Cody picks at his teeth. Both thinking hard. Finally, Laser nods slowly and says, "Probably will work. But if we're going to do that we might as well add a few more names to the list. You know, have multiple cronies. Like in comics."

Tyrell asks, "Who are we adding?"

"Just names," says Cody. "It's an illusion. Beef it up so it's like the cats who took Patty Hearst. That was only ever like five people but they made it seem like dozens. Good thinking."

Laser looks at his watch. "We have an hour until sunup. Let's get the gear out and start making sure everything works. I'll type up all the stuff we'll need and get it ready for the press. We need to work on a few other things. Especially Cody's fancy-ass guns. Before I finish, anyone else got any surprises for me?"

No one says anything.

"Fine. I'm gonna close my eyes for a few minutes over in that leather chair." Laser points to a chair in the corner. "You wake me in ten minutes and we'll get this party going. By the way, make sure Earl waits to hear from us before sending that communiqué."

"Right-o." Cody salutes.

An hour and five minutes later they're on the roof of the building across from where Leigh is being held. They're crouched down, clad in black with black ski masks on. They're silhouetted against the orange of the morning.

"I can't believe we're actually doing this," Tyrell whispers.

"Believe it," Cody says.

"I just hope they're on their normal fucked-up schedule."

"You're sure Leigh's by herself at the pool?" Rufus asks Tyrell.

Tyrell says, "One hundred. But we only have twelve minutes."

Cody has his antique guns in holsters under his arms. They catch the rising light and Rufus notices. He nods to Cody and mouths, "You. Look. Fucking. Rad."

Laser has a stopwatch. He says, "Three minutes and we go."

Tyrell whispers to Rufus. "Why can't we talk about the horse?"

Rufus whispers back. "He doesn't like talking about it."

"Yeah, but it was the most gnarly thing ever."

"True. Now shush."

Tyrell had spent the day working on his bio and he wrote at least ten drafts but none of them seemed right. He wrote it out longhand in a cheap notebook his brother had gotten him for Christmas last year and the paper kept tearing because he was writing so hard and so fast. Tyrell scratched out his childhood, the skate parks and how he was in a photo in *Thrasher* once. He bulldozed through his parents' messy divorce, how his dad used to beat his mom until she lay dazed in a corner of the bathroom. He spent maybe two minutes on his art career. Heavily exaggerated his tracking skills. Decided to spend more time on his fascination with boxing, wrestling and guns and how he took his middle name after boxer Tyrell Biggs. Then he chucked it all. Tyrell knows he isn't really in this for the fame or money. He's here because he's looking for the most radical form of expression he can find.

When Tyrell was out at the Ute reservation he spent a good deal of time shooting guns. He'd plugged a few squirrels and one time he got a marmot. There was something about handling weapons that had him jittery with excitement. Wasn't sexual, though any time he talked about it, that was the reaction he got. People saying, "Gun's just a penis replacement. You must have a micro." Tyrell brushed that away. For him it was the precision and the power. The fact that he could dispatch something—anything, really—from a hundred yards away with a bullet the size of his thumbnail was breathtaking. Past few months he's been working on gun-related pieces. All of them exploring the dynamism of gunfire. His profs at Allstrom College of Design aren't as happy with the work as he is but they've never fired a gun. Never felt that sting of muscle.

Crouching on the roof, ready to go, Tyrell knows that in a few minutes he just might be able to put his artistic imagination to work.

CHAPTER FOUR
Go time

1.

Leigh is on the deck as the light is fading.

It's timeless, this scene. It's something Leigh imagines has played out around the wrecked ship for millennia. And she's uncomfortable at the thought that it will be the same around the wreck of the *Lucinda*. The *Lucinda* will be just a rusting hulk in a matter of years, the weeds eating away at its hull. The crabs scouring the last bits of sustenance from her bones.

The thought actually makes her laugh and for a second, no, less than a second, the derelict is gone. In its place is a couch, a brown leather couch that's covered in dust and desiccated palm fronds. Leigh leans forward, eyes as wide as bicycle wheels, and just as she sees it, the vision is gone. The derelict is back.

Leigh smacks herself. She smacks her cheeks hard.

And when she does, her sight wobbled and watery, the couch is back again. It's not sitting in a continent-sized chuck of drifting seaweed. It's on the edge of a pool. Gathering dust on the edge of a murky, filthy pool. And when Leigh looks down at the

Lucinda, she sees not a yacht but an inflatable pool raft. A yellow pool raft that she's lying naked in. Her eyes go wider, threatening to bust from their sockets.

It isn't often that Leigh breaks out of her delirium for more than a few seconds. When she gets lucid the sea fades away and walls of the room become obvious. The *Lucinda*'s shining white bow slowly turns back into the inflatable raft. The mess of seaweed surrounding the ship just the flotsam of paint chips and dried leaves floating in the pool. Just like last time, Leigh's first thought is trying to remember where she is. And more importantly, how she got here.

These memories tumble in fast and furious, and every time this happens Leigh has to fast-forward through them. They're scattered, these memories, and totally unreliable. But the core events are there. The kidnapping. Being drugged and bound. Hustled into the back of a van and off into the night. Some of the memories are romanticized. Leigh never really gets a clear picture of the faces of the people abducting her. These images, they are like bits of film with no coherent plot. The storyline is about a kidnapping and possibly a ransom but who's involved (outside of Leigh) and why is a complete mystery. Of course, realizing these things—even as intangible as they are—means that Leigh is waking up from her drug-induced fantasy and that means that soon, very soon, she'll be visited by someone ready to knock her back into la-la land.

Today is the same as always.

Leigh on her inflatable raft, nude in a skuzzy swimming pool. Kidnapped and held against her will atop a decaying apartment building somewhere in an industrial wasteland. The thing is, her eyesight's blurry. Her hands are shaky and she's weak. Very weak. When the man comes, and he does quickly, he injects her with what Leigh guesses is a funky ketamine cocktail and it's only a matter of minutes before the *Lucinda*'s bow has reformed beneath her and she awakens once again in the vast emptiness of the Sargasso Sea.

Sure enough a man's hand appears. It comes down out of the sky almost as soon as Leigh's recalled something. Almost clockwork. She sees a flash of a hotel room and a woman's face. The needle goes in Leigh's left arm. Right below her wrist, it slides smooth into a hole that's already there. There is a drop of blood, dark red against her skin in the fading light. And then she is out.

Black.

How it started was that Leigh imagined the pool was a sea.

The ketamine helped. Leigh'd been in the k hole in college once before at a rave. It lasted a few hours and when she got out she was in an orgy. Not a good experience and had she known that her captors were going to use this particular anesthetic she would have protested.

Whatever else was in the syringe helped too.

Leigh had never shot up. Never wanted to though she knew a few people who had really gotten into it. There were a few times she'd walked in on them with the needles bouncing lightly in their arms. She thought it looked disgusting but the serene expression on her friends' faces was enough to see the appeal. She longed for that peace so many times. After the first two injections she didn't even notice the needle. It was like having someone run fingernails along her arm

Soon Leigh was seeing the South Pacific. She'd been to Bali. To Tahiti. To Indonesia. The ocean there was so blue and soft. It was soft like the silver sand that would accumulate between her toes when she hung her feet over the side of her dad's yacht, the sand like ash that would vanish as soon as she touched it.

The first two days Leigh sat on the steps at the south end of the pool and just put her feet in. It was Bali again. She was surprised to find that the water was warm. The third day she waded in, her dress bunched up around her hips. Just like in Tahiti. The fourth day she swam in her dress. The fifth and sixth days she shed the dress and swam in her bra and underwear. Indonesia. By the end of the week Leigh was swimming nude, fully aware of the man watching her as she did slow laps. There was a yellow raft in the pool and Leigh took to lying in it, staring up at the ceiling and imagining she was on vacation.

The atrium was large, at least two hundred feet in length. Outside she could only see rooftops. Black tar bristling with smokestacks and antennae, the roofs stretched off into the horizon like stark geometric lowlands. There was no detail there that suggested anything other than industrial wasteland. It could have been New Jersey as much as Philly. Beyond the rooftops, nothing but sky and the distant billowing phosphorous clouds of some remote factory. Leigh was, for all intents and purposes, nowhere.

An ocean floating in the sky.

The Sargasso Sea fantasy came pretty naturally. Leigh had read about it in high school. Her dad had loaned her a book by a nineteenth-century writer about a family trapped on a ship in the Sargasso for decades. The parents died; their children grew to middle age on a boat surrounded by weeds and dangerous animals. It was a lonely, sad story and it haunted Leigh.

No one checked on her except to give her the drugs and when they did she was usually asleep. She'd feel a slight tugging and would open her eyes to see someone in a black ski mask standing over her whispering something. Soon she didn't even bother opening her eyes. Leigh'd feel the warm rush of the drugs and fade out.

The city below the sea disappeared.

The walls vanished.

She was alone in the water and her raft became a ship. The sun beat down heavily on her and she'd shield her eyes to watch the wreck drifting so close by. Days passed until all was lost.

2.

Three minutes is a very long time under certain circumstances.

Laser Mechanic never understood that until this very moment. Sitting on the rooftop with the adrenaline of a hundred men pumping in his veins and he's only been up there two minutes. The last minute, that third one, feels like an eon away. For Laser, it feels like it will never happen.

He maintains his breathing.

He does not sweat or even blink.

But something inside his head is spinning. And when he goes over the plan, how they will get in and get Leigh, he can see nothing. Laser's usually good about visualizing. Whenever he flies he sits at the gate and closes his eyes and envisions the entire flight. Walking the tight aisle and putting his carry-on above his seat. Sitting down and fiddling with his seat belt and then pulling out the airline magazine and giving it a once-over. As the plane taxis and the flight attendants begin their in-flight safety presentation, he follows along with them in the tri-fold instruction manual in the seat pocket in front of him. He looks for his nearest exit. He says a few prayers. And sitting at the gate, Laser visualizes more. He envisions the crawl of the beverage cart. The one time he needs to take a leak and how his knees feel when he stands up. He sees the landscape come into focus below him and the stewardess coming by to tell him to bring his seat to the upright position. The feel, the twin bump, of the landing. He sees all of it. It comes easily.

But here on the rooftop, he can't see anything.

He has no idea what this means but he tries hard not to let it get to him.

Laser looks to Cody and nods.

The game is afoot.

They move quickly across the rooftop. Just the crunch of their shoes on the pebbles. The jump from the roof they're on to the Abako Apartments roof is a matter of three feet. Tyrell is first across. He barrels over the space between the buildings and slams down hard, a bit too hard, on the other side. Rufus is next; he's a bit less dramatic. Then Cody. Laser takes a deep breath and then runs toward the gap. He jumps and sees the alleyway below him and then a second later he's on the rooftop.

They move curled over, slowly, to the maintenance shed and then Tyrell pulls lock clippers from his backpack and cuts the silver lock off the door. They're in. The staircase down is narrow and metal. Despite this, it squeaks and squeals like it's made of wood. Cody says something about wishing they'd thought to bring a can of WD-40.

Bottom of the stairs is a door. This is locked. Cody steps in front of Tyrell and counts to three and then kicks the door down. He's good; it goes down quick. They are in a small hallway and ready for anything. There is no one there. All is quiet.

Rufus turns to Laser and gives him a look that says, *We okay?*

Laser nods. He whispers, "I don't hear anything."

They open the door to the pool and they are flooded with light. Sunrise. Everywhere on everything. It's like they've ascended to heaven. They're standing on a cloud, motes of dust swirling centimeters from their noses.

It takes a few seconds for their eyes to adjust.

Then they see the pool. It's different from the drawings.

"Rufus, your colors were all off," Cody says.

"The windows were filthy outside," Rufus says. "There's no way I could have guessed it was this blue."

"You had it orange," Laser says. "Orange like a bad shag rug."

The pool is big. It's five lanes and tiled blue. A few scattered chairs and a beaten-up couch sit at the north end of the pool. Cigarette butts litter the tiles by the couch. A few beer cans drift lazily in the cloudy water.

In the middle of the pool is a bright yellow raft large enough to accommodate two people. On it is Leigh Tiller, naked except for a pair of cheap sunglasses and a white visor. Leigh's obviously unconscious and a small puddle of drool sparkles by her right cheek.

"How much time?" Cody asks.

Tyrell says, "Five minutes max."

"Good enough. Let's roll." Rufus makes his way to the windows on the south side of the pool. "This shouldn't take me more than two minutes," he whispers to himself. Reassures himself.

Laser and Cody wade into the pool from the north end where it's shallow. The pool gets deep quick and they find themselves treading water twenty feet from the raft. When they reach it they both take a side and swim the raft back to the shallow end. Leigh is beautiful close up. Her eyeballs move frantically beneath purple eyelids.

"She's dreaming," Cody says. "More beautiful in person."

Laser watches Leigh's chest move up and down peacefully like ocean swells. He says, "She is amazing . . . but she embodies everything wrong with this country. Her father is the Antichrist and she's done nothing but spend millions on outfits for parties and premieres and turn up in some shitty movies and garbage music videos."

"Still beautiful."

"Three minutes, people," Tyrell yells. He adds the "people" because it sounds right. "Captain is due up here in three."

Laser and Cody haul the pool chair up onto the side of the pool. Then they wait. Tyrell is by the elevator doors and looking at his watch. There is a low rumble as the elevator comes to life and begins its slow climb to the tenth floor.

"He's on his way!" shouts Tyrell.

Laser pulls a syringe out and fills it with a clear liquid. He taps it twice, squirts. Then he puts the needle in Leigh's arm and she moans. Tracks dot her arms like ants on the way to a picnic. Rufus is over by the window scanning the street below with binoculars. "Nothing," he says to no one in particular.

"One minute," Tyrell shouts.

The elevator lights blink on to seven and then eight.

"He's two floors away."

Leigh is covered with a blanket and they're moving her to the stairs when Tyrell goes to open the door and it doesn't budge. "Locked. Shit." His face is blanked out with panic.

Tyrell tries the door again.

"I swear it wasn't locked earlier."

Laser groans. Cody says, "Kick the fucking door in, then."

That's when the elevator doors open and the Captain walks out, speargun in hand. Tyrell hisses, "It *is* a speargun."

The Captain stands there stunned for a moment. Laser and Cody, Leigh draped between them, Tyrell and Rufus standing by the door. "Get those guns out," Laser says. Cody pulls one of the silver revolvers from the holster. He points it at the Captain, says, "Don't even fucking think about it."

The Captain raises the speargun.

Cody says, "Don't. Fucking. Think. About. It."

The Captain, his bearded face breaking out in a smile, jolts forward; there is a whoosh and the spear arcs across the space between the elevator and the door to the stairs and slips with a twang through the blanket covering Leigh. Cody drops Leigh's legs and fires but misses. A window shatters.

Laser falls backward on the tile, his hands reaching under the towel, desperately feeling for a spear embedded in Leigh's flesh. He sighs when he finds the spear on the floor having passed cleanly through the blanket and missed Leigh entirely. "She's okay!" he shouts to no one in particular. "She's fine."

Tyrell kicks at the door.

The Captain comes running. Eyes wild. The soles of his sneakers squeak on the wet tile floor.

Laser pushes Leigh across the tile toward Tyrell and tries to stand. Cody fires again. A clang of metal as the bullet ricochets off the elevator.

Tyrell kicks at the door and something in it splinters.

Laser says, "Take her . . ."

The Captain leaps, his shaggy beard and bloodshot eyes making his face a mask of terror like something from before time began. He lands on top of Cody and the two of them roll across the tile floor and into the pool in a furious explosion of froth and filth.

Underwater, Cody sees only a kaleidoscope of bubbles and hair. Feels the Captain's fingers digging into his lower back. Cody doesn't panic until he feels teeth biting down on his shoulder. He kicks. Spins. Left leg breaks the surface. Back of his head crunches against the bottom of the pool.

The Captain gurgles. Teeth sink deeper.

Pain rockets into the dry spaces behind Cody's eyes. He bucks against the weight of the Captain. Pushes back against the straining form wrapping around him. Cody's throat burns. Lungs spasm.

He kicks again, feels the Captain tear loose.

Cody bursts out of the water. Gasps and screams, "Shoot this fucker!"

He's there only moments but long enough to see Tyrell finally kick the door in and Laser leaping into the pool looking heroic.

When Cody breaks the surface again, dry-heaving, the Captain floats facedown beside him. Laser grabs Cody's uninjured shoulder and gives it a squeeze.

From somewhere over Cody's shoulder Tyrell shouts, "Damn, dude, he pummeled you!"

"Fuck off, Tyrell," Cody shouts back. He turns to Laser. "You do a death pinch on him or something?"

"Clamped down on his arterial baroreceptors." Laser looks at Cody's bite wound. "Hope you had a tetanus shot."

3.

The Serologist enters the run-down lobby of the Abako Apartments and takes a seat on an achingly loud wooden bench across from a bleached blonde in a power suit with a walkie-talkie.

She sees him but ignores him and shouts demands into the walkie. "Garfield, you need to pick up immediately!"

She adds, "You don't get how super important this is right now."

The Serologist smiles at her. Waves.

The blond woman doesn't know what to make of it. She shakes her head, looks worried. Says into the walkie-talkie, "Garfield, can you please just radio down? Please?"

The Serologist stands up. He clears his throat. "Where is she?"

"What?" The blonde freezes.

"Where's the girl?"

"I don't know what you're talking about."

"You do."

"No, I don't. Sorry."

She goes back to her walkie. Almost frantic now. "Garfield! Garfield!"

The Serologist says, "Garfield isn't going to answer."

The woman drops the walkie-talkie and pulls a pistol from inside her jacket. She points it at the Serologist. She shouts, "Who the fuck are you?"

The Serologist smiles. He chuckles. He says, "I'm here to get the girl."

The woman fires. The Serologist doesn't flinch. The bullet misses by a yard and blows a chunk of plaster out of the wall. The woman screams into her walkie, "Garfield! Backup, quick!"

The Serologist walks toward her and she fires again and misses again.

She screams something unintelligible before he grabs her by the throat and knocks the gun from her hand. He squeezes her throat hard and she starts to shake uncontrollably. A man's voice comes on her walkie-talkie in a squelch of static. "Jessa?" She bucks like she's being electrocuted. Then she goes limp and the Serologist lets her fall to the ground.

He sits down on the couch where she was sitting and picks up the walkie-talkie. The man's voice comes on again, "Jessa, I'm just outside. I heard shots. I'm coming in."

The Serologist crosses his arms and waits.

Two minutes later a dark-skinned man runs into the lobby. He stops when he sees Jessa on the floor and then looks at the Serologist. There is panic on his face. He reaches into his coat to grab for something but the Serologist throws Jessa's walkie-talkie at his head and the man is momentarily stunned. Stunned long enough for the Serologist to put a screwdriver deep into his left ear canal.

The screwdriver in his ear, the man's eyes flicker, then grow dark like a television set turning off. The Serologist watches this happen and he closes his eyes and wonders what, if anything, the man felt. He lets the man fall to the ground. The screwdriver protruding from his head makes a plastic clack.

The Serologist sits back down on the couch and pulls his cell phone out. He dials and then leans back and sighs. Olivier answers the phone. "Hey, boss."

"Hey there."

"What time is it?"

"I think it's close to five."

"Anything wrong?"

"You remember that guy in Westchester that I did with the chain saw?"

"Sure. Couldn't forget that."

"He had this peaceful thing in his eyes, didn't he? I mean, right at the very end, there was just something so peaceful that came over him. I can't even describe it but it was like I saw his soul ascending to heaven. I think I just saw that same thing again. Do you believe that?"

Olivier pauses. Then he asks, "Are you asking if I believe in heaven?"

The Serologist says, "I guess so. I do. I also believe in souls. Not the whole ghostly mumbo jumbo but something more ephemeral. You know Maimonides, the twelfth-century rabbi and scholar, said that the soul is intellect. You can't weigh it or anything. I always liked that."

"I'm not sure. I used to believe in those things. But lately, I think I've been doubting."

"Why's that?"

Olivier coughs. "Seriously?"

"Yes."

"Well, you did just cut me up really, really badly. I thought I was going to die."

"And that made you doubt?"

"I don't know why. There were a few moments, when I passed out, that I didn't see anything. No light. No stairway. Didn't hear any angelic choir or anything."

"After this," the Serologist says, "I think I'm going to retire. This is my last job, Olivier. I just don't think I can take any more. It's just too profound. It's as though when I'm working I step into another place. A holy place maybe. Some place incredible, sacred. All I'm saying is that I just don't think I can do this anymore."

Olivier says nothing.

"I've got to go now, Olivier. I'll call you in a few hours."

The Serologist hangs up the phone and drags the bodies down the stairs into the basement. He doesn't bother cleaning up any of the pooled blood. He walks outside, gets into his car, and has a cigarette.

4.

While Leigh is all of one hundred and twenty pounds and gangly, they are surprised at how difficult it is carrying her down the stairs.

Rufus and Cody have to keep shifting her back and forth from each to the other. The Captain's nasty bite wound is freaking Cody out. He says, "It's like burning. Is that normal?"

"Maybe if you're bitten by a dog." Rufus laughs.

"Should have just let me shoot that dude," Tyrell says.

By the time they make the second floor they're shocked they haven't encountered the other two kidnappers.

Every floor Laser asks, "Where are they?"

He directs his comments to Tyrell. Tyrell says, "This is working like clockwork, Laser. They're downstairs. I'm sure they're just kicking back sipping coffee and chatting. You know. Exactly the way they have done for the past forty-eight hours. Don't stress."

But Laser does stress and with each floor his stress increases.

"Osama and The Former Mrs. Stallone should be here," he says. Every chance he gets he says it. "What the fuck is going on?" he says.

They get to the lobby and there's still no sign of Osama and The Former Mrs. Stallone. But there is blood.

"Jesus," Rufus says. "What is that?"

"Blood," Cody says, crouching down over one of the puddles.

"Whose?" Tyrell asks.

They drape Leigh across one of the couches in the lobby; the towel barely covers her naked body but her hair is drying and there is color coming into her cheeks. Tyrell lights a cigarette. Laser shakes his head.

Tyrell says, "Fine." He stubs the cigarette out on the bottom of his shoe and then drops the butt. Laser picks it up and puts it in his pocket. "This is evidence, you dumb shit."

Cody says, "Honestly. I don't care what happened here or where Osama and The Former Mrs. Stallone are. Let's just get out of here."

Laser says, "What if they're waiting outside?"

"I doubt it," Tyrell says. "This is bizarre. Maybe something went down. Maybe they cut and ran or there was some fight or something."

"What if they're waiting outside?" Laser says again.

Cody says, "Fuck it." He leaves the huddle and before anyone can shout or say anything or run and stop him he's out the front door. It slams closed behind him. No one breathes. Laser looks to Tyrell. Tyrell looks at Rufus. Rufus is craning his head to hear something. Anything. There is nothing.

And the door opens and Cody walks in and says, "Nothing doing. Street's empty."

Tyrell laughs. So does Rufus.

They're heading out of the apartment complex into the sunlight, Leigh between Laser and Cody, when they see a man walking up to them. He's about a half block away, coming around the south side of the building, and he has a twisted face and a trench coat and a rifle.

"Ho there!" he shouts.

"Shit," Laser whispers to Cody. They exchange glances. "Who is this?"

Cody shakes his head.

They pick up speed, dragging Leigh across the street to their car. Her bare feet on the pavement, kicking up pebbles. They ignore the man in the trench coat. They pretend not to hear him. Just keep walking. Eyes on the prize.

"Hang on!" the man shouts.

They don't. They reach the car and Laser goes to put the key in to unlock it and the driver's side window explodes. A shower of glass. Laser and Cody fall to the street. Leigh falls with them and Cody catches her head in his lap. They turn to see the hideous man running over, the rifle smoking.

"Don't fucking move," he says.

"Fucking move!" Laser shouts to Cody.

Cody drags Leigh around the car and leans her up against the passenger-side door. Her head hangs down, hair in her face. Eyelids fluttering. Laser stands up and Cody throws one of the silver pistols over to Laser and Laser points it at the man running toward them. "Stop right there," he says in as commanding a voice as he can muster.

The man with the rifle raises his hands. He holds the gun above his head. He's laughing and he says, "You've got some balls."

"Who are you?"

"Representative from the family. I need the girl."

"Like hell you do."

"No, really. I do."

The man lowers the rifle. Laser doesn't move but he closes his eyes and braces for a blast. It's all happening too quickly. He has no time to react other than to just be invisible. He closes his eyes and keeps the gun pointed out and waits for the deafening noise that will end his life.

The noise comes but not a bullet. The car is hit again. The rear tire facing Laser gasps and explodes. Laser opens his eyes and the man is closer now. He's smiling.

"You are either really fucking stupid or . . ."

Laser keeps the gun pointed forward. As the man approaches he fires and curses himself for not knowing guns well enough. The man doesn't slow. As though he knows he won't be hit.

Laser's errant bullet zings down the street.

"You better get out of the way and give me the girl," the man says. "I'll spare you. Just give her here. This doesn't involve you."

He's almost on top of Laser now.

"She's mine," the man says.

Cody shouts from behind the car, "He just wants the reward money!"

"We're just bringing her back," Laser says. "Her dad, her family. They want her back. That reward is ours. We got her fair and square."

"I don't give a shit about the money," the man says. "Go ahead and shoot her. Save me some ammo."

"We're just bringing her back to her dad," Laser replies.

The man says, "Shoot her. I'll let you live."

Laser, backing up faster, says, "She's going home. Back to dad."

The man chuckles. "Who do you think hired me?"

Laser blinks, takes the gun and points at the man and squeezes off another shot. Another miss.

The man keeps moving forward. He says, "If you're not going to shoot her, then you better hand her over or you'll be eating pellets."

Laser says, "You can't have her."

The man shrugs. "Fine. I'll kill you with her."

He raises the rifle but before he can fire he's knocked to the ground. The man falls before Laser hears the echo of a gunshot. He turns to see Tyrell running from the apartment complex, gun in hand, shouting, "That was incredible! I picked that dude off with one shot."

Laser looks at the guy on the ground. He's not moving.

Tyrell runs over to Laser and pats him on the shoulder and

says, "Got that fucker. Who is this Quasimodo anyway? He a cop?" He shoots the man again. The bullet tears into the guy's left thigh. The guy doesn't move.

"Shit. Shit. Shit," Laser chants. He grinds his teeth. "Wasn't supposed to—"

Tyrell fires again. A hole smokes on the guy's chest.

"You can stop that now, Tyrell!" Laser shouts. "What the fuck just happened here? Who the fuck is this asshole?"

Cody stands up from behind the car. "Can we just fucking go?"

Sirens squeal in the distance.

"You need to get back to your spot," Laser says to Tyrell. "Meet Rufus. I'm sure he's waiting."

Tyrell nods. Before turning to go he says, "I saved your ass, dude."

"Thanks," Laser grunts. He throws the silver pistol inside the car, right through the blasted-out window and onto the seat. Then he runs around to the side and takes a look at Leigh. She's still passed out. "I don't think she'll be waking up anytime soon," Cody says.

Laser gets in the car and bangs a fist against the steering wheel. "God damn it, who was that guy?"

"Fuck it!" Cody says. "Let's go. The car'll still run on rims. We can ditch it and take Ru's."

Before sliding Leigh into the backseat, Laser takes off his hoodie and wraps it around his hand and then sweeps the backseat clean with it. He wipes all the glass down onto the floor and then helps Cody put Leigh in. They roll her with her face against the seat and then Cody says they shouldn't put her in like that. That she might puke and choke on it. "Just like Led Zeppelin's drummer," he says.

Laser shakes the glass out of his hoodie and drapes it across her. Cody gets in and Laser walks around the car to the driver's side. The sirens are getting louder. The sun higher. Laser takes a look at the man Tyrell shot and he's shocked to see the guy sitting up reloading his gun.

Laser's eyes go super wide and he scrambles into the car. "That fucker's still alive!"

Cody sits up, propping himself on the dash, and looks out the shattered driver's-side window to see the man in the street leaking blood and loading the shotgun. "We really need to leave pronto."

Laser starts the car when another blast of the rifle shakes the vehicle. It's the trunk this time. Laser hits the gas. He plows straight and slams the car into a parked van. Leigh falls to the floor and groans. Air bags go off. Laser pushes the bag out of his face and looks in the rearview.

The guy with the messed-up face is limping toward the car. His expression is hard to read but Laser knows it isn't good. It's like pain and anger and it's like something from a nightmare.

Cody seems stunned. He's sitting there staring into the air bag.

"We gotta go," Laser says and turns and points back at the man approaching.

Cody looks and sees the guy loading his rifle again.

"Jesus, is this guy a fucking robot or something!" Cody shouts.

Laser feels for a pulse on Leigh. It's shallow but there. He grabs his pistol, pissed as all hell. Veins ballooning with adrenaline. "You get her out of here and take her to the rendezvous," he orders Cody. "Do it and I'll meet you there. I'm gonna end this fucker."

Cody nods and climbs into the backseat and props Leigh up.

Laser kicks open the car door and steps out and just starts shooting. The man with the rifle drops to the pavement. Cody drags Leigh out of the car and hefts her up onto his shoulder and stumbles with her down the street as fast as he can. Laser fires and fires. The last four rounds zinging in the general direction of the man with the puzzle face.

Laser keeps shooting until he's out of bullets. Until the barrel just spins.

That's when Laser runs. Running, like this, right now, it's like he's running in a dream. He runs faster than he ever knew possible. The feeling is pure elation. Laser tells himself that this must be a dream. That this kind of thing only happens in dreams. It's enough to make him laugh.

He looks back and sees the man with the rifle struggling to get up.

Laser's clearing parked cars when Tyrell runs up to him and puts an arm around his waist. They swerve over the sidewalk and around a corner to where Rufus's car is waiting. When they get to the car, Tyrell shoves Laser into the backseat right on top of Leigh. Leigh groans again but doesn't move. Rufus is in the driver's seat. Cody is in the passenger's seat. They both look panicked.

"What the hell is going on?" Rufus asks. "I thought we had this in the bag."

"I don't know who he is," Laser moans.

Cody says, "Nearly indestructible is what."

Rufus shouts to Tyrell, who is standing outside the car reloading his gun, "Are you getting in or what?"

Tyrell says, "I wanna finish that guy off. He saw us. He knows the deal. We gotta end him."

"Are you fucking crazy?" Rufus shouts. His voice high-pitched. It would be embarrassing in any other situation.

"No. We need to stop that guy," Tyrell says calmly.

"Where is he?" Laser asks. He's still lying on Leigh.

Rufus turns and looks in his rearview. He sees a man stumbling toward them a few cars back. "Holy shit!" Rufus says. "That guy's right behind us."

Tyrell looks up. His face becomes a red splotch. He falls and then they hear the report of the rifle. Rufus leans out the driver's-side window and looks down at the sidewalk where Tyrell is twitching faceless.

"Fuck!" Rufus shouts and starts the car. He grinds the gears and the radio blasts.

There is another shot. The trunk is hit again and the rear windshield is pockmarked but doesn't shatter.

Cody says, "You've got to be fucking kidding me."

"Is Tyrell dead?" Laser asks as they tear down an alleyway.

"Yeah," Rufus says. "Jesus."

Laser asks, "Are you sure?"

"We can't go back regardless," Cody says.

"His friggin' face was shot off," Rufus says.

"This wasn't supposed to happen," Laser says. "Not like this. No one was supposed to get hurt."

"He's not hurt!" Rufus shrieks.

Laser moves Leigh's legs and sits up. He looks back down the street at the apartment complex and the man standing in the middle of the street. He mumbles, "Who the fuck was that asshole?" to no one in particular and watches as the man removes his coat and peels a bulletproof vest off and throws it into the street.

5.

From: Strategic Art Defense
To: All media outlets

What you hear is true.

That whisper in the streets, the energy in the air, it is very real.

Leigh Tiller is free. She is safe and she is secure.

Strategic Art Defense has performed a mission in Newark, New Jersey, at approximately five AM today

EST. Not only did our operatives find Ms. Tiller but they successfully freed her without the assistance of local law enforcement or the Federal Bureau of Investigation.

Thank us later. Celebrate later. Now is the time for action.

This, dear citizens, is only the first of Strategic Art Defense's upcoming Revolutionary Actions. The wheels are turning, the rust has been cleared, and the world will change in only a matter of days.

We have five goals:

1. Art is/as communication—Art as/is insurgency
2. Freedom from oppression in all its forms and in every medium
3. Defeat of corporate rule and the embracing of All Access
4. Elimination of all static space
5. Ninja, by design, practices unorthodox war

From here on out you will see us. You will know us. Remain calm and enjoy. After all, we're doing this for you.

Your humble servants,
Strategic Art Defense

6.

The Serologist drags himself to his car three blocks away. He's leaking blood furiously but moves as quickly as he can; the cop cars are only a few hundred yards away now.

He settles into the passenger seat and opens the glove compartment and pulls out some gauze and a syringe and a small glass bottle with a clear liquid in it. He opens the packing on a needle and affixes it to the base and then stabs it through the rubber stopper on the bottle and fills it halfway. He taps the syringe and then pushes the plunger and squirts some liquid into the air. The way it looks, it's the same as every time someone does it on television.

Then he pulls down his pants and plunges the needle into his right thigh and pushes the plunger all the way down. He grimaces though it's hard to see beneath all the scars. He cracks the door and throws the used syringe out onto the street. Then he sighs and takes a look at the wound on his left leg. Where the bullet went in the skin is charred and black and purple. There is no exit wound.

The Serologist grabs a cell phone from the glove compartment and then leans back and closes his eyes.

"Dale?"

A thick voice on the other end of the line says, "Dr. Rousseau?"

"Yes."

"It's been so—"

"I need your help, Dale. Can you help me?"

"Sure. Of course."

"Can you meet me at the clinic?"

"Yes. Okay. When?"

"In fifteen minutes."

There is a pause. Dale sounds confused. "What's going on?"

"Can you meet me in fifteen minutes?"

Another pause. "Yes. I will."

"Good. Fifteen minutes."

"What are we doing?"

"Bullet removal."

"Where?"

"Left leg. Thigh. Inner aspect, lateral side. No signs of vascular injury. No thrill."

"Active bleeding?"

"Yeah."

"I'll see you there. You okay to drive?"

"Yeah."

The Serologist hangs up and puts the phone back in the glove compartment. He can hear the sirens and actually see lights of cop cars cruising to the scene of the shooting. He pulls his belt off and bites down hard into the soft leather of it and then moves over to the driver's seat and starts to drive. The car is an automatic so he keeps his left leg immobile but even the smallest of bumps jars it and the pain is incredible. By the time he gets to the clinic he's bitten his way through the belt.

Dale is waiting in the parking lot. He's thin and has gray hair. He opens the Serologist's driver's-side door and helps the injured man out.

"Thanks, Dale."

"Sure."

As he's walking the Serologist into the clinic, Dale looks closely to read the doctor's face. The Serologist notices Dale staring at him hard and says, "You knew about the accident, right?"

"Yes. I just didn't expect—"

"Me to look this bad? Hmm. My face is the least of it. You should see what happened to my soul."

Dale says nothing.

Dale unlocks the back door to the clinic and helps the Serologist to a room. He helps the shot man take a seat and then goes to get some supplies. He returns with gauze and dressing. With a scalpel and a stapler.

The Serologist tells him, "Don't ask me how this happened."

Dale laughs. It's a slight laugh. He says, "Why's that?"

"Because I will have to kill you."

Dale doesn't laugh. He looks at the Serologist and half smiles. "Let's check this leg out."

The Serologist pulls his pants down. The wound looks worse. It's pulsating.

"Looks terrible," Dale says. "What kind of weapon?"

"Handgun. I didn't see it."

"Did you see who shot at you?"

The Serologist says nothing.

"Right, no questions," Dale says. "Well, let's get to work on this."

A half an hour, three towels, and five packets of gauze later the bullet is out, resting in a metal tray, and the wound is sewn up. The Serologist admires Dale's work and says, "Excellent job. I should pay you for this."

"That's okay." Dale smiles. His gloves are coated with blood.

"You still working with the Pace Clinic?"

"Yup."

"And Dr. Hammond?"

"Indeed."

"You were the best nurse . . . Are the best nurse I've worked with. Ever."

"Thanks, Dr. Rousseau. That means a lot to me."

The Serologist pulls his pants back up. Dale hands him a bottle of pills. "You know you should really take these, just to ward off infection. It was a clean wound, but still," Dale says.

The Serologist nods. He gives Dale a hug. Dale smiles and says, "Hope to see you again. It's been a really long time, and after the accident I was really worried about you. None of us heard anything. There were all these rumors going around. You just kind of dropped off the face of the Earth. Right?"

The Serologist puts a finger to his lips. He makes a *shhhhhhh* sound.

Dale shakes his head. He says, "I can't just let you walk back out there, Dr. Rousseau. If you're in trouble, you need to talk to me. I can help you. Really. I can make some calls and—"

Dale stops midsentence. His mouth hangs open. A droplet of drool tinged with blood hangs like a pearl on his lower lip. The Serologist leans over and whispers in Dale's right ear, "I tried to warn you." Then he backs away and pulls a scalpel from Dale's left ear. It doesn't come easy, as deep as it was.

Dale slumps to the floor, his mouth still open.

The Serologist drops the scalpel on the floor and looks down at Dale's prone form. He says, out loud, "I really hate myself sometimes. Really. Really. Hate."

Then he turns and leaves.

CHAPTER FIVE

Drive

1.

They drive to Laser's apartment and he runs upstairs and gets a few things. Rufus leaves the car running. Leigh unconscious in the backseat.

"Tyrell was a good guy," Cody says, picking at his teeth.

"He was." Rufus nods. "Changes things, doesn't it?"

Cody angles the rearview down, smiles into it. "Contingency plans, Ru. That's why we have them. Tyrell signed up for this just the same as you and me and Laser did."

"We didn't prep for that, though."

"True."

"Tyrell was a good guy."

"Let's not talk about his flaws, Ru. He was a strong soldier."

Laser gets back in the car, tosses a duffel bag to Rufus in the backseat. "Earl sent the communiqué. Already, he fucking sent it. He was supposed to wait for us to call."

Cody shrugs. "I told him."

Laser, eyes burning. "You did?"

"Yes. Of course."

"You sure?"

"Fucking yes I'm sure."

Laser shakes his head. "Well, that asshole is fired for sure."

"What's it mean?" Rufus asks.

"Means that plans have changed. We've set this up in advance to run smoothly and I'm sure it will. We'll just cruise in. Make pit stops, pick up cars, stay with the Irregulars, and then head for Vegas. We need to be furious, less than a week. Other thing is that Leigh is coming with us, at least for a while. . . ."

Cody's jaw drops. "What?"

"Yeah."

Rufus says, "Can't we just drop her somewhere? I mean she's safe now."

"No," Laser says. "No. She's not. That cat we just shot it out with, that fucker that didn't go down after how many rounds? He's still out there. And her dad hired him. Fucked up but true."

"How . . ."

". . . do I know?"

"Yeah."

"He said it. Said he was there to kill her and anyone in the way."

"So . . ."

"So, Kip Tiller is one of the richest, most corrupt motherfuckers alive and if he wants his daughter dead, you can sure as hell bet she's going to wind up dead, regardless of whether we turn her in or not. She's as good as marked. We take her with us."

Cody says, "And that's not even the half of it, right?"

"Right. Your buddy Earl's communiqué. The cops are showing up at the Abako Apartments right now, finding Tyrell's body and trying to figure out who he is. They're finding the Captain and wondering who did him in. Finding rifle shells and blood spatter on the pavement outside the complex. But they're not finding Leigh. Not only is that hit man still out there but the cops are coming to gun for us as well—and we just released a statement that will make us look like fools."

Rufus says, "Looks like we're fucked."

"The anvil is hot," Cody answers. "White hot. This couldn't be better."

"What about her?" Rufus asks, thumbing toward the backseat.

"She comes along," Laser says.

"What if she doesn't want to?"

Cody says, "I guess we're kidnapping her."

Laser says, "Wait until she wakes up. Maybe she'll be down."

"Maybe," Rufus says.

"Cody, I want you to call Gary and make sure he's expecting us, make sure that everything in Mason is rolling. Rufus, you're on Boulder detail."

"What about you?" Rufus asks.

"I'm fucking driving."

Laser isn't driving by the time they get to Harrisburg.

He's passed out in the backseat next to Leigh with Cody's cowboy hat down low over his eyes. Leigh is snoring and Cody watches her nostrils flare ever so gently in the rearview mirror. Rufus is sketching in the passenger seat. Something resembling a deer.

"You're going to have to explain that to me, Ru," Cody says, craning his neck to look at the sketch.

"Just imagination."

"A deer?"

"I think it's a fawn."

"So when you close your eyes and just let your imagination run wild that's what you come up with. A baby deer."

"I guess so."

"And to top it off, Rufus, you're using the wrong fucking pencil again."

Rufus stops sketching and puts the pad of paper on his lap.

Cody says, "Ah, come on now. I didn't mean for you to stop. Don't have to throw a fit. It's great that you're practicing. Even better that you can work in the car. Me? Too carsick. I'd be puking my guts out within the first few pencil strokes. Listen, Rufus, take a look in the backseat there."

Rufus sighs, turns around.

"See that woman?"

"Leigh?"

"Yes."

"Uh-huh."

"We've got a fucking superstar in the backseat snoring right now. She is not only an heiress to one of the wealthiest families in the world but she's a bombshell. Smart too. I don't know how much you know about her but we're talking Gloria Vanderbilt brilliant here. This could be so much bigger than we even comprehend right now."

"What if she wakes up and goes nuts?"

"And?"

"I don't know. Just freaks out on us."

"I think there's a fairly good possibility that will happen, Rufus."

Rufus groans. "People screaming . . . Whew. That makes me really tense."

"Maybe she'll wake up and be totally cheery but I'm doubting it."

"Just saying it will make me really uncomfortable."

Cody scoffs. "Better practice plugging your ears."

"No. No. No, no. Don't ever do that. Worst thing you can do."

"What?"

"Plugging your ears. Worst thing."

Cody screws up his face. "What are you on about now, Ru?"

"You should just never plug your ears. See, your mind needs to receive all signals. Even those you don't like. Those that make you uncomfortable. Stop getting those signals and it can really screw up your energy. Energy gets screwed up and suddenly you're barely functioning. Like a sleepwalker."

"Didn't you just tell me you hope she doesn't scream 'cause you hate that?"

"Yeah."

"But you need to hear it?"

"If it happens. Front and center. Got to keep sharp."

"I don't know whether to smack you now or wait to hear what other crazy thing comes burbling out of your mouth. This, this is the type of stuff that drives me nuts."

Rufus shrugs. "There's science behind it, Cody. Lots. I ever tell you about my friend Jake?"

"No. Do I really want to know?"

"Probably not but it will help you."

"Help me what?"

"Break out of that rationalist prison."

Cody groans.

"Jake's this ecoterrorist cat from Oregon. He's figured out how everyone is being monitored and brainwashed with these wires. Part of me even thinks that the reason he bailed Jersey was 'cause some of the Feds caught on. I mean he probably had to split to save his life."

"Sounds heavy. What wires?"

"Here's the scoop: you know those wires that you see on the street. Black wires going across all the lanes. Usually they are connected to these silver boxes the size of toasters. They look like someone is running some power cord across the street. You ever seen those? They can just pop up overnight and within days they'll be gone."

"Those cables are for monitoring traffic, Rufus. It's how they can tell if the roads are congested."

"Yeah, that's what they want you to think. But if you actually get one of those metal boxes and crack it open you'll be shocked at what's really in there. It's not a bunch of gears and clickers.

No, if you get a real one, it's got a fucking human brain in it!" When he says this, Rufus's face turns bright, beet red. It's like he's held his breath up to this moment and when he says "human brain" it's like he's exhaling for the first time in minutes.

Cody goes wide-eyed.

Rufus misinterprets Cody's reaction as surprise. He races on. "The real ones are hard to come by, see. Thing is, most of the little boxes you see out there are decoys. Just a bunch of machinery chucked into the box. That's the way they keep the whole scheme on the down low. You've got to get ahold of the right ones. Then you'll find the brains."

Cody says nothing for a few beats. And then, "Why on Earth would they have brains in those boxes? Makes no sense, Rufus. None. Zip. I can't tell you how scared I am to be sitting next to you right now. I'm praying I'll wake up from a really bad, lame nightmare in a few seconds."

Rufus ignores him. "They're probably the brains of terrorists. Maybe convicted criminals. All I know is that Jake told me it has to do with mind control. Those brains, they're most likely psychically beaming stuff to brainwash us. Every car that drives over that cord, wham!, brainwashed."

"How does any of this help me, Rufus?"

"You start seeing behind things. You know, see the wizard behind the curtain. Changes your perspective on life. I think that you're just afraid to broaden your horizons. I think that somewhere along the line you were taught that thinking outside the box isn't cool or maybe not masculine or something."

"You're right, Rufus. Got me dead-on. The problem must be that I was raised in some freakish household where people didn't believe in ghosts and goblins and energy crystals and crop circles and Bigfoot and Atlantis. I'm glad you're setting me straight."

Rufus shakes his head. "Don't have to be a dick."

Cody sighs. "Can we please—"

Then he hits the brakes. Rufus looks around. "What?"

"There." Cody points to a planter in a parking lot. It's about the length of the car and has one scraggly tree poking up from the middle of it thin as a fish rib. "I'll get the gun from the trunk," Cody says, popping out of the car.

He reappears at the passenger-side window with what looks like a flare gun.

"You load me?"

Rufus reaches under his seat and pulls out a gallon plastic bag. Inside are paper-towel packages tied off with threads. They look like dumplings. Rufus hands two of the paper-towel bundles to Cody and Cody stuffs them into the barrel of the gun. "Lock and load," he jokes. "Think I can make it from here?"

Rufus looks over at the planter fifty feet away. "No."

"So little faith. You believe in brain boxes but not my skills. Shame."

Cody loads a shotgun shell into the back of the gun and then holds it out, aiming it at the planter. "Bombs away!"

The gun belches smoke and the paper-towel packets go flying, arcing into the sodium light and then down into the planter with a plunk.

Rufus claps.

Cody, getting back into the car, says, "Rationalism at work, my friend."

2.

Dr. Levi Rousseau dreams.

It's the first time he's seen himself in a dream in many months. It's the first time he has had a dream where he isn't broken. A dream that takes place before the accident.

He almost doesn't recognize himself.

He's looking in a mirror and he sees, behind him, his old

house. He also sees his wife and his daughter sitting on the couch talking. They are sitting and talking the way women sit, turned to face each other, eyes wide and heads nodding. His daughter is talking about something she learned at school. Something about a book. His wife is nodding and saying that she read that book as well and that she got the same impression. Dr. Rousseau is not sure what the book is or what it is about. He doesn't recall the name of his wife or daughter.

In the mirror he sees that his face is whole. Unblemished. And he sees that he is handsome. He sees something of his father in his thin nose, though his memory of his father's face is blurry. His eyes are bright. They shine like polished stone. His lips turn up. It is as though he is always smiling. Laughing.

He smiles and prays he will always look this way, this good. But after a second he realizes the absurdity in it all. He frowns and turns from the mirror and looks at his family.

Dr. Rousseau's wife and daughter are locked in conversation. They don't notice him. His daughter's brown hair is done up and his wife's is graying. She is wearing a blouse that he recalls buying her in Allentown. His daughter is wearing a tracksuit. Her skin glows.

He says nothing and walks upstairs. His home was old. Built in the thirties and remodeled twice. Once in the eighties when the former owners added the deck, and then once by Dr. Rousseau just after they'd moved in. His wife wanted to expand the master bath, add a whirlpool. He never once used it but he enjoyed sitting on the side of the tub and watching her read in the bubbles. She only read nonfiction, lots of stuff about people overcoming drug addiction and people reconnecting with families they never knew they had.

In the bedroom Dr. Rousseau pauses by his dresser. He picks a photo album off the top and flips through his daughter's childhood. In his mind he sees her first wobbly steps and he sees her swinging in the backyard and blowing out candles and running track and diving into his sister's pool in Santa Monica. He puts the photo album down and is troubled by his lack of emotion.

He goes into the bathroom and looks at his face again in the mirror and he expects to see some emotion there. But there is nothing. His face is a void. Soon he can see the cracks. They aren't in the skin. His eyelids are still symmetrical. But they are there under the skin. He can see them beneath, wispy spider lines of damage.

He leaves the house and walks down the street to the corner and comes upon a car accident. His car accident.

Dr. Rousseau walks up to the three-car pileup and looks first in the overturned green SUV. His wife is in the passenger seat. Her eyes are shut and she looks like she's sleeping. Sleeping but not breathing. His daughter isn't in the backseat. She's on the street a few yards away. She is lying facedown and he doesn't want to get any closer. He can tell that she too is sleeping. Deep, deep asleep.

The steam from the wreckage is caught in the air. Nothing moves. This silent tableau is so very peaceful. Dr. Rousseau stands beside the wreck and just breathes. He wants to cry. He wants the tears to just well up and stream down his face but nothing happens. He kneels down beside the wreck and grabs a handful of shattered glass on the ground. He palms it, feels the glass biting into his skin. That's when the first tears begin to form. That's when he wakes up.

The Serologist is sitting in his beaten-up Volvo station wagon across from Kip Tiller's house with his eyes closed.

There's a metal taste in his mouth. He pulls down the visor and looks at himself in the small mirror there. He puts the visor back up when Kip Tiller walks across the street in his smoking jacket. He has a pipe and his hair is down, shaggy on his shoulders.

The Serologist rolls down his window.

"How did that go so God damned wrong?" Kip asks.

"The unexpected."

"I thought you were the best. I was led to believe that paying you to kill someone was as good as seeing their corpse. That it was that simple. No going back, right?"

"Right."

"So where is the body?"

"Just a delay. Better this way, frankly. If I were a liar I would tell you that I planned this out. That this was just all part and parcel of my grand scheme."

"I'm worried. Can you tell me just what the hell happened? Television says there were other people there. Some body they found. That yours?"

"Yeah." The Serologist chuckles. "Some kids. I think they found your daughter and were attempting to rescue her themselves. I kind of got in the way."

"I'm very worried."

"Don't worry."

"Who are these kids? Any ideas?"

"Yeah. I have a few."

"They take her?"

"Yes."

"Where?"

"Not sure. I'll figure it out. Not too worried about it."

Kip just stares hard at the Serologist. "Not too worried, huh?"

"I suspect the cops will be releasing the name of the kid I laid down at the scene. That body, he'll lead me to the others. Happens every time. Chances are, they've left. Kids, they always run."

"Any ideas on that?"

"West is my guess. All the better, honestly."

"How is that better?"

"They are on the run. Lost in the wilds of America. Anything can happen out there. Here. The city. There are simply too many eyes. Too many ears. Everything is seen and eventually everything comes to light. Can't tell you how many times a body will float back up."

Kip nods. Chews the end of his pipe.

"And out there"—the Serologist looks over Kip's head—"out there people can be swallowed up by the landscape. Whole caravans can vanish and never be seen again. At least not until future archeologists start digging around."

"How do you know they've left? Maybe they just went upstate."

"Like I said, kids always leave."

"You actually make it sound reasonable."

"Reason. A good thing."

"And when do you expect to finish this?"

"When I stop bleeding."

3.

They pull over for gas in Clearfield, Pennsylvania.

Laser fills up the tank. Leigh and Cody sleep in the backseat. Rufus is switching the dial on the radio. He pauses a few times. Oldies. Hard rock. He finds nothing he likes and shuts the radio off and rolls down the window and tells Laser, "That guy back there freaked me out, Laser. Freaked me bad."

"He was interesting. . . . I'd like to know how he found us."

"With that cat out there we're going to need some serious guns. I'm thinking we should stop somewhere and get machine guns or something."

"We'll be fine, Ru."

"Still think I'd be happier with something automatic."

"You surprise me. I'd have thought you'd have a different take on this. . . ."

Rufus shrugs. "Nothing in New Thought about not using guns when you need them."

"You ever heard of Tsukahara Bokuden?"

"Nope."

"He was a famous Japanese swordsman in the 1500s. There's a story about him being challenged by this punk who teased Bokuden about his 'no-sword style' of fighting. Bokuden suggested that they go to a secluded island in the middle of a lake to have their battle so they wouldn't disturb anyone. The punk agreed. Bokuden rowed out to the island and when the punk jumped out onto the shore with his sword drawn, Bokuden pushed the boat off and rowed back to shore. He said, 'That's my no-sword style.'"

"Badass!"

Laser finishes pumping the gas and he goes into the station to pay. The kid behind the counter has a WWF cap on and a halfhearted beard. He asks, "Where you off to?"

"Nowhere particular," Laser says.

"Just curious."

"You have any fresh coffee?"

"Sure." The kid points over to a coffeemaker in the corner near the bathroom.

Laser buys two cups of black coffee. As he's heading out, the kid says, "You probably shouldn't be on I-78."

"Why's that?"

"Lots of pigs on the road tonight."

"How do you . . . ?"

The kid points his thumb back at a police scanner sitting on the counter behind him. Laser nods, smiles. The kid says, "Just not a big fan of pork. I could tell you guys weren't exactly fans either."

"How's that?"

Kid shrugs. "Look at you."

Laser looks down at his clothes. He can see.

* * *

Leigh wakes up just outside of Zanesville, Ohio. She jerks awake and screams.

Screams.

Screams as though she's being cut or burned.

Cody veers off the highway onto the shoulder and kills the engine and the lights. Laser plugs his ears with his fingers and Rufus awakens out of his sleep like someone just kicked him in his head.

Leigh, eyes bloodshot and knuckles white gripping the edges of the blanket, says, "What the fuck is going on? Who are you?"

Cody lights a cigarette and steps out of the car. Rufus does likewise.

Laser turns around to face Leigh. He asks, "Do you remember where you were?"

"Pool."

"Right. You were kidnapped."

Leigh nods, her hands shaking. "I remember that. You . . . ?"

"We rescued you."

"Where are we?"

"Ohio."

Leigh looks anxiously around the car, ducking to see out the windows as though she might recognize something in the shadows that line the highway. "Why?"

"We have something we need to do here."

Leigh begins to cry, her eyes blinking furiously. "Why? Why didn't you take me to my father? The police? What do you want with me?"

Laser says, as calmly as he can, "We won't hurt you. We don't want anything."

"Why am I here? I want to go home."

"You can't go home."

"I want to go home." Leigh's lips tremble. "I want to go home."

"Leigh, I don't know how to tell you this . . ."

"Please," Leigh sobs. "Please, just take me back."

"Your father . . ."

"Please."

"He doesn't want you back."

"Please."

"Leigh, listen . . ."

"Please, please, please." Leigh collapses in sobs.

Laser isn't sure of what to do. He hesitates, uncomfortable. Sweating. Grinding his teeth. Cody leans in the window and mouths, "Do something." Laser shakes his head.

Leigh tries to rub away the tears. "Why are you doing this?"

Laser pauses before answering. He thinks hard before speaking. "I'll admit that rescuing you was selfish on our parts. The cops were moving in but we wanted the fame of getting you ourselves. The money. We never meant to hurt you in any way. We still don't."

Leigh clears her throat. Sits up. "Listen, I'll give you whatever you want if you just take me to the airport or even the nearest police station."

Laser shakes his head.

"Come on."

"Can't."

"Why?"

"Your father doesn't want you back, Leigh. He wants you dead."

Leigh stifles a laugh. "Are you fucking with me? Come on, let's just go by a bank and I'll get you money and then you can just drop me off somewhere."

"Sorry, Leigh. We can't do that."

Leigh scoffs. "And why the fuck not?"

"I just told you that your dad wants you dead. He hired a hit man to kill you. This scarred-up guy we had a shoot-out with . . ."

"Scarred? Like how?"

Laser looks out at Cody. "His face. It was like he'd been taken apart and then stitched back together. Frankenstein-style. And he was a professional. Unstoppable. Took at least six bullets and when we left him he was still standing."

Leigh cringes. Holds her hand to her mouth.

"You know him?" Laser asks.

Leigh nods.

"Who is he?"

"I don't know his name. I've seen him with my dad a few times. Business associate but I always just assumed he was a crony. So many cronies."

"You believe me now?"

"I don't know."

"If we leave you somewhere that guy is going to kill you. And if that guy doesn't, then it will be some other guy. I don't need to tell you how powerful your father is."

"But . . . why?" Leigh cracks. Sobs. Crumples again.

This time Laser climbs into the backseat and pulls Leigh into his lap. She struggles at first but quickly shudders into place. He strokes her hair and says, "You're fine here. We're not going to hurt you."

Cody and Rufus smoke three or four cigarettes. Two or three cars pass. The heavens spin and the forest sounds croak. When Leigh stops crying she asks Laser if he has anything she can wear.

"The duffel bag," he says.

"My lips really hurt. Do you have any ChapStick? Lipstick?"

"Sorry." Laser climbs out of the car and Leigh dresses under the blanket while Laser, back turned to the car, stretches and rubs his eyes.

"What a fucking day," he says to Cody.

Cody, sitting on the hood of the car, says, "Wouldn't miss it for the world."

Laser puffs on his albuterol.

Rufus asks, "How much farther?"

"Couple hours," Cody answers.

Rufus says, "I'm praying Cincinnati goes without a hitch. Moon is gibbous, it's our time to really channel some of the energy."

"What energy, Ru?" Cody asks.

"The goddess energy. Creative force. Seriously."

Cody smacks him upside the head.

Leigh rolls down the window and says, "Get in."

The guys get in the car, Laser behind the wheel and Rufus in the backseat with Leigh. Leigh wraps her arms around herself in Laser's hoodie and jeans that fit surprisingly well. She asks, "Who are you guys exactly?"

Laser turns around, points to Rufus. "That's Rufus. I'm Laser. This is Cody. We're Strategic Art Defense. I am the chief operations officer."

"Is that like performance art?"

"Not really."

"What, then?"

"We're guerilla artists. You haven't heard of us?"

"No."

"S.A.D. We've done several highly publicized actions. One in Maine last year, Miami more recently."

"No." Leigh shakes her head. "Like what? What do you do?"

Cody clears his throat. "In Miami we overnight remodeled a McMansion. It was only just finished when we hit it. Two hundred Irregulars showed up—each with a particular, single repetitive skill that they'd been working on for several weeks—and then when we'd placed them just right, the place came together. Like a human assembly line. A smart-mob machine."

"I don't really . . ." Leigh shakes her head.

Laser says, "It doesn't really matter."

"Where are you taking me, Laser?"

"Cincinnati."

"Why?"

"We've got an action planned there. Your rescue just kicked off, essentially, our national tour. Three cities, five days. It's something we've been planning for nearly a year now. Several million dollars are—"

"I can pay you several million dollars if you just let me do my own thing. I'm not sure I really want to go on your tour. Sorry."

Laser shrugs. "I'm afraid there aren't any other options. Not if you want to live."

"You going to shoot me if I run for it?" Leigh asks. "You killers?"

"No," Laser says. "That guy will."

"We don't even know that guy is after me. I'll bet he's not outside right now. He's not clinging to the bottom of the car or in the trunk or anything."

Laser says, "We won't shoot you."

When Laser flicks the headlights on is when they notice the truck idling twenty yards away.

Facing them, the truck's on the wrong side of the road.

It's red, junked and shaking.

"Was that there when we parked?" Cody asks.

Laser shakes his head. "Nope."

The truck's headlights come on, dirty yellow, and it begins to creep toward them, the gravel crunching as it nears.

Rufus says, "That totally looks like that truck from *The Muppets Movie*."

"Lost farmer?" Cody asks.

The truck picks up speed. The crunch of gravel grows louder.

"We should move," Cody says.

That's when Leigh gasps, as though she's been hit in the chest. "In the cab!" She points at the truck getting closer, at the three figures crouched inside the cab. She screams, "Move it! Move it now!"

Laser starts the car and pulls it out onto the highway. The truck swerves over onto the road to block them. Laser grinds gears and punches the accelerator. The truck speeds up. Laser can see the figures in the cab of the truck now. A monkey, a penguin, a bear, all shabby suits made menacing in the sickly blue light of the truck's dash.

"Who are they?" Cody asks

Leigh says, "The ones who took me."

Laser glides the car past the truck, narrowly avoiding sideswiping it. As the car drifts by the truck in a cloud of dust, the bear sticks a tatty paw and a gun out of the passenger-side window. Cody shouts, "Down! Down!"

The gun reports twice, the windows in the backseat of the car shatter and the inside of the car is like the inside of a snow globe as bits of glass, suspended for only a hundredth of a second, rain down.

"Fuck! Anyone hurt?" Laser cranes his neck to see into the backseat.

Leigh and Rufus answer at the same time. "No."

Cody brushes glass out of Leigh's hair. "What the fuck is going on?" he asks.

"They're part of it too," Leigh says. "We've got to move."

Honking. The truck, billowing soot from its stacks, comes roaring up behind the car. The animals inside gesticulating wildly. The occupants of the car can hear their animal shrieks over the roar of the engine.

Cody says, "They're fucking rabid."

"How far are we from someplace?" Laser asks Cody.

Cody flicks on the dome light and looks at the map. The truck's horn blares, a rampaging beast behind them. "Maybe fifteen miles."

Laser pushes the pedal to the floor but the car maybe speeds up another five miles an hour. The truck, however, is moving faster than that. It's kicking up so much dust that in the rearview it looks like it's surfing in on a storm cloud. The animals in the front seat hoot and holler. The car barrels over a hill and below they see lights, an exit ramp. A gas station.

"There!" Cody shouts, points.

"I see it," Laser says. He pushes on the pedal but it's already down as far as it can go. His eyes burn holes into the lights ahead, blazing out through the darkness. He can practically feel the hot exhaust of the truck on the back of his neck.

"What are we going to do when we get there?" Rufus asks.

"No plan," Laser says.

Cody says, "Lose them."

"How's that?" Laser asks.

"I don't know, side roads and shit. Turn off the lights and just cruise."

"We won't shake them," Leigh adds. "They're right on our ass."

They hit the off-ramp going seventy-eight and screech out onto a dirt road that curves into a thicket of pines and shadows. "Still behind us," Rufus says. The road widens and joins up with a paved road and then suddenly, as if bursting out of the night, they see sodium lights and closed-for-the-night strip malls. Laser veers into the parking lot of the closest and scans the storefronts.

Rufus says, "They're getting closer now that we're off the dirt."

"What's the fucking plan?" Cody asks.

"Cody, where are those antique pistols?"

"I don't know. I haven't seen them since Newark."

Laser says, "There." He points across the street to another strip mall, to Bob's Guns & Ammo Superstore in the middle of it, then he floors the pedal again and the car screeches out, plumes of rubber dust clouding up behind. The truck follows and there are popping sounds, gunshots. Rufus and Leigh in-stinctively duck though the car isn't hit.

Laser shouts, "Brace yourselves!" He pushes the car up and over a median and then into a parking lot and then through the plate-glass front doors of Bob's Guns & Ammo Superstore. The car smashes into the checkout counter and the registers go flying. Rufus and Leigh roll out of the backseat and scramble down an aisle. Laser crawls out of the car with Cody, shouting, "Everyone grab something!"

Laser eyes the front doors and wonders why he isn't hearing an alarm blare. The truck idles in the parking lot. The animals remain inside and for the first time look calm, almost collected. Laser, over his shoulder, shouts, "You ready?"

Leigh, somewhere, says, "I have no idea what I'm doing."

"Just grab something."

"Everything is locked up."

Cody shouts, "Smash and grab!"

Glass shatters, display cases topple. Rufus yells, "I got a shotgun, someone find me some shells!"

Leigh asks, "What exactly is the plan?"

The truck stalls, lights go out. Against the backdrop of the sodium lights, Laser can see the animals getting out. The bear is still clearly holding the gun. The penguin, waddling over goofily, has a baseball bat. The monkey, what looks to be a stun gun or a cattle prod arcing brightly.

"They're coming," Laser says. "Get ready."

"What are we doing?" Leigh asks, crouched down behind a display case.

"Just shoot."

"But I have a machete."

"Then chop."

Laser ducks behind the front of the car. He cannot see where Cody is but Rufus is to his left behind a bookcase. Rufus gives Laser a nod; it's supposed to be reassuring but Laser isn't quite sure Rufus believes it. Rufus holds up a gun.

"Is it loaded?" Laser mouths.

"What?"

"Is. It. Loaded?"

Rufus nods.

Laser motions for Rufus to hand it over and then reaches out

along the floor. Rufus puts the gun down and spins it over to
Laser. Laser inspects it and then takes a deep breath and peers
up over the hood of the car.

The bear is first, stepping into the shop gingerly, the big,
bobbing head turning slowly, eyes fixed like its paste-on smile.
The penguin peeps over the bear's shoulder, then raises a flip-
per and points over in Leigh's direction at the back of the
store. The bear heads that way first, kicking at bits of shelving,
and as it passes, Laser can hear the person inside the costume
breathing hard. The monkey keeps watch from the doorway.

When the penguin passes close by the bookshelf Rufus is
crouched behind, Laser looks to Rufus and nods.

Rufus, not sure what the nod means, shrugs, mouths, "What?"

"Shoot. Him," Laser mouths back.

"What. About. No. Sword. Style?"

"Fucking. Shoot. Him."

"Which. One?"

"Penguin."

"What?"

"Just. Fucking. Shoot."

Rufus leans back against the bookshelf and wipes the sweat
from his brow. He looks back at Laser and shakes his head. He
mouths, "I. Can't. Do. It."

Laser's eyes widen. He bares his teeth. "Fucking. Shoot."

Rufus shakes his head. "No. You."

Laser mouths, "Fine."

He grips the gun, takes a deep breath and thinks about target practice. About the gun kicking holes into those paper sil-
houettes. About how easy dropping the big, ratty bird would
be. They are in a tight spot. None of them ready for this. None
of them prepared. But using the gun would be agreeing to defeat.

Laser puts the gun down by his side and looks over at Rufus.

Rufus, eyes bugged out, mouths, "What. Are. You. Doing?"

Laser closes his eyes and takes a long, deep breath. He wishes he could take a few hits from his albuterol inhaler but knows it would be too loud. With his nerves steeled and something akin to calmness coursing through his veins, he begins to crawl steadily forward toward the person in the penguin costume. Rufus, grinding his teeth, watches Laser's transformation and panic wells up in his lower intestine.

Then the pop of gunshots.

The penguin falls backward, puffs of cotton and lint ballooning out of its chest.

Cody comes running out of the darkness, shotgun blasting bitter fire. The penguin is hit twice more and liquid arches out of where its beak had been. The bear runs, firing randomly into the ceiling, before Cody fells it with a smack of buckshot and it crashes into the display case Leigh's crouched behind. Cody does a war whoop and spins toward the door where the monkey drops the stun gun and makes a run for the car.

Cody chases after, pumping and firing the shotgun and screaming into the night.

Laser shouts back to Leigh, "You okay?!"

Leigh says, "Yeah."

Rufus stands and stretches, his hands shaking. "How come you wanted me to shoot? Were you testing me or something, Laser? That was fucked up."

Laser looks to the parking lot where Cody has gunned down the monkey and stands gloating over the sprawled-out form. It's a sick and ridiculous image. Cody gives the shotgun one final pump and then raises it into the sky and blasts shot up into the heavens with a delirious roar.

Before they leave Bob's Guns & Ammo Superstore, Leigh removes the big costume head of the penguin. Underneath they find a woman, her hair slicked back, eyes closed, looking as though asleep. Rufus asks, "Do you recognize her?"

Leigh says, "No. She's nobody."

He asks Laser.

Laser says, "No. I haven't seen her before."

They do not bother with the bear or monkey.

Rufus is able to back the car out of the storefront and it runs smoothly as it rocks out into the parking lot. "That's why this is Quartz," he says. "See, nothing but a bit of grill damage."

When they pile in and pull out, Rufus turns to Laser. "You could have dropped all three of them with a flick of your finger, right? You were just testing us. We're the acolytes, right?"

Cody chirps up. "Laser could have dropped them just thinking about it."

Laser says nothing and it is only then that he hears the distant scream of cop cars.

It is immediately clear to Laser that Leigh has had some ninja training.

While she is not a ninja—she does not have the breathing down, she twitches in her sleep, and her eyes roll around like crazy in her head, which Laser chalks up to her coming down off the drugs—there is something notably controlled about her. Laser likes that.

In the backseat, wedged up against Cody's bulk, she looks frail but healthy at the same time. The way a bird looks all light-boned but honed. Toned. Maybe it's the time she spent floating in that mucky pool, but her skin shines. He decides she's studied Seido meditation. It's the measured breathing. Laser thinks back to when she was awake a few hours earlier, how controlled she was; he's sure it's Seido.

When Leigh awakens, Laser watches her in the rearview for a few minutes. Her eyes open and close slowly; she chews at her bottom lip. A few beats and Laser says, "How's it going?"

Leigh says, "I don't know what I'm supposed to say."

"Whatever you're feeling."

Leigh says, "Betrayed. Exhausted. Hungover. Sick. Hurt. Surreal."

Laser says, "Sorry."

"I was on a ship."

"Huh?"

"In that pool, I had these visions I was on a ship. They drugged me."

Laser's eyes move to Leigh's left arm, just below the wrist. The track marks. Leigh covers it up with her right hand. She says, "What drug does that, do you think?"

Laser shakes his head. "Some psychotropic drug maybe."

"You ever done acid?"

"'Shrooms once."

"This wasn't anything like that, like acid. This was Technicolor and so real."

"Where was the ship?"

Leigh smiles. "The Pacific, near Bali I guess. Just floating on this bed of seaweed and there were these beautiful little crabs. Their shells were like mirrors."

"Sounds beautiful."

"It kind of was but creepy too."

"You been to Bali?"

"Yeah."

"Nice?"

"Incredible."

"That's what they say, that when people are in danger or feeling threatened that sometimes the mind can just override everything and transport them to a comfortable place. You make up a place inside your head to hide in. To escape."

Leigh looks wistfully out the window at the dashing trees. "Tell me about your name. It's unusual."

"Dad's an engineer. Geoff Mechanic. He's friends with one of the guys who worked with Theo Maiman at the Hughes Research Lab in Malibu. Maiman was one of the guys who built the first working laser. Flashlamp and ruby crystal. Pretty basic. Anyway, my dad idolizes this guy. Wishes he could have been there. Been him. That's why the name."

"And the ninja thing?"

Laser doesn't blink, eyes stony in the rearview. "What about it?"

"Is it a joke?"

"Why?"

"I just don't associate ninjas with anything but nine-year-old boys and bad movies. I mean, do you creep around and assassinate despots or something?"

"It's a way of life. It's about finding your primal self."

"Oh."

"Our lives, we're just living through mirrors. Kind of like the crabs in your hallucinations. We've got these mirrored facades that show the world everything it wants to see, wear our selves on the outside. But to be a ninja master is to look beneath the mirror—beneath all the mirrors—and find your root self and embrace it."

"What's your root self, Laser?"

Laser pauses. His eyes focus out on the highway. When they return to the rearview they are softer, warmer. "To really know yourself you need to be aware of your failings. To embrace them. Deep down, for a long time, I was scared. Weak. The only way I overcame that was to accept it."

"Scared of what?"

"Failure, mostly. My dad."

"Scared of your dad? What, is he like mine?"

Laser laughs. "Sorry. No. No. He's a failure."

"You don't want to end up like him, right? Well, I can already tell you're nothing like him. I mean does your dad rescue heiresses?"

"I can see him in me sometimes. Sometimes when I'm talking to my mom or I'm just going about my day, I think like him. The way I handle my friends. Sometimes, the way I look at women is the way I know he looks at women. I hate that."

Leigh screws up her face. "How do you look at women?"

"Sometimes. Sometimes, I just think of the physical. Detach myself."

"Isn't that what most men do? Doesn't sound very unusual to me."

"I guess so. But it doesn't jive with me, with who I want to be."

"You a romantic, Laser?" Leigh leans in, her arm on the back of Laser's headrest. "A romantic ninja?"

Laser doesn't laugh. "You'd have to know my dad to get it."

"Tell me."

"It's a long story."

"Come on. What else do we have to talk about?"

"My dad gave up on my mom after twenty years of marriage and ran off with this porn actress he'd been wanking off for. He's kind of a slob. You know, the engineer with coffee stains on his trousers. But this chick, she's from Ukraine and doesn't know anyone here and my dad is like harmless. Totally harmless. He's also got money. It's all about her dragging him around like a puppy on a leash and the saddest thing is that my dad is totally willing. He's begging for it because she's got a hot body and she gives him sex. That's it. My mom's just a shell of herself. . . ."

"That sucks. What's the porn star's name?"

"What?"

"The porn star. What's her name?"

"Shira Rosenberg."

"Yikes. That's not a very good porn name. Shouldn't she be like Candy Busters or Rocky Bulges or something?"

"What about your dad?"

"You mean why's he want me dead?"

"Yeah." Laser looks back, eyes searching Leigh's face.

"I don't know. I'm an embarrassment. I can't think of why. Why would anyone . . . ?" Leigh starts crying again, shaking.

"Let's talk about something else," Laser says. "How about—"

"No. No. I want to talk about it. What did the man tell you when you rescued me, the man who my dad hired to kill me? What did he say?"

"Just that. Just that he was there to kill you."

"Those exact words?"

"No. I told him he couldn't take you. He said fine, he'd kill you with me."

Leigh slumps back in her seat. "I think I want to sleep now."

"Sorry."

"For what?"

"Everything."

"Don't be. It's just what it is. Everything's fucked."

Laser switches with Cody two hours later and he passes out with his head at a seemingly impossible angle against the passenger-side window.

Awake, Leigh asks Cody about the ninja thing. "Laser takes it pretty seriously, doesn't he?"

Cody nods. "He does."

"Do you?"

"Yeah, I've seen some pretty impressive stuff. Laser is like metahuman or something."

"You mean cold and standoffish?"

Cody chuckles. "He's just a badass. That's how they are."

"He just seems full of himself."

"You'd be full of yourself if you could do the things he can do."

"Oh, really?"

"For sure."

"Like what? What can Laser the ninja do that's so mind-blowing?"

"He can kill a horse just by looking at it hard."

Leigh busts into a heavy laugh, spittle hitting Cody's seat back. "You're shitting me. Maybe when you guys were tripping . . ."

"Oh, no. No. Dead serious."

"He killed a horse by looking at it?"

"He did."

"That's the most ridiculous thing I've ever heard."

"Believe or not. I've got a video of it."

"A video? Now this is a getting a bit sick."

"Kuntao. Korean martial arts. He can focus his energies on something and change their properties with his mind. When he killed the horse, afterward he was in almost a coma for three days. Almost stopped his own heart. Reverb is what he called it."

"I don't believe it."

"We've got a video. Him standing in this field in front of a perfectly healthy, normal horse. He stands there for nearly four hours just focusing his mind on this poor horse's heart and then, after about four hours and eleven minutes, the horse just goes down. Legs buckle and it's on it's back. Fucking craziest shit I've seen in my life. I mean, I didn't believe it either but I was there."

"That horse was probably sick. Just a random thing."

"You'll just have to watch the video."

Leigh laughs to herself, looks out the window. After a few seconds her smile drops and she finds herself scrunching up her eyebrows and praying to God it's not true.

"The man is a machine," Cody says. "A fucking machine."

4.

Kip Tiller is lounging in a hot tub, a joint smoldering in suds on the edge of the bath.

He sighs, puts a hot washcloth over his eyes. He's like this for maybe fifteen seconds before he flips the washcloth off and hollers for Marcus. Marcus appears, sneakers skidding and slipping on the tile floor.

"Yes, Mr. Tiller."

"You see that show today? The animal-rescue one, I had it recorded."

"No, Mr. Tiller."

"Don't. Very, very disturbing. I'm shaking here just thinking about it. Fucking people make me so sick sometimes. The things they can do to these harmless pups. Anyway, went down in Arkansas or some shit-stained state. We need to get some funds to the people down there. You know which people I'm talking about right?"

"PETA. Right, Mr. Tiller?"

"Yes, Marcus, the only people doing God's work these days. I want them to set something up in Little Rock if they haven't already. Get them whatever they need and remind them of the rules. I'm not in any mood for foolishness."

"Yes, Mr. Tiller."

"While you're at it, I'm going to need my Rolodex and a phone."

"Yes, Mr. Tiller."

"That scramble-faced dumb shit is going to fuck this up, I feel it."

"Yes, Mr. Tiller."

"We can't have that, Marcus. Shit has hit the literal fucking fan and unless this whole crapathon is locked down immediately, then heads are going to fucking roll. You got me?"

"Yes, Mr. Tiller."

"It's time to call in a few favors. See what the jackals can do."

"Yes, Mr. Tiller. The jackals."

* * *

Momma Gash has a pompadour, tattoo arm sleeves of pin-ups, Dolly Parton freak tits, and a nose ring.

She is sitting on an idling blue and white 1961 Harley-Davidson Topper Motor Scooter and smoking a nub of a cigarette across from a phone booth outside Timmy LaRue's Diner in Belleview, Missouri.

Momma Gash isn't there long when the phone rings.

She lets it ring twice and then turns off the scooter and ambles over to the phone. She answers, "Yeah."

The voice on the other end is deep. "You know who this is?"

"Luanne gave me a heads-up you might call."

"You want a job?"

"Sure, Mr. Tiller. This similar to last time?"

"Yes."

"I heard you had someone working already. That old Frankenstein you keep around. Where's he at?"

"Let's just say I've been disappointed."

Momma Gash spits onto the floor of the phone booth. Rotates the heel of her leather boot in the saliva splash. "What are you offering?"

"Anything."

"I want two hundred."

"Done."

"How many girls am I gonna need?"

"How many you have?"

"Five at the moment."

"Fine."

"I'm guessing this has everything to do with your MIA daughter."

"Sure does."

"You want her alive?"

"Not particularly."

Momma Gash laughs. "This is getting interesting. I won't ask."

"Good."

"How many in the party?"

"Four last I checked."

"Headed?"

"There was a shoot-out in Ohio a few hours back, some morons in animal suits were blasted. Cops haven't said anything yet about the deceased but it's a fairly good guess they were the folks who kidnapped Leigh in the first go-around. My guess is they are headed west. I've heard they always run west."

"Fax me over photos, whatever you have on them."

"These people won't be hard to spot, babe. Just turn on the television. These people, they love the fucking limelight. They're basking in this shit. Small-timers. Freaks. They don't know what they're fucking with here."

"I'll get her at the border, no worries."

"I'm not worried."

Momma Gash hangs up and struts out of the phone booth just in time to see three more tattooed pompadour women ride up on scooters. Momma Gash waves the women over. "Girls," she tells them when the engines have stopped puttering, "we've got a cunt to catch."

A cell phone buzzes inside Cleveland "Dookie" Richards's jeans and he pauses the DVD of *Cannibal Holocaust* he's watching to answer it.

"What?" he answers, snorting back snot from the sinus infection he's had for the past two months.

"Where's Rail?"

"He ain't around. He out with Perry."

"Rail isn't answering his cell, bitch. Find 'em."

Dookie flips the phone down and snorts and tells the young woman fellating him that she needs to split. "But baby," she protests. He shows her the back of his hand and she splits.

Dookie's cell rings again on his way out to his Mustang. "What?"

"Where's Rail?"

"Shit, you need to calm it down, nigga. I'm going already."

"We got a big deal, motherfucker. Somethin' that could make some real difference for the Black Sultans."

"That right?"

"Fuck yes."

Dookie starts the car, eyes his gold grill in the rearview and then peels out. "Las' time you had somethin' it almost cost us fifteen grand. Wha' da fuck you got now, cuz?"

"Gots a call from Tiller."

Dookie snorts. "Fuck that white fucker."

"Nah, this time he's legit."

"That fucker still owes us."

"He paid up."

"That right?"

"Yeh."

"How much?"

"Fitty-two."

"What's the extra fo'?"

"Interest."

"Shit's right. I'll call you when I gots Rail."

Rail is lanky and has a lopsided Afro. He's wearing baggy jeans and a Lakers jersey. His eyes are bloodshot, nostrils flaring, when he walks out to Dookie's car. "What the fuck you doin' here, nigga?" Rail spits. "Thought I tol' you to keep your shit indoors."

Dookie snorts, rolls his eyes. "Got a call, nigga."

"Who?"

"Tiller."

"Fuck that white prick."

"That's what I said."

"What's he want?"

"A job, I guess."

"He balanced?"

"Orlando says so."

Rail nods, cracks his knuckles. "Git Orlando on that cheap-ass phone."

Dookie dials, hands the phone over to Rail and then leans back in his seat and picks at his nose. "Git yourself a fucking tissue too, nigga. Shit's disgusting," Rail says, watching Dookie.

Orlando answers, "Rail?"

"Who the fuck you think it was gonna be?"

"Tiller says he's got some serious money."

"How serious?"

"Hundred maybe."

"Maybe?"

"Yeh."

"What the fuck he want to give us a hundred for?"

"Kill his girl."

"That kidnapped bitch?"

"She's out, running round with some artists or somethin'. Tiller wants the bitch dead somethin' desperate. Old fucker prolly jus' smokin'."

"Where's she at?"

"He said she's in Ohio."

"Fuck, nigga, we ain't in Ohio."

"Yeah, but he said she's headed west, prolly on I-78."

Rail runs his tongue along his teeth. His eyes narrow. "When?"

"Soon as we can."

"Jus' wants her dead is all?"

"That's what he said."

"Sick fucker don't want her head or nothin'?"

"Didn't say."

"Aight, call Tiller. Tell him the Black Sultans is down. Tell him that if his information is correct and all that shit checks out that we'll have the bitch dead by end of the week."

Rail throws the phone back to Dookie. "Sick fucker," he says. "What type of man wants his own girl killed?"

Dookie snorts. "Desperate man."

"Sick fucker."

Before Dookie rolls up the window he asks Rail about his birthday. "I gots you a sweet gift, Rail. Somethin' special for the big one four."

"Shit." Rail snarls gold. "I'm turning thirteen, motherfucker."

CHAPTER SIX

Action

1.

Cody and Rufus are the only ones awake as the car slides through Dayton.

The day is hot but they've got the AC cranked and the car is running loud. Laser has his head on Leigh's shoulder and has been mumbling something that neither Cody nor Rufus can make out but that they think may be either "shrunken" or "shuriken." Cody fiddles with the radio but finds nothing. Rufus raids the glove compartment and comes up with a Hall and Oates cassette. Cody shakes his head and Rufus tosses the tape under his seat. After a few moments of silence Rufus says, "I've made this list."

"Yeah." Cody is picking at his goatee.

"It's something I'd been thinking about for like two years but never got around to doing until right before we left. I didn't write it down but I think I have it memorized."

"And what, Rufus, is this a list of?"

"The most dangerous things I've ever done. It's organized year by year in a least to most dangerous format and it starts with my earliest memories. You know, when you're a kid the most dangerous thing you could do might look silly or worse, not at all dangerous, to an adult. So I factored that sort of thing in too. Not sure what to call it but it seems—"

"That would be perception."

"Okay. Right. That works."

"I should be worried about this, right?"

"No," Rufus says, offended. "Wait, why?"

"Let's hear it."

"Starts with when I was six. That was putting my tongue on a nine-volt battery to test it. Of course it's harmless. Just a buzz. But as a kid, then, it was like Russian roulette. At ten it was jumping off the roof of McClaren Elementary. First broken leg. Eleven was skiing in Colorado with my friend Warren Ostermann and his family and going straight downhill, skis straight, and slamming into a tree. First broken arm and last use of spleen. Thirteen was skateboarding and while I did some serious stunts that got my ass bruised, it was making out with Christina Schipper and her massive cold sore that makes the list. Fifteen was sex with Christina Schipper and, well, we won't get into it but let's just say dental dams weren't available at—"

"I get the picture. Moving on."

"Seventeen was serious Atman damage. . . ."

"Atman?"

"Soul. Self."

"New Age bullshit?"

"Hinduism. Nineteen was when I settled down physically but shit got tense emotionally. There was the Lisa Targatt debacle and nearly ruined me. Kissing her is one of the highest on the list. Twenty was telling my mother to fuck off. You see how it's changed, going from these very physical things to more psychological, almost spiritual stuff?"

"Right."

"So it ends here with this. This is all of it wrapped up together. Everything pales in comparison to what we've done. To what we're doing."

Cody stops picking and puts a hand on Rufus's shoulder. "I'm proud of you, Rufus. You've somehow been able to cut through the claptrap clutter of your addled mind and put this whole thing in perspective. It's a nice list but what does it mean? What do you do with it, my friend?"

Rufus shrugs. "Nothing, really. Just a list."

"See, that's the problem—"

"Hang on." Rufus turns around to see Leigh awake sketching in his notebook with a 4B pencil. She looks up at Rufus briefly and smiles. Rufus faces forward, stiffly. "She's sketching in my sketchbook."

Cody looks back. "What are you drawing?"

"I'm sketching," Leigh replies.

"What?"

"You two."

"Let me see that."

Leigh hands the sketchbook up to Cody and Cody hands it over to Rufus. Cody says, "This is actually pretty fucking good. I love how you captured Rufus's sheep back with those waves."

"Sheep back?" Leigh asks.

"Yeah. His hair. Looks like a sheep's back."

Rufus doesn't laugh but Cody does. Leigh says, "I took classes in college. Always loved sketching things. Mostly on vacation. I filled this one notebook with all these sketches of coral I did. Haven't really thought about it until recently."

"It's a good thing to sketch," Cody says. "Adds something rich to your life. Rufus is a fine artist. There are some things he needs to learn about the composition of his work but he'll catch on. You've got a good line. An eye. That's innate. Can't be taught that skill, Leigh."

"Thanks, Cody."

Rufus groans but says nothing and then Laser wakes up. "How close are we?"

"Close. Hours," Cody says.

"It wasn't supposed to happen that way, you know," Leigh says to no one in particular. She just says it.

"What?" Laser asks.

"The rescue. It wasn't supposed to happen like that."

Rufus snaps out of his stupor, "What do you mean?"

"That wasn't how it was planned." Leigh sighs and says, "It was a setup. I had myself kidnapped."

Cody slams on the brakes. The car comes to a stuttering halt on the side of the road. There is the telltale scatter sound of pebbles flying off into the night. And then just the hum of the engine. Laser looks to Leigh and his mouth is hanging open. He looks back at Cody. At Rufus. Both of them stunned.

"What did you say?" Laser asks.

"It was a setup," Leigh says straight-faced. "You weren't sup-posed to be rescuing me. At least, I don't think you were. The cops were. The FBI. "

"Did I miss something?" Rufus asks.

"I'm being serious," Leigh says. "Totally serious."

Laser asks, "How could that be a setup? You being drugged up and kept floating in a filthy pool? You're telling me that you wanted that to happen?"

"I didn't know how it would go down."

Cody says, "This is fucking ridiculous. You saying Tyrell died for nothing?"

"Not for nothing!" Leigh shouts. Her eyes are red, starting to tear up. She's shaking.

"How?" Rufus ask. "How could that have been set up? This is making me seriously anxious. I'm jittery."

"I paid for it," Leigh says. "I was looking for something. Some way to get my dad to notice me again. Love me again. I was at this party in Montreal. I met someone there and we hung out and were talking and I joked about how if I was kidnapped, maybe then my dad would be interested in me again. It was a joke at the time but this person I was talking to said he knew a way to make it happen."

Cody groans, "You're making it up, Leigh. No way that happens."

Rufus turns to Cody and says, "She's fucked up or something."

Leigh says, "No. No, I'm not. The more I thought about it the better it sounded. I called this guy I met in Montreal and he sent me to this random address in Brooklyn. It was crazy. Knocked on this door and then was led to a black car idling in an alleyway. Blindfolded and then taken to some basement. I knew it was a basement 'cause of the smell and that's when they told me how the whole thing would work. It just sounded foolproof."

"We're the fools, right?" Cody scoffs.

"No. No."

"How did it work?" Laser asks. "How did they possibly sell it to you?"

"It cost me one point three million dollars. And I paid it. They told me that I would be safe. There would be drugs involved. They said it was most likely some opiate. Maybe heroin. Anyway, this was all decided and paid for in secret. I never saw the man who designed it. Never talked to him directly. They called the whole thing a black-box operation. Black box because you can't see how it works inside.

"The deal was for me to be picked up, somewhere, sometime. Grabbed out of my car or my apartment or even on the street. I wouldn't know when it was coming. That bit was nerve-wracking. And I was told it would be real. No holds barred. I might be hurt. Had to sign a waiver about that. The deal was for me to be picked up and then held, maybe for as long as three weeks. And the deal was for me to be released, either that or rescued. I'm not supposed to tell the cops. Or anyone, really. I had to drop off a cherished possession—I settled on my grand-mother's engagement ring—and I'll get it back when this is over. So long as I don't talk, I'll get the ring back."

"Who was going to rescue you?" Rufus asks.

"They didn't clarify who would do the rescuing but it wasn't supposed to be you guys."

Laser asks, "Why? Why'd you do it?"

"My dad," Leigh says. "I want my dad to love me again."

The car is silent.

Rufus says, "That's heartbreaking."

"He hasn't loved me in years," Leigh says. "I'm nothing but a bother. Another box to check on his list. Visit daughter. Check. Pay daughter's bills. Check. Ignore daughter. Check. Used to be that I'd do almost anything to get his attention. That worked. It worked for so long. All the slutty bitches he used to date. I was the one who found them for him. All those women. He liked me then. When I was helping him get laid he liked me. But then it all changed. Dad just doesn't look at me the same way. He's checked out. He's finished. I want to have him back."

"Well, I think you got his attention just fine. Especially after today," Cody says.

Cody starts the car, says nothing, and pulls back onto U.S. 83.

Leigh buries her face in her hands, crying.

Rufus leans back in his seat, looks outside at the darkness and says, "You're better off with us anyways. Laser is like a super-hero and we're channeling some serious yin energy when we're all together."

Leigh knows something has changed looking over her sketches of Rufus and Cody.

The lines are different. There is nothing indistinct in them, nothing severe. She doesn't know if it's the pencil but there is something soft, almost wistful, in the images. One, a profile of

Cody at the wheel, has the edges so rounded out and clean that it looks like watercolor. At the back of the sketchpad are several sketches of Laser. A few slight ones, just outlines really, of him sleeping. But also two of him awake, these from Leigh's imagination. In one he is standing, facing the viewer, with his right hand at his brow, shielding his eyes. Leigh doesn't know if she's actually seen Laser in this pose but she imagines she has.

Looking at the sketch, something in Leigh breaks with warmth. The only way she can describe it is like when someone pretends to break an egg on your head with their fist. The way it tickles so deliciously. That feeling, it's in her chest. Around her heart. She doesn't get the same feeling when she looks at Laser (his head wedged up against the window, neck craned, face pinched); what she feels is something like sibling rivalry. Or at least what she thinks sibling rivalry should feel like. It is tight and funny and oddly competitive. This feeling reminded her most of sketching itself. Liberating. Frustrating. Mesmerizing.

Leigh started drawing in college. Never took art classes but studied art history for a while. She had a friend named Nastia who was a consummate art snob. They'd spend the night in Rhinebeck, dinner at Leonardo's and then a movie at Upstate Films, and have long, winding conversations afterward about the meaning of art. Leigh showed Nastia her sketches on one of those trips and Nastia, surprisingly, was quite impressed.

"There's something childlike. Primitive. Very nice."

"Primitive, huh?" Leigh found that a bit off-putting.

"Sells for loads these days. Everyone's buying it."

"I'm not drawing to sell my stuff. It's for me. It's hard to explain but it's something that I just do automatically. It's like a way of processing things, a way for me to kind of sort out how I feel. I do a lot of drawings of my dad."

"Yeah, those ones are creepy."

"I don't even want to know what you think that says."

"They're good creepy, though."

"I never actually sit down and think, right, now I'm going to do this sketch of my dad or of this guy I met in Econ. It's more like it happens on its own. Organic, in a way. I think way too much, constantly trying to process things. Conversations mostly. And when I do it my hands just start moving like on automatic. Like a trance. I never see the picture until it's at least half drawn."

"Like a Ouija board or something? You channeling spirits?"

"No. Just me. Me wrestling with . . . You know, the drawing has just become part of the process. In a way it keeps me sane. But it's irritating as well. It's weirdly impersonal. I've filled drawers with them."

Nastia said, "I'd love to see those."

"I don't think so. Sorry, I couldn't."

"We each have our own ways of creating the world."

And that was just it. Looking at the sketch of Laser standing heroic, Leigh realizes that what she's feeling is the giddy rise of something new. The way a sketch unfolds on the paper, the way the lines come together out of nothing, this is the same. Leigh is drawing her way into Laser's orbit. At the same time she's creating a space for him in her life. She has the overwhelming thought that she doesn't want this trip to end, that she can't imagine not being with Laser.

The thought makes her sick.

"He's such a douche."

2.

Olivier has to wake the Serologist up.

"Your cell's been ringing for the past half hour," he whispers.

The Serologist just groans.

He's passed out on Olivier's couch with a hypodermic needle bouncing in a lopsided vein in his arm. He's been asleep for the past five hours and Olivier has been cleaning the apartment around him.

It has been years since Olivier gave the place a real good cleaning. Despite the Serologist laid out on the couch, Olivier has been vacuuming. He's been spraying bleach around the kitchenette counter and the bathroom. The place smells cleaner than it ever has. Olivier never realized how musty and dusty things could get. He found dust bunnies the size of apples in the hallway closet and mildew rotting away the grout on the tile floor behind the toilet. He scrubs it with a toothbrush and despite the fact that he's missing fingers, he finds the experience rewarding, downright refreshing.

Both ears gone, it took him a while to hear the cell phone ringing. At first he ignored it. But now it's buzzed at least fifteen times since he noticed it and he's sure it's important.

The Serologist is difficult to wake. Olivier has to shake him and he's afraid to do it. "Your cell is ringing off the hook. I think this is really important. Come on."

With a groan and a spasm, the Serologist's eyes open. "What?"

"Your phone. I think it's important."

"Where? What's going on? Why does it smell like a pool in here?"

"I'm cleaning."

"What?"

"My apartment. I'm cleaning my apartment."

The Serologist sits up and looks around. "Nice," he says. "Looks good."

"Thanks."

Olivier hands him the cell. "I didn't recognize the phone number."

The Serologist takes the phone and looks at it. Eighteen missed calls. All from the same number. No voice messages. The Serologist stands up and stretches. The syringe falls out of his arm and rolls under the couch.

"How long have I been out?"

"Since two. It's nearly seven."

The Serologist nods. "I think I needed that."

He sits back down on the couch and asks Olivier if he has something to drink. "Just water is fine. Maybe with some ice."

Olivier brings him a coffee mug with ice water and a lemon slice in it. The Serologist takes two sips and closes his eyes as he swallows. Then he nods to Olivier and says, "Nice touch. Hits the spot."

The Serologist picks up his phone and dials the number of the missed calls.

Olivier sweeps around the couch, making sure to get the syringe, and listens in on the conversation. The Serologist paces as he speaks. He lights a cigarette and ashes it on the floor and Olivier dutifully sweeps it up, following. When the Serologist hangs up, Olivier puts the broom down and asks, "So?"

"'They're headed west."

"Who?"

"The kids that took the girl."

"You going after them?"

"No," the Serologist says. "I'm going after her. Olivier, how much do I owe you?"

"For what?"

"This gig. Last gig. When did I pay you last?"

"You gave me a credit card. I've just been using that."

"Right." The Serologist nods. "Right. I think I remember that."

"Should I stop using it?"

"No. Go right ahead. It's paid for. I have a strong feeling that this is going to turn into something more. I'm assuming it's my last run."

Olivier frowns. "Why?"

"Just in the air. The situation is pregnant with possibility. I don't like the way it's gone so far and I'm not expecting it to get any easier. I haven't left the East Coast in a long, long time, Olivier. Getting out there. Hunting on that scale. It's not going to be easy. Truth is, I don't think I'm cut out for the chase anymore."

"You don't think you're coming back?"

The Serologist looks hard at Olivier. Smirks. He says, "Yeah."

"I'll miss you."

"Really?"

"Yeah. And not just the paycheck. I don't know why."

"I'm an evil bastard, Olivier. Look what I did to you."

Olivier reaches up and touches where his ears were. He smiles. "You are an evil, evil man. And you've been horrible to me. But I guess I'll miss that attention. You noticed me. Let me run with you. That means something."

"It does."

The Serologist thinks for a second and then reaches into his pants pockets and pulls out a set of keys. He puts them on the couch. Says, "These are the keys to my apartment. The place is paid for."

Olivier quietly says, "Thank you." He pockets the keys and nods. Just as the Serologist opens the front door, Olivier clears his throat loudly. He says, "I got a call today from Marcus."

"And what's your boyfriend have for us?"

"Tiller's called out a favor. He doesn't think you can do this."

"Of course he doesn't."

"You're not worried?"

"Not at all."

"But he's made a lot of calls, some people I've never heard of."

"Just the running dogs, Olivier. And you know what I make of dogs, right?"

"Right."

3.

They crash with Gary and Elise, street artists with a thing for murals, in the Main Street neighborhood of Cincinnati.

Gary is more than welcoming. "Right, sorry. Hey man, heard about what went down. What a loss. Never met Tyrell but, you know, I'd heard about him before."

"He was a good guy."

"Yeah, shit. Heavy."

Gary is tall and awkward, wears hoodies and seems to be perpetually trying to grow a goatee. Elise is thin, partial to baby-doll dresses and black jeans. She has a tattoo of a sparrow on the back of her neck. They argue constantly but are friendly apart from each other.

"We didn't expect you until dinner," Gary says, walking them in. Elise helps a stumbling Leigh upstairs to a spare room furnished with a futon and a mirror. Gary adds, "We've been in the middle of a major argument so the house is kind of a mess. Sorry."

The front room, the couches are covered in clothing, takeaway food containers from Whole Foods and Lou's Organic Pizza, and comic books. Gary says, picking up and piling things in his arms, "She basically emptied out my closet, all these comics, old magazines, tattoo catalogs. Stuff I was saving for my kids she just unceremoniously dumps out here. Got her back last night and threw her porn collection in the recycle bin. Not sure if she's seen that yet."

Lasers asks, "You sure it's cool that we're staying?"

"Yeah, totally."

Cody says, "We don't want to impose . . . seeing as how . . . you know."

Gary stops picking up stuff, smiles. "Dudes, I cannot tell you how psyched I am that you're here. Elise is thrilled too. Promise that we won't fight around you guys. While you're here, we bury the hatchet and get to work. Speaking of, your e-mail was cryptic."

Laser says, "Plans have changed slightly."

Gary laughs. "Only slightly, huh? I expected to see you roll in here in style, all sorts of fanfare on the news and shit. Guess things went super wrong."

Rufus says, "Like Laser says, plans have changed."

Elise comes downstairs. "I can't believe we've got Leigh Tiller sleeping in the spare room. How crazy is it that this billionaire fashionista is totally crashed on the futon that Gary and I have make-up sex on?"

Gary grins ear to ear.

Elise shakes her head, turns to Laser. "I don't get it. Why?"

"She had nowhere else to go."

"Didn't sound like that from the press release."

"That was a mistake."

"What part?" Elise scoffs.

"The timing. It wasn't supposed to happen this way but—"

Gary interrupts, "Whatever. Doesn't matter now. Does it? Let's just move on."

"Just saying," Elise says.

Gary says, "Fine."

"Kind of a big deal and all . . ."

Gary says, "Fine!"

"I wouldn't have—"

Gary says, "Would you please shut the fuck up?"

"We're going to just go get some stuff out at the car," Laser says. Cody and Rufus head out with him and they sit on a neighbor's stoop and have cigarettes. "They've gotten worse," Laser says. "Could this get any more fucked up?"

Leigh is still asleep when they sit down to a dinner of lentils and soy burgers. Laser answers questions and slowly brings the conversation around to the plan of action for Cincinnati. "So what have you heard?" Laser asks.

Elise says, "Craziness. As you might expect, the cable news is covering this thing every fifteen minutes. There's some new breakthrough every hour. Honestly, the jury's still out. No one can decide if you guys are worse than the kidnappers or just more of the same."

"Not better, though?" Rufus asks, chewing.

"Sorry."

Gary says, "They don't have your photos up or anything. They've only figured out who Tyrell was this afternoon, got his mug up on there in the corner of the screen like he was some sort of fucking terrorist or something."

"Things are going to heat up," Laser says. "This is just beginning and I would be lying if I told you that by the end of this we won't look like maniacs."

Elise puts her wineglass down. She looks concerned. "What exactly do you mean?"

"This is a revolution," Cody says. "Eggs will be broken."

Gary laughs nervously. "Okay. Eggs. That's fun."

Elise says, "Maniacs how?"

"The straight and narrow aren't going to see the whole picture right off. They'll maybe catch a glimpse here or there. Maybe see one side of what we're doing. You ever heard of Moses Elias?"

Gary shrugs. Elise shakes her head.

"What Elias Moses did in the late seventies was a revelation. He took art out into the street, made it almost impossible to tease out from reality. It was action. It was movement. It was edgy and it was obsessive. His most infamous piece, *Lost Among the Hours,* consisted of ten manila envelopes delivered, seemingly at random, to four media outlets. The contents of the envelopes were photographs of various network executives in compromising positions with typed-up death threats and in one

case a severed finger (later determined to have come from
Moses's own left hand). Moses served two years in prison for the
stunt. Three surviving envelopes were sold in 1992 at Sotheby's
for approximately six million dollars. *Calling All Submarines* was
a film, ninety-eight minutes long, shown only once to five people (all well-known art critics who paid five thousand dollars
each to see it) in 1986. The one condition of the screening was
that the people in attendance could not tell anyone what they
had seen outside of a single word. The five words were 'phantas-
magoric,' 'carnivore,' 'disorienting,' 'furious,' and 'post-apocalyp-
tic.' Moses burned the print and original camera negative in the
parking lot. Many times, with Moses's exhibits, people thought
they saw his art but hadn't. One piece, *WALL-k Around* in 1978,
was a walking tour of Pittsburgh. Attendees got tickets and were
led by Moses down an alleyway, through a construction site and
finally up a fire escape for wine and cheese on a rooftop. When
asked what pieces they noticed along the way, most pointed out
graffiti or random junk objects, none of which were Moses's.
He would nod and smile and take notes. Every week the tour
changed, a different location, different people, but he never
had any work on exhibit during any of the tours. The whole
thing was a hoax. Moses said, 'People don't really see art. They
just think they do.' Same here, but in reverse, the people who
will see what we're doing won't think they're seeing art but they
will be."

"What you guys pulled off in that lunchroom was stellar,"
Gary says.

"Thanks."

Cody says, "That took weeks of location work."

"Mason took months," Laser adds. "How many people have you
been able to pull together?"

Elise looks to Gary. Gary says, " 'Bout half."

Laser frowns. "It'll have to do."

Elise says, "We've been every day this week since we got your e-mail. Mostly it's people shopping, businessmen on their lunch hours. Let's hear it."

"It'll be a whiz mob, like Miami. Only this time we won't be celebrating."

Elise screws up her face. "Whiz mob?"

Gary says, "She wasn't around for Miami."

"We're in the Age of Symbiosis," Rufus adds. "House of the Unconscious."

Cody explains. "You've heard of flash mobs and smart mobs. Same things. Essentially a group of people who spontaneously gather together. In Tokyo kids will text each other when a starlet is rumored to be at a club and then hundreds of them will suddenly show up. Smart because the mobs are using high tech to get the info out. Lot of performance art is done this way, interactive stuff. It's all about the loss of the individual, hive mentality, and most of the time the stuff the mob can accomplish is pretty simple. It's not really that smart. But whiz mobs are the next step up. They're genius mobs—they get things done."

Laser says, "We've spent the last five weeks prepping three hundred and fifteen Strategic Art Defense Irregulars for this. Tomorrow morning, early, at around four, they show up. Teams will assemble and I'm sure that by eight they'll be done and scattered. Then the reenactors come in and they'll be there until the cops can shut it down, which will undoubtedly happen by midday but not before the camera crews have been there."

"Gary mentioned something about sewage," Elise says.

"Raw," Cody says. "Only the best for America."

Leigh wakes up at two in the morning and it takes her a few seconds to remember where she is.

She hears snatches of conversation downstairs. Hungry, she heads down cautiously. Every step she thinks about escaping but knows she can't. Knows, somehow, she shouldn't. Laser is asleep on the couch. His eyes closed softly, he looks serene. Leigh pauses for a second to watch him and chuckles seeing how tightly he's holding the edges of the blanket. Like a baby.

Cody, Rufus, and Gary are sprawled out in the kitchen, surrounded by beer cans and ashtrays with smoldering butts. They are laughing when she walks in but quickly stop. Leigh waves, then shrugs and has a seat in the one empty chair. Without speaking Cody pops open a beer and slides it across the table to her. She takes a sip and coughs. Cody smiles.

"Hope we didn't wake you."

"No, you didn't."

Gary says, "Sorry, that mattress kind of sucks. We need a new one something bad. Can't tell you how many times we've left the house with the express purpose of picking one up but it just doesn't come together. . . ."

"It's fine." Leigh takes another sip. "Don't let me interrupt."

Gary says, "Cody was just telling us the best place to meet women. He says he gets his best dates and best lays at Target."

"I'll admit I'm intrigued," Leigh says. "I'll regret it, right?"

Cody nods.

"Can you at least tone it down for me?"

Cody says, "I'll try."

"Let's hear it, then. Best places to meet women."

Rufus adds, "And get laid."

Leigh nods slowly. "Right. This is totally going to amaze me."

"First is Target," Cody says. "Second is Whole Foods. Third is probably Kmart, and I'll get to why in a minute. Fourth is Albertsons. Fifth is definitely Costco. You see it's really a personal preference thing. It all depends on the type of woman you like to hit on. Me, I'm partial to the overeducated, understimulated type. That type frequents Target and I'm speaking specifically here about the Target Greatlands stores. The ones with the supermarket attached. It's a bit overpriced but it's trendy in a way that none of the others are. There's just something hip and edgy about

Target. Not hip and edgy in the sense that it's exclusive, mind you. Just enough to feel exclusive. At least exclusive compared to Wal-Mart."

Rufus says, "So far, so good."

Leigh snickers.

Cody smiles. "Let me give you an example. I met Lucy at a Target in Pennington about five months back. She's thin, long black hair tied up all hastily and half of it hanging in her face. Really nice pouty lips and a butterfly tattoo on her neck. She looked just trashy enough to be wealthy. That or overeducated. Turns out she had a PhD in physiology and was barely scraping by. We chatted over Starbucks about leg cramps and ended up fucking in the back of her '89 Civic. A really good lay and she didn't expect a callback."

Rufus shakes his head. "You kill me."

Leigh groans. It's audible, but neither Cody nor Rufus responds.

"Whole Foods is kinda like Target but on a whole other level," Cody continues. "The women there are certainly well-to-do and overeducated. That's a given. They're stay-at-home moms itching for something more interesting in their lives than cookouts and yoga. Women dying for conversation that has nothing to do with diapers or retirement plans. They drive nice cars and wear sunglasses indoors on cloudy days. Either that or they're vegans who spend their entire paychecks at Whole Foods and live in really tiny apartments. Really tiny apartments that reek of self-pity and pain. I know 'cause I've fucked both."

"And Kmart. Please tell me how that fits in." Leigh is shaking her head.

"Ah, the other white meat. Kmart, as you may have already guessed, is the domain of the trashy woman. She's cheap because she dropped out of school and can't afford any better or she's slumming looking for gifts for people she doesn't really like. She's slutty and punky and doesn't give a fuck who sees her browsing the inexpensive undergarments. I met a woman, a Latina woman with huge tits, at a Kmart in Detroit once. She had two kids and worked at the post office. I took her from behind and the whole time we screwed she called out other men's names. Really surreal."

"But worth it?" Rufus asks.

Leigh groans again.

"It's always worth it, Rufus. Everything I do is always worth it."

"Everything?"

"Truth."

"How about number four?" Rufus asks.

Cody says, "Sure, Albertsons. That actually might be even more shocking than Kmart but it makes perfect sense. You see, Rufus, the woman who shops at Albertsons is looking for more than discounts. She's not looking for anything trendy, she's not looking to stock her shelves with organic food, she's just looking for something wholesome and fresh. Take Val. I met her at an Albertsons in Princeton Junction. She was a systems analyst at some tax firm in the city. Mid-forties and single. Had two cats and a cheery townhome. She liked walks on the beach and romantic comedies. Val invited me home with her and I rubbed her feet and kissed the nape of her neck. That's as far as it got. I couldn't have asked for anything better."

"Romantic," Gary says.

Leigh sighs. "You guys are killing me. Why did you have to rescue me?"

"And number five?"

Cody chuckles. "Rufus, my friend, Costco is a place to save money. You're shopping for blue-collar bitches. Now, there are tons of suburban moms as well. But my advice is to go for the women who work there. Unbefuckinglieveable. Really, my friend. You get these brawny women built like trucks. And they fuck like you wouldn't believe. Nothing beats after-hours anal on a pallet of Grisham novels. . . ."

Cody wakes around eight to find Laser doing sit-ups on the floor beside the couch he's crashed out on.

Rufus is snoring under a blanket on a beaten leather chair. Laser does maybe ten reps before Leigh appears at the base of the stairs in shorts and a gray sweatshirt. Her hair is a wild shock around her face. Even now, her eyelids drooping, her skin flushed, she looks angelic.

Laser stands and wipes the sweat from his forehead with the back of his hand. "Good morning."

Leigh's eyes roam the room. "Remind me where are we again?"

"Cincinnati. At Gary and Elise's. Friends."

"Why?"

"Our road trip o' fun has begun. First stop."

"You going to let me in on any of your plans?"

"Yeah. Sure. Can we trust you?"

"No games."

Laser shrugs and looks over to Cody. Cody says, "I trust her."

"First thing," Laser says. "We need to cut and dye your hair. Something dramatic. Then maybe colored contacts or something along those lines. You game?"

"Okay. I'd really love some makeup too. Any chance?"

"Doubtful."

Laser finds a half-emptied bottle of hair lightener in Elise's medicine cabinet and grabs a pair of scissors from the kitchen. Leigh sits on a stool by the sink and he bleaches and then cuts her hair short. She doesn't ask him about how he's cutting and she doesn't ask for a mirror, she just closes her eyes and lets it happen. His hands in her hair, rough and strong as they are, she can't help but shiver at the little waves of giddiness rising and falling in her stomach like carbonation. Laser's movements are so precise. His hands flutter through he hair like butterflies or the wings of hummingbirds. She is surprised at the lack of sound and the amount of hair drifting down around her. The haircut is over before she knows it.

"Come on, take a look."

Leigh follows Laser upstairs to the bathroom. Along the way they pass Rufus, who is sitting lotus-style on the couch, sipping tea. His eyes go wide and he nods slowly. Gives Leigh a thumbs-up. She cracks a smile but isn't sure if she should be worried.

"You look great," Laser says, pushing Leigh into the bathroom.

She hasn't had her hair this short in many years. When she was a junior in college she freaked out after being dumped by Harris McCarthy and chopped her hair down to nothing and sat on her bed and ate chips and sobbed until her roommate took her to the movies. Leigh thinks of that, staring at this new, bleached-blond, younger-looking self, and laughs.

"I do a good job?" Laser asks.

Leigh sees where he missed, where the hair falls irregularly, and shrugs. "Last time I had a haircut this inventive the stylist was flown in from Buenos Aires. All told, it was several thousand. . . ."

"This is on the house."

"I like it," Leigh says. She turns to him. "But you're a terrible stylist."

"It's not about style."

"I know, but you're the artist."

"I think you'll need a hat too."

Gary and Elise appear at the doorway. They both grin and clap.

While they pack, Laser hands Gary a check for twenty-four thousand dollars. "For a new car."

Gary asks, "Why? I just got my car last year."

"We're taking your car."

Gary looks to Elise. Elise says, "That works."

Laser yells to Cody, "Get a press release ready!"

Twenty minutes later they leave Gary and Elise's, Leigh in Gary's Che Guevara–style camouflage cap. The drive to Mason is brief but intense. They stop three times for Laser to use a payphone that he barks into. Each time, when he gets back into the car he's flushed. Eyes hardened. Each time, he shakes his head at Cody. "We've only got three rides," he says. "Where do we get this help?"

"It's all for the love of art," Cody replies.

They smell it before they arrive at the town center.

An odor attacks Leigh nearly a block away. Stink comes charging in through the AC, blasting in the vents. It is, Leigh knows, the smell of death. Of decay. She's smelled this once before: India. Bodies being burned and bodies wasting on the muddy banks of the Ganges. The smell is rot.

She pinches her nose shut. Her eyes water. "Please tell me they don't have corpses out here."

Cody chuckles. "No corpses."

"But the smell is part of it, right?"

"Right-o."

At the center of town is a square where normally children would be pushing scooters and mothers rocking strollers. Normally there would be flowers and sunlight but when they park the car and walk over the half block to the square, and the stink of death or whatever is stronger and stronger foot by foot, they notice only black and brown and clouds of soot.

"They burn the place down?" Leigh asks.

Cody says, "You'll see."

Come around the corner and Leigh is literally knocked back by the sight of it. The Mason town square, the whole luxury-car-parking-lot whole of it, has been transformed into a third-world slum. A filthy river of oil runs thick over the cobblestones. In it Leigh can see feces and flotsam. In some places, it's deep enough that a person could fall in and be lost. Around this central stream are shacks. Literally dozens of them. Each made of cardboard and plywood and fencing and tin. The soot, it bellows out of the greasy holes in the roofs. Children are there, dark-skinned children, running over planks across the shit canal, chasing chickens, and dragging half-toys. Adults too. Reed-thin men lifting cinder blocks or hawking mercury run out of computer parts and derelict hospital equipment, reed-thin women with baskets on their heads and squealing infants on their backs.

"What is this?" Leigh asks, scanning the scene.

"This is a mega-slum. Okobaba to be accurate."

"Where?"

"Lagos, Nigeria. Everything you see and smell is real. This is not a reenactment but a slice of Okobaba transported to Mason. The people are all from the slum, the houses, all the materials. I don't want to say they're replicas 'cause they're not. They're real. We didn't fly them over but we 'treated' them so they are indistinguishable from the real thing."

"It's horrible. That water, those children . . ."

"That's shit."

Leigh looks around, nose pinched. "Is this legal?"

"That's not the question. The question is: is it moral?"

Leigh doesn't have an answer. "Why did you do this?"

"Like I told you. We have volunteers, Irregulars, part of the network who, in this case, function like a hive mind. They each learn one particular skill, sometimes even just one motion—the swing of a bucket or how to reload a nail gun—and it's all independent. But when you get them all together, they function seamlessly like an organic machine. We got this up and running before dawn. The genius part was getting a tent over it while they built. Getting approved permits for 'reconstruction' work. Got the local bureaucracy, town council, committees involved. It's so messed up, this town doesn't know its head from its ass."

"It's unbelievable."

"Hang tight for a few minutes. I'm going to make some announcements and we're going to film some stuff before the media and the cops shut it down."

Leigh looks over toward the far side of the square just behind the instant slum to see two sheriff's cars pull up, lights flashing. "Looks like you're a bit late. I'm not surprised, what with the smell and everything. . . ."

Laser smiles. "Those are Irregulars."

"Seriously."

"Sure, being a cop is nothing but getting hold of a uniform. Hang tight."

Leigh sits on a bench and watches the slum dwellers go about their daily routine. Watches as they try and avoid slipping into the shit river, as they change and feed their children in hovels that are little more than packing crates and cheap cement, as they burn tires and plastic and release plumes of toxic smoke out over the town.

Laser in sunglasses and a straw hat, followed by a camera crew that has suddenly materialized, tours the slum and speaks into a bullhorn. Photographers crowd the uneven streets and the flicker of flashes makes it look like a movie set. Leigh is reminded of the paparazzi that used to follow her around L.A. and London, of the swarming masses so eager to see her teeth, to smell what perfume she had on.

Laser's voice booms out across the slum, "One million people live within this one square mile. . . . This water kills. . . . The people here pick through the garbage. They are prostitutes. They are desperate. They are being killed by America. . . ."

Leigh sees a woman emerge from a hut and slaughter a squealing piglet.

Laser says, "These are the shadow cities, the hidden

economies. . . . These illegal communities are the future of and they will one day replace our suburbs. . . . Furious capitalism, human rights be damned. . . . Citizens of Mason, this is the product of your comfort. . . ."

Cody walks over to Leigh, smiling. "What do you think?"

"This is crazy."

"It's brilliant. Revolutionary. Maybe last fifteen more minutes before it's shut down."

Leigh says, "People need to see this, though."

"They will."

"But they'll just turn the channel. This, this will upset them. You can't eat dinner and see this on the news and want to watch. It'll turn them off before they even get the point."

Cody shrugs. "What do you suggest?"

Laser climbs atop one of the fragile roofs. He shouts, "Here there is no hope! The population will double and the run-off from our hunger for objects will choke the rivers and spread like plague. . . ."

Then he looks to Leigh, points to her, and holds up the bullhorn.

Leigh looks to Cody. Cody asks, "Well? You all talk or what?"

Leigh walks through the maze of cracked concrete and shit and burning drums and with the help of several of the cameramen climbs up onto the roof beside Laser. She takes the bullhorn. "What should I say?"

Laser hands her a script. "Read this."

Leigh, voice shaking at first, reads: "This is the voice of Strategic Art Defense. We have brought the world to America's previously impenetrable heartland. Here, in Mason, we have shown some of the wealthiest, whitest Americans what the rest of the world looks like, smells like, feels like. This is Revolutionary Action Number One on our tour of the United States. Three more days, two more events. Brace yourselves."

By the end Leigh's voice has been roused. It's like she's on a film set reading something dramatic. Something that encapsulates the whole of the story. Her voice is authoritative. It is alive. Leigh turns from the camera, her face flushed.

She hands Laser the bullhorn and says, "I can't believe I just did that."

"How'd it feel?"

"Crazy."

"Crazy good?"

"Yeah."

As Leigh climbs down off the roof the air is broken by the wail of sirens.

Laser says, "We've got another car. Cody and Ru are waiting."

4.

The Serologist stops at Wal-Mart first.

He grabs a duffel bag and loads it with shotgun shells and a pair of pliers and a hedge trimmer. He throws a gas canister in the car and some donuts and heads out onto the road west through Pennsylvania.

It's night when he gets on I-80 and the whole drive past Mercer, Ohio, he sees cop cars with lights flashing. He decides on a detour using the Beaver Valley Expressway. Even though he's going the speed limit he's pulled over outside of Belmar Park. The road is nearly empty. Just the two cars humming on one side of it. The cop walks up to the Serologist's window and looks at him funny and asks, "Where you headed?"

"West to Wyoming. Visiting family. What's going on?"

"Police business."

The cop takes out his flashlight and checks the Serologist's backseat and then shines the light into his mismatched eyes and asks, "Mind if I check the trunk?"

"Nope. Be my guest. I'll have to unlock it for you though. Doesn't work from in here."

"Fine."

The Serologist gets out and walks to the back of the Volvo. The cop follows him, his left hand on his holster the whole way back. He shines the flashlight on the truck and the Serologist pops it open and stands back.

"This about that heiress's kidnapping? Heard about a shoot-out on the radio."

The cop says nothing. Just digs around in the trunk and pulls out the hedge trimmers and looks them over and then he puts them back.

The Serologist says, "Crazy the stuff going on these days. I considered emergency medicine for a while and the stuff that I saw then, I knew I wasn't ever going to forget it. Thing was, I thought that this was the worst of it. Mid-eighties. The whole crack cocaine epidemic and black kids shooting the shit out of each other. Saw some horrible stuff. But what's happening today, that takes the cake for sure."

The cop grunts. "What's in the duffel bag?"

The Serologist says, "Tools."

"What tools?"

"Tools I work with. I'm in reconstruction."

"That so?"

"That's so."

"Reconstruction, huh? Can I have a look?"

"Be my guest."

The cop leans into the trunk and pulls the duffel bag out.

The Serologist says, "These days, people just don't even think about the repercussions of what they're doing. It's like acting on instinct. Everyone is just crazy and they all have hair triggers."

The cop unzips the duffel and pokes his flashlight inside.

He sees the shotgun and steps back from the bag, going for his gun.

The Serologist says, "Comes to be you just can't trust people."

The cop spins around and holds the gun up, his mouth open to say something but nothing comes out. His mouth open and it's like he's yawning. Still nothing comes out. Cop's gun clatters on the asphalt. The Serologist has his hand in the cop's stomach and he lowers him slowly to the ground and pulls his hand out and it's red. The knife he's holding is red too. The cop spasms. Dies.

The Serologist gets back in his car. He starts it up, grabs a Gordon Lightfoot disc from his glove box and heads west.

5.

From: Strategic Art Defense
To: All media outlets

Leigh Tiller has joined S.A.D.

She denounces the tyranny of corporate America and embraces our unstoppable mission. Today America flails wildly just as the baby screams when it is pushed from the birth canal into the cold, clinical reality of capitalist life. The founding members of Strategic Art Defense have found America's capitalist society guilty of the most grievous and horrific cultural crimes. From the debased breeding ground for poverty that is Wal-Mart to the xenophobic morass of cable television, America is in dire need of a reality injection. Only art of the most extreme kind can provide the necessary inoculation against the terrorism of our culture. To save ourselves from the base aggression of capitalism we must use aggression. Not violence. Not hate. Only creation can defeat mindless destruction. There is a Japanese legend about Issun-boshi, a tiny boy with a knitting needle for a samurai sword. In the story he is swallowed by a giant but does not despair; he defeats the giant from inside by pricking him with his needle. Like Issun-boshi we will prick the stomach of the United States until the goliath lies in crippled ruin.

From the belly of the beast:
In art, we find struggle.
In struggle, we find art.
Love to Mizmoon.

Yr. Humble Servants
Strategic Art Defense

6.

They take back roads out of Ohio. Slow roads.
Leigh sits in the passenger seat while Laser drives.
Cody has his headphones on.
Rufus is just staring out into space.
Her head bobbing in sleepy nods on the seat, Leigh watches the moon hanging distant and tiny above waves of trees. She thinks about her mother. Not her dad's latest girlfriend. The one who calls herself Momma but is only thirty-eight and has never given birth. No, she thinks about the one who pushed her out. The one who died nearly thirteen years ago. The one who

haunts her late at night, when she's singing to herself in the shower, the one she sees on the subway trains and near Madison Square Garden.

Leslie Marcel Tiller.

Leslie, who passed away from cervical cancer, was wafer thin, smoked long cigarettes and drank obscene amounts of wine. Ten glasses a day, sometimes two bottles an afternoon. She was always drunk and spitting and falling down, and outside of three meaningful conversations she and Leigh had when Leigh was in elementary school, Mom was absent from her life. Leigh used to call her a "vulgar ghost." She was either rattling glasses in the hallways or stumbling down the stairs in her heels at seven in the morning. Or she was moaning in the bathroom at three. Or she was passed out in the garage, an unconscious and disheveled shadow drooling on the concrete. Anytime she tried to straighten up, tried to act like any other mother might, she lasted maybe ten minutes. Ten minutes at the soccer game, ten minutes at the awards show, ten minutes at the school play, ten minutes until she started complaining about being thirsty. The fact that she died of cancer was something of a fluke. It was the easiest way out imaginable, the one that let her drift off without having to apologize or make her shame public. Not that she had any shame.

To combat Mom's "habit," Dad took lovers. Lucille was the first Leigh could remember. Leigh was still in diapers when Lucille was taking her to the zoo and MoMA. Lucille was nice and pretty but she couldn't play the game and Dad let her go. Next was Giselle and she was a haughty bitch, just out of college, who showed no interest in Leigh. Mom went into rehab twice after Giselle and the effort was enough that Dad stopped seriously seeing other women, at least for two or three years. Those years, middle school, were particularly hard on Leigh. She missed Dad's lovers, these exotic women who blew in from nowhere. Mainly it was because Dad seemed so happy, each new shiny girlfriend a new lease on life. They wanted his fortune. He wanted their youth.

Kip Tiller was something of an emotional vampire, the kind that feeds off youth and beauty. For Kip, just being around these women took years off his life. Sure, fucking them was great. He never denied that. But it was basking in their vivacity that he craved most. Just watching them be young and act silly provided him those few remaining essential nutrients that being wealthy could not buy. And as silly as it sounds, Leigh played Renfield to his Dracula.

In high school she was the one who lured the women in. Being an heiress and socialite meant that Leigh was at the right places. The parties, the shows, the openings, she soon started seeing them as something other than easy social outings and good press face—these were traps. Innocence traps. These were women looking for men like her dad. Women looking for someone to sweep them off their feet and adore them. The thing with Leigh was that she could sniff these women out so easily. And when she brought them over, arm in arm, giggling, to meet her dad he would give her a quick wink and it meant the world to her. That wink, that approval, was the "I love you" and "I appreciate you" that Leigh never heard. But Laser, she can tell by the way he's been eyeing her that he appreciates her.

They camp out in an empty lot behind a supermarket. Take turns sitting awake, wide-eyed in the dark while the others sleep uncomfortably.

When Rufus and Cody switch, they bring out the flare gun and paper-towel packages again. They launch a few packets into the space between the supermarket and a gas station. It's loud enough after the first shot that Leigh wakes up and watches.

"What the fuck are you doing?"

Cody walks over to the car and leans on the roof, his smile filling Leigh's window. "We're planting."

"Planting what?"

"Seeds."

"Huh?"

"Native plant seeds. A mix of joe-pye weed, purple loosestrife, marsh milkweed, some others. Rufus makes the concoction based on where we're traveling. We're fixing the motherfucking planet while we work."

"What's with the gun?"

Rufus puts the gear into the trunk and closes it carefully before getting back in the car. He turns to Leigh and says, "It's a seed gun. Made it myself. We launch these seeds into desolate spots, improperly used planters, medians, anyplace where there are non-native plants struggling to survive or just empty patches of dirt. Each paper-towel bundle is totally biodegradable and contains enough soil and moisture to get the seeds up and running."

"You've been doing this awhile?" Leigh asks.

"Couple years now. Not officially part of S.A.D. Laser likes the idea of it but it's hard to call it art. More like guerilla topiary work."

"It's clever," Laser says from the backseat.

Laser gets out and stretches and Cody takes the wheel. He's been eyeing a truck-stop diner across from the supermarket. He tells Cody, "I'm just going to run over there and pick something up. Just a snack or something."

Cody says, "You sure that's a good idea?"

"We're in the middle of fucking nowhere."

"Yeah, last time we were in the middle of nowhere those freaks tried to run us down with a shotgun."

"I'll be like five minutes."

"Your choice."

Rufus says, "Get me a chocolate something."

Leigh says, "Me too."

Laser runs over to the diner and sits down at a booth with a sigh. He orders a coffee from the haggard waitress and then cracks his knuckles and closes his eyes. He opens them when he hears someone slide into the booth across from him.

It's the man with the face of shattered porcelain.

The man asks, "How's it going?"

Laser freezes.

The man smiles with too many creases.

Laser swallows hard. "Good to see you again."

"I'll bet."

The waitress brings the coffee and the scarred man orders a short stack. "You have blueberries? I'd love blueberries on it."

When the waitress leaves, Laser says, "She's not here."

"I know."

"So, why are you here?"

"I want to talk to you. Give you an opportunity to get out of this."

Laser says, "I didn't get into this by accident."

"I know that too."

"I won't let you take her."

"What does Ms. Tiller mean to you? Is this for your 'art'? Is this a statement?"

"Maybe."

The man nods. "I did a little digging around. You are a fairly well-respected warrior of sorts. I'm familiar with some of the masters you've studied under. Jacques Valley. Bertrand Dock. Then again, there is the other stuff too."

"What do you want?"

"You're a worthy opponent. Knew that from when I saw you at the apartment building. Terrible shot but there's something steely in you. I can sense these things."

"You're not getting her back."

"No. You're right. I'm not getting her back tonight. I want you to know that I'm a worthy opponent as well. We're cut from very much the same cloth."

"Somehow I doubt that."

The waitress comes over and delivers the short stack and syrup. The Serologist looks happy. He offers Laser a bite. Laser shakes his head. "No, thanks."

"You see," the Serologist says, forking a bite of pancake into his mismatched lips, "I'm not the only hound on your trail now."

"The cops."

"Forget the cops."

"FBI."

"Sure, but I'm talking desperate people. Crazy people."

"Who?"

"Mr. Tiller has put a bounty on his daughter's head and you've got all manner of slime climbing out from under their rocks to get a fat paycheck. These people are mercenary. Very mercenary."

"I'm not too worried."

"I found you very quickly, my friend. Very easily."

"Are you offering your help?"

"Not at all."

"Then why tell me this?"

"I want the girl. I'd be extremely disappointed if one of these dogs got to her before I did. You understand, right?"

"No. You're here right now. Why not now?"

The Serologist nods, takes another bite of his pancakes and chews slowly. When he's finished he leans back and says, "I like the chase. The fear."

"You're an unhealthy bastard. I don't know what your story is but I hope you realize what side of this thing you're on."

The Serologist is puzzled.

"Tiller's blood money. You know what his company is responsible for? You know how much damage the Tiller empire has inflicted on the world for the past century? You are the most blatant symbol for all that. Like the poster child or something."

"Oddly enough, this is the second time I've had this conversation this week. I don't attach any meaning to the money. Frankly, it's means to an end. I would think you'd be understanding of that. Surely your little games aren't self-financed. You're not charging this on Mommy's credit card. You don't have to answer that, doesn't matter to me."

"It should. You're just a cog in the machine this way."

The Serologist snickers. "Think you're big, bad revolutionaries, don't you. Out to change the world one city at a time. Is that right?"

"We're doing our part."

"I think you, your crew, are a bunch of fakes."

Laser narrows his eyes. He can feel the muscles in his jaws tensing. "How's that?"

"You're just kids playing around. The media's all whipped up into a frenzy over these ridiculous little shows you're putting on and while they might be entertaining, there's nothing revolutionary about them. The scale is larger, the effects long lasting, but you're not really changing shit."

"What would you be doing? Killing people?"

"Not necessarily. But I sure as hell would be using force. Why don't you fuck something up? Just say to hell with it and bomb the system. You guys have more than enough money, more than enough people involved in this thing. Raise a little army and go raise some hell."

Laser shakes his head.

The Serologist continues. "Fuck. It. Up. Burn it down. Go wild in the streets. Get your thousands to bring thousands more. Take out the power grids. Target the television stations. Bomb the malls. The water supply."

Laser says, "You don't have to tell me how to run Strategic Art Defense. We create situations. What you're talking about is madness. Ends in death. Ends in nothing."

"I guess you're more the laid-back type. Let things happen on their own."

"We're not the Symbionese Liberation Army. Not Red Army Faction. This isn't the sixties. That sort of revolution went down the tubes. Can't solve anything with violent anarchy. This is about creation. Giving people options. Choices."

The Serologist shrugs. "Boring."

"We're not killers like you. Since you're on Tiller's payroll, I'll just leave the check here for you." Laser gets up and leaves the blemished man and makes his way back to the car quickly. Cody is awake and eyeing him. Rufus and Leigh are sleeping soundly.

"You didn't bring anything?" Cody asks Laser as Laser gets in.

"No, sorry."

"They're gonna be pissed. Went to sleep talking about chocolate."

"What can I say?"

"That you'll go back."

"No. You can go. I want to stay here."

"You look kind of flustered. Everything okay?"

"Yeah. Yeah. Everything's good. Just looking forward to getting back on the road."

7.

Kip Tiller is pacing his kitchen, shouting into a speakerphone hanging over the counter.

Two pit bulls drag behind him in tight circles. They yelp occasionally and he leans down and smothers them with kisses and they, likewise, smother him with drool.

Kip says, "Since when have I ever not thrown you a bone?"

The voice on speaker is young and haughty. "You ain't given us shit in like two months. We've been struggling out here."

Kip laughs. "What are you saying, Rail? That I'm edging you out?"

"Sometimes kinda seems like thas the truth."

"And where else would I go?"

"Sure there's lotsa motherfuckers willin'."

"Not for this. Not the way you do it."

"I ain't even gonna get into this whole daughter thing you got us jammin' but we been talking and a hundred ain't coverin' it."

"This is about money, then?"

Rail pauses. "Here's how I got this shit figured. It's cool for you to pay us piecemeal an' shit for dogs. We cool with bustin' dogs outta fightin' rackets. Gives us a leg up too. We can collect double when we fuck up some ring that's got cash on hand. But this shit is a whole 'nother deal and unless we gets paid right, shit could start lookin' ugly. Ain't no niggas care 'bout some filthy dogs gettin' ripped to shit so long as they makin' bones off it. An' you come across as some fuckin' hero with your peoples. All good, right? But this here shit is sick. It's ugly. Even I know that."

Kip stops pacing. He cracks his neck and then takes the phone off speaker and picks up the receiver. "Rail, you trying to blackmail me?"

Rial laughs. "Nah, chief. Why would I do that?"

"Sure sounds like you are."

"Jus' tryin' to get me and the boys what we feel we due."

"Uh-huh. Right. Listen to me, you nappy-headed fuck. I have taken care of you and your fucking boys from the time you were shitting in diapers. Your dad and his Sultan crew were friends of mine. Busted our first dogs out, us two. He was there when the shit went down and all the white pussies at PETA made a fucking run for it. Your pops knew how business was done. He was a soldier in this war. Clear to me already that you've inherited none of his brains but almost all of his balls. That's not a good thing, Rail. I know you're a bunch of desperados, fucking cold-ass killers. Chafes me to think you're so young. So corrupted. Can't even imagine what the fucking world has come to to have you shits running around the streets. . . ."

"Ain't just running around the streets, we running the streets."

"Whatever. You fucking listen to me 'cause I'm saying this shit once: I own you. I own your fucking crew. Sultans? I made the Sultans. All those gats, all your gear, all your drugs. Where do you think the money comes from to buy all that? Isn't coming from you. I only ask a few things and I pay you well. Don't fuck with me, Rail. Don't you ever fuck with me or you'll see your whole world come tumbling down. Think you're the only street punk I've got? I have a whole Rolodex of replacements. Killers that make you look like a fucking jaywalker. You understand me? Am I clear?"

Rail is silent. Kip can practically hear him biting through his tongue. "Yea, we're clear."

"Good. You do this job for me and you do it well and we'll talk more money."

"Aight."

"Don't fuck around with me again, Rail."

"Sure, boss."

"Excellent. If I'm feeling generous I might even send you a birthday present. You're what, fifteen, sixteen?"

"Somethin' like that."

"You should be in school, you dumb fucker."

"School's the streets, Mr. Tiller. If I was in school ain't shit be getting done."

"I always hated school myself. Go get her."

8.

The Serologist is driving past cornfields.

He's driving slowly; appreciating the way the moonlight is filtering down through the clouds and painting the roofs of the farmhouses in the distance.

There is something so tranquil about it. Calming.

Something otherworldly.

He is not surprised to hear his daughter's voice. "Dad?"

The Serologist turns and sees his daughter sitting in the passenger seat. She has her hair pulled back and she's wearing her school uniform. She's smiling. "I thought you were zoning out," she says. "Isn't it beautiful out here?"

"Yes it is," he says. The way the moonlight is playing on his daughter's face reminds him of standing in the light of an aquarium. It shifts in soft focus. The light spills out over her nose, those sparkling eyes, her hair. "I've missed you so much."

"I've missed you too, Dad."

"Where have you and Mom been?"

"You wouldn't believe me if I told you."

"Tell me."

"You think you can handle it?"

He looks at her. She smiles, turns toward him. She says, "We're living by the beach. We've got one of those houses on stilts. It's made of driftwood and palm fronds—that's what Mom calls them—and there are all these tide pools just outside. There are these beautiful fish and amazing mirrored crabs. You'd love it, Dad."

"Sounds wonderful," the Serologist says.

"It really is. I don't like when it rains but the rain is warm and it doesn't last for long. You should come and visit us. We can take a walk down to the village at the end of the beach. There is a shop there where you can buy painted conch shells."

"I will visit you soon. Soon."

"Mom says that this is your last job."

"It is."

"And what's next?"

"I retire."

"Like how Grandpa did. You're going to live in an apartment? Get a job at Wal-Mart?"

The Serologist laughs. "No. I'm going to come and stay with you."

"And you won't leave us ever again?"

"No. Never again."

"Promise?"

"Promise."

"What are you going to do when you find the girl?"

The Serologist looks at his daughter. He shakes his head. "I don't want to tell you."

"Why?"

"It's bad."

"You're going to hurt her."

"Yes."

"Why, Dad?"

"That's what people hire me for. That's what I'm good at doing."

"You used to tell me that you were good at making people feel better."

"I was. Things have changed."

"What changed?"

"There was an accident. Do you remember it?"

"Yes."

"I hurt my head in the accident. Something got broken inside. My face. Who I was changed. It's not unusual. Sometimes something so terrible can happen to someone that when it's over, they aren't the same person anymore."

"Who are you now?"

"I'm a bad, bad person now."

"Why?"

"I don't know. It's just who I am now. Like a switch that got switched on inside me. You know, we're just chemicals. Just big bags of chemicals and sometimes the chemicals get mixed up. That's how it happens. That's how I changed."

"Are you evil, Dad?"

The Serologist laughs. "No. I'm just not good."

9.

"What the hell is going on?"

Laser digs his nails into the cheap leather on the wheel as they crawl through Bedford, Indiana, the Limestone Capital of the World according to a sign they passed on Highway 50.

"Parade on 12th," Cody says. "If that heavily decorated cardboard poster tacked to the telephone pole on 10th is to be believed. Then again, it was heavily glitterized and the font they used was Curlz MT so maybe it's a hoax."

Laser groans.

Leigh says, "It's going to be like this the whole drive, isn't it?"

Rufus says, "Yup."

They pull the car over hear a Laundromat and watch the parade go past. Laser says, "I guess we can make the time up. We don't technically have to—"

"Can't you just relax for a few minutes?" Leigh interrupts. "Please?"

Horses, beauty queens, children with balloons, the parade is standard fare but a smile slowly but surely creeps onto Laser's face when he sees the Limestone Capital of the World float. While Laser's moment of joy is fleeting, Cody notices it and elbows him. "Should we bust out the costumes?"

"Is there a band?"

Cody says, "Bedford–North Lawrence Stars, to be precise."

Laser thinks for a second. Rufus pokes his head up between them, "You guys thinking what I'm thinking?"

Laser says, "Twenty minutes."

"Yes!" Rufus shouts. "Let's get frivolous!"

"Should I be worried?" Leigh asks as the guys get out and pop the trunk.

She gets no response but then they reappear three minutes later decked out in bright orange marching-band uniforms complete with epaulettes, baldric, cummerbund, cords, and feathered vanguard helmets. Cody has a ghetto blaster on his shoulder.

Laser leans in the back window, his white feathers brushing the roof. "What do you think?"

Leigh smiles. "There one for me?"

The paradegoers aren't sure who the four marchers in orange are but they applaud them anyway.

A woman holding a small dog says, "They certainly are enthusiastic."

The Bedford–North Lawrence Stars think the four new band members are students in on some prank and they go along with it for a few minutes. Eventually the short kid with the tuba says, "Who are those assholes?"

And that's when the band notices that the orange-suited marchers have sequined skulls on the backs of their uniforms. That they're waving American flags that are upside down and seem to show the stars as dollar signs.

The music stops, with individual instruments falling out of line. First the horns and then the drums. The marching stops.

A man on the street shouts, "Get out, pranksters!"

An old woman screams, "Not funny!"

Laser walks over to a media platform and grabs the cordless microphone from a woman with bulletproof hair and painted cheeks. He says "excuse me" and then walks out into the street. "Fellow Americans," he says into the mic. "You are being joined today by members of the country's most elite underground art squad. Before you today stand the directors of this program. We are only stopping in Bedford for a few, brief moments. We do not want to crash your parade. We're here to celebrate with you."

Laser looks around at the stunned and silent crowd. "What are we celebrating anyway?"

"Football team!" an older man with a hat yells.

"What team?" Laser asks him.

"Stars."

"Right, then. Go Stars!!"

One person claps. Then two. Applause and Laser bows. Leigh is laughing so hard she's shaking. Cody puts the ghetto blaster down on the street and looks to Laser. Laser shrugs, says, "Okay."

Cody presses play and turns the volume up. Japanese hip-hop comes pounding out of the cheap speakers and the crowd backs up. Laser drops the mic, jumps up onto the platform, where the plastic woman reacts with horror, and begins to break-dance. He is surprisingly good, moving from windmills to butterfly kicks and handstands. After three minutes and twenty-eight seconds he freezes on the downrock, tongue out and left foot extended in a kick.

Only Cody claps.

Then Rufus whistles.

Leigh, like the audience, stands stunned. Slowly applause creeps out and spreads until everyone is clapping loudly and some are even whistling. Laser bows and then walks over to Leigh and kisses her full on the lips. She is frozen to the spot, hands at her sides, lifeless. "Sorry," Laser says. "Just pumped up."

Leigh backs up. "Uh, okay." She can't think of what to say next. Laser stands there, sweaty in his uniform, his cheeks flushed. She asks the first thing that comes to her mind. "Where'd you learn to break-dance?"

Laser smiles, winks. "Wasn't always a ninja."

10.

Kip Tiller is sitting in a limo near a beach on Fire Island.

His hands shake as he pours whiskey into a tumbler. Across from him sits an elderly man on oxygen, his portable concentrator making sucking sounds every few minutes as though it needs the air as well.

This older man asks, "Have you given much thought to karma?"

Kip chuckles. "I don't think about voodoo nonsense."

"Hindu nonsense."

"Any nonsense," Kip clarifies.

"Perhaps you should consider it."

"Why's that, Nathaniel?"

"Just looking at the stormy forecast here, Kip. You assured us, you assured the board as well, that the picture was rosy. I believe that was the very word. Rosy. I was quite taken aback by your assumption that this would be easy. I've never understood how you can qualify things so very easily."

"Experience. Up until now my instinct hasn't let me down."

Nathaniel lights a cigarette and puffs away, his oxygen concentrator making several high-pitched whines that are tempered by some fiddling with its various dials. Nathaniel says, "Maybe it's that I'm not saying it right. When you first told us she'd been kidnapped, you seemed quite concerned."

"I was."

"And then you gathered yourself together and came to us with the proposal."

"Right."

"How did that happen, Kip?"

Kip sips his whiskey and looks out at the rolling whitecaps. He sighs deeply. "Have you ever killed someone, Nathaniel?"

"No. Have you?"

"Several."

Nathaniel asks, "In 'Nam?"

"There and here."

Nathaniel closes his eyes. "I don't need to know this."

"You do. You see, there are only two reasons that you will ever kill someone. The first is self-defense. It just plain makes sense, no use in going into it. The second is a bit more complicated. It's more philosophical than anything. Not karma, not religion. I'm talking rationally."

"Okay."

"There are moments in life where the clouds break free and you can see the landscape around you, below you. These are moments of extreme clarity. They're as close as we can get to the divine—to the ineffable fabric of the cosmos. You see, there are moments in a man's life when he understands why we're here. The questions are all answered. In these moments, a man can see both backward and forward in time—he can see the impact of his actions as clearly now as in a thousand years. Fate, perhaps."

"What does this have to do with murder?"

"Well, sometimes that clarity highlights problems. Obstacles, if you will."

"Competitors?"

"Please, Nathaniel, that's putting it very, very crudely. The Tiller brand has survived and thrived for as long as it has not because a few competitors were eliminated along the way but because whole generations were changed, the nation was redirected."

"By murder?"

"Yes. You just need to know who to kill. Take a fictional man walking his dog on the beach just a mile from here. This guy might be some lawyer at a small firm, he's getting paid, things are looking up. There is nothing in this man's life to suggest that killing him would be a good idea. That it would benefit me or you or society as a whole. But thinking that way is simplistic. Who knows, this man might rise up the ranks and become a government lawyer. Maybe he'll oversee some budgetary line item that authorizes the destruction of several villages in Southeast Asia, a line item that condemns fifteen thousand innocent civilians to death by 'accident.' Killing that man now would spare those people. . . ."

"You're talking about divination, Kip. We cannot see the future. It is not in the best interests of Tiller Industries to make business decisions based on horoscopes or crystal balls."

"No, of course. But instinct, yes."

Nathaniel smirks. "Your gut tells you to kill people?"

"No. No." Kip Tiller chuckles. "These days I don't kill them. My men do."

"And your daughter."

"My gut tells me that she should have died in the kidnapping or in the rescue. My gut tells me that not only is her surviving going to ruin our brand but that she will take the final plunge and divorce herself from her heritage because of the fact that she lives."

"It says that, huh?"

"It does. One of the moments I was talking about. I saw two separate futures. One in which she dies and the stock skyrockets out of sympathy, we are reborn. The other, I see everything plummeting. I see it all burn."

Nathaniel rolls down his window and chucks the cigarette out. "And what of self-fulfilling prophecies? Do you ever think that maybe these thoughts, visions if you will, have led you to create the very future that you are afraid of? I have been there, Kip. Waking up in the middle of the God damned night sweating my ass off from a nightmare about a business rival or partner choking the life out of me. Used to happen nearly every week in the early days. Now, it seems as though it was wasted energy—I am glad I never carried through on any of those delusions. The emphysema will be the one getting me."

"That would be nice, wouldn't it?"

"How do you mean?" Nathaniel coughs.

Kip raps on the one-way mirror behind him. A few seconds later the passenger door opens and two pairs of gloved hands reach in and drag Nathaniel from the car. Kip watches as Nathaniel is pulled down to the beach, his oxygen tank dragging behind him, and his head is held underwater until his feet stop kicking.

Kip raps again on the one-way mirror.

He says, to Marcus behind the wheel of the limo, "Call that scarred dog. I want an update and I want it now."

11.

None of them can drive for more than ten minutes without starting to close their eyes.

The past five hours all they've done is talk and laugh about the parade gag. And about Laser's moves. Leigh is shell-shocked. She doesn't mention the kiss but finds it hard to believe that Laser could dance. At least like that. Rufus and Cody go on and on about how relaxed and playful Laser seemed. Laser chuckles but quickly reverts to All Business Mode. His mood doesn't deflate the others until he starts yelling at them to keep it down. Leigh says, "Yes, Daddy Mechanic." Cody busts a lung laughing over that. The laughing wears them down quickly with all but Laser asleep after a meal at a convenience store. He tires as well and after a call at a pay phone in Effingham, Illinois, opts to pull over at a motel managed by an Irregular named Custer.

Custer is cockeyed and has a wispy moustache.

He is overwhelmed that they're staying at his motel.

"This is just unbelievable," he tells Laser. "I've been waiting for something like this for almost a decade. Ever since I signed up, really."

"I'm glad you could be of assistance."

"Really, anything you need, especially if it involves something dramatic."

"Dramatic, huh?"

"Yeah. I'm a cold-ass fighter."

"Good to know, Custer. I'll get back to you if anything should arise. By the way, the place looks pretty quiet."

"You're the only customers tonight."

"Excellent."

Cody and Rufus play craps on the floor of their small room. They share a bottle of vodka. Laser asks them where they got it but neither Cody nor Rufus answers. Laser says, "We're going to get a super-early start so I suggest turning in."

Cody shrugs. "We just need downtime."

"Fine. But be up and ready at five."

Rufus says, "We're cool."

Laser does some sit-ups and then lies on the bed and reads a community newspaper he picked up at the front desk, before falling asleep next to Leigh. Leigh files her nails and then hangs out in the bathroom looking at her haircut, examining the rings around her eyes and the acne that's sprouted on her forehead. She takes a long, hot shower and then lies back down on the bed. Cody and Rufus are passed out. She turns out the light on the dresser and then sighs in the darkness.

Laser is awake. He says, "You're doing fine."

"How's that?"

"You're in one piece mentally, emotionally."

"As far as you can tell."

"I can tell a lot. You're a strong woman."

"That's what people tell me."

"It's true. And beautiful."

Leigh rubs her eyes. Without opening them she asks, "What was that back at the parade?"

"Break-dancing. I know it's out of character."

Leigh opens her eyes, shakes her head. "That was ridiculous but not what I'm talking about."

"The kiss?"

"Yes, the kiss."

"Don't know. Just came over me. Just wanted to."

"Any other situation, some other circumstance, and I would have slapped you. Or maced you. Or maced and then slapped you."

"I can understand that."

"So, the dancing just brings out the animal in you? Some special ninja technique to get a girl into bed?"

Laser says, "Not at all. The break-dancing I picked up in Tokyo. A fluke, really."

"Don't get me wrong, I *loved* that. That was incredible. It's like you became a whole other person. Or maybe the mask slipped just enough for us to see the real Laser deep down. And surprise! He's a b-boy!"

"Just a fluke, really . . ."

"What's your next move?"

"No more break-dancing. Time to get back to serious."

"Oh, back to boring. You know, you can lead a rag-tag group of freedom fighters and still maintain a sense of humor. No point in getting all fascist on us all the time. Really, it's unbecoming."

"I'll consider it."

"If you ever want to kiss me again, you'll give it some good, hard thought. I'm not the type to just run and—"

The room is suddenly awash in light, a car or cars in the parking lot outside. Laser sits up. "Cody, Ru. Wake up."

Cody groans. Rufus says, "Turn off the light."

Laser, looking at the bright curtains, says, "Someone's here."

Then there is a knock at the door. A methodical rapping.

Laser hisses, "Get the fuck up, you two."

He turns to Leigh. "Head for the bathroom."

She's stepping out of the bed, the hideously patterned duvet wrapped around her, when the door comes crashing in. There, framed in the doorway like some mythical creature, is a woman in sunglasses with a pompadour atop a scooter. The woman has a Molotov cocktail in her hand. She says, "Wake up, assholes."

The fiery bottle comes spinning into the room and hits the television, where it bursts into an octopus of flames.

Laser dives out of the bed and runs toward the doorway, his legs a blur of pale flesh in the bright light of the scooter. The woman revs the bike and pulls it out of the doorway and back into the lot but Laser is quick, a flash, and he's on the front of the scooter with his right fist in the woman's mouth. There is the sound of bone cracking, and teeth scatter like sparks.

The woman falls backward. The bike spins and topples.

In the parking lot wait three more women. All of them with pompadours, all of them tattooed, and all of them sitting on scooters. Laser, standing half naked, looks feral. His taut face etched heavily in the bright headlamps.

"Mechanic," one of the women says. "Welcome to hell."

Laser says nothing. Clenches his fists.

"You some sort of superman?" the woman asks. Her fake tits cast huge shadows.

"Let me take him, Momma Gash," a tall redhead to her left says. "I want to taste his blood." The redhead swings a chain around her head and revs her scooter.

Cody comes barreling out of the room, the pistols stretched out in front of him, their silver barrels glinting. He fires wildly, the whole time screaming obscenities. The women duck behind their rides.

"I thought you the lost the guns!" Laser shouts.

"Found 'em just now."

One of Cody's bullets hits home and a scooter squeals in

alarm, front tire deflating. Cody is out of bullets soon. Before he even realizes it he gets a bottle to the head.

Laser doesn't see who threw the bottle but Cody staggers and curses.

"Where's the girl?" Momma Gash asks.

Laser says, "Me first."

Leigh and Rufus are trying to beat flames out of the bed but they're losing the fight; the fire explodes and crackles up onto the cheap mantelpiece and then it's licking the ceiling. An alarm goes off but it's shallow and weak; there is no way anyone outside the room can hear it. Rufus, holding a blackened pillow that he's been smashing into the flames, says, "We need to bail. Is there a window in the bathroom?"

Leigh looks. "Small one. Real small."

Rufus says, "Will have to do. Smash it down."

Leigh runs for the bathroom but is tripped up by a heavy chain that someone has left lying around the hotel room floor. At least that's Leigh's first thought until the chain moves, pulled by a woman crouched by the shattered television set. The woman says, "You're not going anywhere, hot stuff."

The smoke thickens, blown low. Leigh struggles with the chain, calls for Rufus but he doesn't come. The woman holding the chain walks over, her leather boots as slick as water and her miniskirt a leopard print. The woman's eyes are bloodshot and a tattoo on her neck says Tiger. The woman snarls, "You've been a bad, bad baby. . . ."

She flicks the chain and Leigh's ankles collapse. She screams in pain.

". . . it's going to be a real pleasure. . . ."

The smoke changes direction and the flames dance high, lighting everything in hell colors. Tiger pulls a butterfly knife from her back pocket and flicks it around, snapping and clicking. She says, "I've never gutted a superstar."

That's when Rufus appears with the skeletal box frame of the television set. He hovers over Tiger for a split second, only long enough for Leigh to see him deliberating, before smashing her over the head.

Tiger stands there confused, her face warped in the wavy glass, her head framed as though she's on the television, the stuttering of the flames strobe-lighting across her features. Then she falls.

Rufus pulls the chain from Leigh's feet and drags her up and out into the parking lot. The two of them collapse just outside the door, thick black smoke spilling out over them like reverse clouds.

Between them and the street a strange tableaux: Laser in his boxers standing back-to-back with Cody in a face-off with three pompadoured women who look just like Tiger on scooters. The women are revving their engines; they're catcalling, laughing. Leigh notices a fourth woman lying facedown on the asphalt, still.

"Where the fuck's Tiger?" Momma Gash asks.

No answer.

"Where the fuck is she?!"

Momma Gash looks distraught, her face exploding in rage. Her pointer finger out like a blade, she shouts, "Get that fucking cunt!"

Two scooters move, tires squealing.

Laser, like he's attached to wires, leaps toward one of the bikes. He knocks it over, the rider tumbling into the lot. She screeches. Laser's up fast, his knees raw and gory, and he kicks the woman in the head. Hard. She spasms and coughs. Laser shouts to Rufus, "Get her in the car!"

The second scooter stops just short of Leigh's shins. The woman on the bike, a brunette with a Bettie Page cut and a tattoo on her neck that says Axle, is there only long enough to sneer before there's a crack like backfire and she poofs in a shower of blood.

Custer, in frayed jeans and shirtless, walks across the parking lot with a smoking shotgun and a corncob pipe. He winks at Leigh and Rufus. Says, "Cold ass."

Laser looks to Momma Gash.

She says, "It's not over."

Laser smiles. "Looks like it is."

Momma Gash flicks him off and peels out. Her pompadour casting Gumby shadows across the walls of the motel until she is swallowed up by the night only to reappear, ever smaller, in the pools of yellow light beneath street lamps reaching out into infinity.

"From here on out, it's going to be like this."

Laser leans forward, resting his chin on the back of Leigh's seat. "We're lucky we got out of there without any major damage."

"I don't think I can—" Leigh begins.

"No choice," Laser says. "This is grit your teeth and bear it. No more stopping. From here on out it's drive like hell and when we get to Boulder, we do the action and we turn it around quickly. I want to be in Vegas by nightfall Thursday."

Leigh says, "We're going to die."

"No," Cody pipes in from the backseat with Laser. "Not our time."

"You sound confident," Leigh says, trying to force a smile.

Rufus, driving, says, "We should score some speed or something. After that, my body is slipping."

Laser says, "No synthetics, Ru. Chew khat leaves. I've got an Irregular in Kansas who can hook us up with some if you think you'll need more than just caffeine."

"I will," Rufus says.

"I'm sorry for getting you into this." Leigh wipes her eyes.

"Not your fault," Cody says.

Leigh adds, "Is it wrong of me to be enjoying this?"

She laughs cautiously, scans the car.

Laser says, "That's why we do it."

"Not that I like the constant chase and the almost being killed, I could do without all that. It's the action, the thing in Mason, and me taking the bullhorn. It was so unlike me to do something like that. The way I was raised, my image, my father's image, was paramount to anything I might honestly feel. Being out on that limb, it made me feel, I don't know . . . different."

"Adrenaline," Laser responds.

"How's that?"

"You get enough of it in your system and it's addictive. Changes the way you think, the way your body reacts. The way you feel. With enough of it you can become essentially invincible."

Leigh laughs. "That's what you want, right, Laser?"

"Sure."

"Nothing more, right?"

Laser tugs on his albuterol inhaler. "That's part of it."

"What else?"

"How about we talk about it in the morning? I'm just super exhausted having pretty much single-handedly kicked those biker chicks' asses for you all."

Leigh shakes her head. "You love being the asshole."

12.

Momma Gash is racing the winds on the Interstate.

Every few seconds she curses under her breath and slams her fists on the front of her scooter. Tears form at the corners of her eyes and she grits her teeth. She has decided she will not call Tiller, she will not turn around, but she will ride back to her apartment, load up on weapons and grab Tulia and Jasmine and a bazooka.

Momma Gash has decided that no matter what happens next—no matter if she's paid or not, whether she lives or dies— she will get her vengeance and it will be sweet. It's been years but she honestly craves the taste of blood.

She's so caught up in her manic fury that she doesn't notice the Escalade that pulls up behind her, lights off, rims spinning.

She's caught up enough that when the Escalade first bumps into the back of her bike, she assumes it's just a mistake. A quick look back reveals the truth—two kids with shotguns.

The Escalade pulls up alongside Momma Gash. The kid in the passenger seat, all cornrows and gleaming grill, rolls the tinted window down and asks, "Why you runnin'?"

Momma Gash doesn't reply. She hits the brakes on her scooter and slips behind the Escalade. She searches her ride for a weapon, any weapon. She finds a chain, a baseball bat, and throwing stars. She goes with the throwing stars.

Pulling her scooter up just behind the rear left wheel of the Escalade, Momma Gash readies to throw one of the matte black metal stars into the rubber but there is a firecracker sound and the tire blows out on it's own. Stripped rubber flies. White smoke puffs up and out.

Its all Momma Gash can do to avoid slamming into the back of the SUV. She curses and pulls a hard right and spins off the road and off her bike into a culvert. As she rolls, kicking up dust and gravel, she hears another crack.

She is sure it is the ricochet of a .50-caliber bullet.

Momma Gash lies there silently, trying to count her breaths, before feeling and counting her ribs. She thinks back to her time in the army, thinks back to the first Gulf War and getting smacked by a Humvee and winding up in a ditch with her breath knocked out. That was like dying. Like being buried underwater. She is certain it was a .50-caliber.

When the crickets start up again, Momma Gash pulls herself up and crawls out of the culvert. The Escalade sits in the middle of the road, the engine still running, the back tires flat.

Momma Gash scans the horizon. A few low hills in the west where the first rays of sunlight are creeping. Pines and elms to the south. It is deadly quiet.

The Escalade's passenger-side door swings open slowly and a kid, no more than fifteen, gets out, eyes bugged, with a submachine gun. He hollers and fires the gun into the sky, tracer rounds leaving red arcs into oblivion like neon spiderwebs trailing the heavens. When he stops, stands there panting and sweating in his wife-beater, is when the third crack comes and the kid's chest implodes. He is thrown back against the Escalade and is dead before his eyes roll backward into his head.

Momma Gash curses under her breath. She has no idea where the sniper is.

The only time Momma Gash fired a .50-caliber was years after the war. She was seeing a woman named Patricia, who had a contact who let her "borrow" a McMillian Tac-50 sniper rifle for an afternoon of fun at the reservoir. Momma was able to blast a can off a picnic table at two thousand meters. She wanted to sleep with that gun but wound up having pathetic sex with Patricia.

Momma Gash does some quick calculations; the shooter might not even be visible. He or she could be nearly a mile away. But the terrain isn't great for long-distance sniping. Momma Gash figures the shooter is close. Maybe a matter of fifty yards or less.

She ducks back and watches from the lip of the culvert.

There is another bang. The air around her ears vibrates.

The driver's-side window explodes.

Then another and the hood goes flying off.

Another and the frame of the Escalade shakes, warps.

Minutes pass in silence, just the *tink tink* of liquid dripping out of the bottom of the car. Finally, just when Momma Gash's legs are starting to cramp, a man appears from behind a pine tree two hundred yards from the road. He is tall and carries a .50-caliber sniper rifle. Momma Gash is proud of herself.

The man walks over to the car and inspects it.

From where she's lying, Momma Gash can tell the man's face is unusual. It's shattered, crisscrossed by scars. She has heard of this man, recalls someone telling her about a messed-up hit man who used to be a doctor. The man checks the car, poking his head into each window, inspecting the back.

He walks over to her downed scooter, pulls out a handgun and blows a hole in the gas tank. Then he smokes a cigarette, scans the horizon. And then he leaves.

Momma Gash waits ten minutes.

Just before she pulls herself out of the culvert, another, identical, Escalade pulls up to the wreck. Two boys get out, both of them as young as the dead ones from the other car. They get on their cell phones, shout obscenities, then jump back into the Escalade and burn rubber.

Momma Gash's body aches, her heart broken, her soul seething. She spits on her bullet-riddled scooter and begins the long walk west to a pay phone.

13.

It is early morning and Leigh is running around a field on a frontage road near Jefferson City, Missouri.

She's running in wide circles through waist-high grass, her arms outstretched. She looks like a kid. Some kid gone crazy on a family vacation. She's been running for ten full minutes. No stops.

Laser has just finished doing some high kicks and push-ups. He and Cody are sitting on the hood of the car. Rufus has been peppering the field with some of his seed bombs and is now inside the car fiddling with the radio.

"What are we going to do with her?" Cody asks. "Honestly."

"We use this," Laser says.

Rufus shouts, "Nothing on the radio about last night."

Cody says, to Rufus, "We're in middle fucking America, Rufus. Besides, I think our fifteen minutes are up."

"I wouldn't be sure of that," Laser says. "I think they've just changed."

Leigh is running toward them. She's got her eyes closed. She gets about fifty feet from the car and then turns left, heads back into the field.

Rufus steps out of the car and lights a cigarette; he hands it to Cody and then lights another one for himself.

Rufus says, "Like I was telling you, the people left behind are doubles. Fact is, most celebrities and CEOs and politicians are already on Mars."

Cody asks, "Where did you hear this, Rufus?"

"That's what's funky. In the seventies there was this documentary produced by the BBC and broadcast in England detailing all of it. How scientists and VIPs have been fleeing the planet for decades. We've had a base on Mars since like the 1950s. The Earth is dying and the people who helped kill it are getting out to leave us here to rot."

"You don't seriously believe any of it?"

"Of course I do. Why wouldn't I?"

"You think Leigh here is a double?"

"Maybe. Possible."

"How come I haven't heard of this? If it was broadcast on television to millions of people wouldn't it have become a big public scandal? This would have been blown wide open years ago, Rufus."

"Well, the BBC said it was fiction. The documentary was filmed for April Fool's Day, but everyone is certain that was just disinformation to make people think it was a joke."

Cody nods. "See, Rufus, the answer's been in front of you the whole time. Your problem, my friend, is that you like the romance of the conspiracy. That's what keeps it alive, that's what justifies your hatred of the system. I'm not gonna fault you that. I hate them too but I'm not going to grasp at straws. They've done enough bad stuff that's undeniable."

Rufus finishes his cigarette and leans against the car and says, "What if Leigh is never found? I mean, what if we all just disappear out here. Set up shop in some tiny farm town. No phones. No Internet. No television. Just live out here."

Cody, looking out at the horizon, says, "That's just more myth, Rufus. Maybe thirty years ago we could do that. Not now. Not with the technology these days. Even the farmers out here have broadband connections. They have satellite television. We walk into town and they'll pick us out in a second flat."

"Sucks," Rufus says. "By the way, this field. The road. I think we're following a ley line. I'm guessing, just looking at those trees over there, that there's an underground river of psychic energy beneath us. Just a guess."

Laser shakes his head and walks down into the field.

He hears Cody behind him berating Rufus. Cody saying, "What the fuck are you talking about, Rufus? That kind of shit will get you handed your ass. . . ."

When Leigh makes another lap around the field she stops in front of Laser and sits down on the ground. He sits down beside her. The grasses in the field are tall enough that they have disappeared from view. As if they are underwater. Leigh's breathing hard and sweating and she wipes the hair out of her face and says, "I feel really amazing."

"Good," Laser says, fiddling with some tiny stones in the dry soil.

"Yeah. It's been a long time since I've felt like this."

Laser says, "You know, you and I have a lot in common in the dad department."

"Oh yeah, did yours try and kill you too?"

"No," Laser laughs. He stops. "Sorry, it's not funny."

Leigh smiles. "We do have a lot in common. Both have fathers that have failed us. Dads obsessed with getting their rocks off. Just that mine has money and access to everything and that's what he wants."

Laser says, "Mine gives everything he has to his porn star. She doesn't love him but that doesn't matter to him. He needs to sleep next to her, to have his hands on her, to feel like a man. To feel important."

"See, you're right."

Laser asks, "Why does your dad want you dead?"

Leigh shakes her head. "I don't know. I know you tell me he does."

"He does."

"He probably is just sick of me. This, this whole kidnapping thing, it wasn't the first thing I tried. Two years ago I just ran away. You read about that?"

"No."

Leigh smirks. "It was in the papers. But it wasn't like this. All my friends knew. Everyone was talking to the press after the first week. I went to Barcelona for a month and, not surprising, my dad didn't give a shit. Anyone who asked, he just said, 'Oh, Leigh is just taking a break from it all. She's young, needs that adventure. It's good she does it now.' Clearly, backfired. After that I just did little things. I sent him malicious letters. Not from myself but from fictitious people at first. Just random names. Then it was from his exes. Then my mom. I made these letters and postdated them to make it look like she'd wanted them sent after she died. Like years later."

"How'd that go over?"

"If he cared he didn't say. He probably knew it was me."

Laser says, "What do you want him to do?"

Leigh's mouth drops open, her eyes narrow. "What?"

"Well, what do you want him to do to show that he loves you? What are you looking for?"

"Fuck you, Laser. You don't get it at all." Leigh starts to get up.

Laser says, "No. No. I don't mean it like that, I'm just . . ."

"Just what?" Leigh snaps.

"It's just that you are trying all these tricks. Have you ever just sat down with him and talked? Told him what you want? What you expect?"

There is a pause. Nothing moves in the field.

Leigh stands up, brushes the dust off her legs and says, "You are just like him, Laser. You don't fucking get it. I don't need to tell him what I want from him. He needs to find it in himself. He needs to feel it. Fucking just feel it."

Leigh stomps off. Laser stands up and says, "Leigh, come on."

She flicks him off.

He grabs her left arm and pulls her back.

"I have something I want you to know," he says.

Her eyes spitting venom, she says, "And?"

"I'm the one who set up your kidnapping. You paid me for the black box."

Leigh starts to laugh.

"I'm serious."

"You're a fucking joke, Laser."

Laser reaches into his pants pocket and pulls out a ring. He hands it to Leigh.

She shakes her head, closes her eyes and tightens her fist around the ring.

"Your grandmother's," Laser says.

"I know."

"So?"

"What do you want? You want me to tell you that you're brilliant? You want me to ask you how you planned this whole charade? How you suckered your friends in? I'm not going to do that, Laser. I don't even know what to think."

"I never intended for this to happen."

"Oh yeah, what *did* you intend? Did you get those poor schizos killed for what? For your art? For your crusade? Did you pay them or were they duped too?"

Laser says nothing.

"A lot of people are dead or wounded because of you."

"You're alive because of me. The nation will change because—"

"You really do believe that, don't you?"

"I do."

"And you think that I'm going to have some role in it. Is that what you want?"

"No. That's not it. I just wanted to rescue you."

"And the reward you thought you'd get?"

"I didn't need a reward. You'd already paid me."

"So?"

"Art. Fame."

"Selfish. You going to tell Cody? Rufus? Tell the rest of your comrades? Don't you think they deserve to know the truth behind all this?"

"Maybe. But it doesn't change anything."

"Like what, Laser?"

"Like the fact that you fascinate me."

Leigh slaps him and storms back to the car, gets in and slams the door. Rufus looks to Laser, walking in from the field, and raises his hands. Cody asks, "What happened? You piss her off?"

Laser shakes his head. "Let's go."

14.

Kip Tiller is getting a deep-tissue massage from a young Korean woman with bright blue lipstick.

He is lying on his back and has his eyes closed when Marcus walks in with a cell phone. Marcus is saying, ". . . certainly unexpected. I don't think he'll be particularly pleased to hear that."

Marcus hangs up.

Kip says, "I don't want to know, do I?"

"Most likely not, Mr. Tiller."

"Will it ruin my time here with Hazumi?"

"Perhaps, Mr. Tiller."

Kip growls. "Oh, fuck it. What is it, Marcus?"

"A call from Gash. She had a run-in with the Black Sultans on an Interstate in Ohio. There was a firefight and several Sultans were killed."

Kip chuckles. "What the fuck!? That boy was like a fucking son to me. What about the dogs, Marcus? Our fucking work? Who does that bitch think she is?"

"Rail is fine, Mr. Tiller."

"Then who died?"

"Others, don't know the names. But Gash didn't kill the Sultans. She said a scarred man with a large rifle, .50-caliber I think she said, was there as well."

Kip sits up, pushes Hazumi out of the way. "What the fuck is going on here?"

"I don't know, Mr. Tiller."

"I do, Marcus. I certainly do. I'm surrounded by fucking incompetence, that's what's going on. Here's what you're going to do, Marcus. You're going to get my Rolodex and look up the Bison Brothers. Then you will call them and tell them that I will pay them four fucking million dollars to get Leigh and kill that fucking car-wrecked bastard."

"The Serologist, sir?"

"Yes, the fucking Serologist! And Marcus, I will be going to the casino tomorrow evening and by the time I get there I want this shit all cleared up. You're coming along."

"Yes, Mr. Tiller."

"And get me some fucking scotch."

"Yes, Mr. Tiller."

"And give Hazumi here an extra hundred, I'm going to need a BJ to calm down."

CHAPTER SEVEN

Convergence

1.

In Overland Park, Kansas, they pick up a new car from an Irregular called Gear.

The man is five foot four and has an orange beard and an Insane Clown Posse tattoo on his right forearm. His eyes are hidden by mirrored sunglasses and he coughs when he speaks. Gear leads them to a garage behind the auto body place he owns and opens the door slowly, savoring the mystery. "You're not going to believe this shit," he says before the garage door rocks to the top. "This will blow your mind."

Inside the garage sits a green BMW.

"Looks nice," Laser says.

Gear coughs. "Nice, you haven't seen shit yet." He walks up to the car and runs his hands over it, says, "This mother is state-of-the-art. I took what you sent me and got it tops. This vehicle, ain't no cop going to catch you from here to China."

"What's on board?" Cody asks.

"Lidatek LE-30 laser jammer, Beltronics Vector radar detectors, Cheetah GPS mirror, police radio scanners, thermal cameras, thirty-gallon reserve tank . . ." Gear looks to Laser. Laser's face is a blank. Cody's as well. Rufus shrugs. Leigh shakes her head.

Gear says, "Don't matter. I'll drive."

"Whoa there, homes—" Cody starts.

"That's fine," Laser interrupts with a wave of his hand. "Gear can come along."

"We leave at dusk," Gear says. "There's a cot and some snacks in the back of the shop. It's nothing pretty but you're more than welcome to crash there for a few hours."

They do.

Laser sleeps fitfully; when he turns, the cheap metal frame the cot is on squeaks and rattles. Cody goes out to buy smokes but winds up lounging in the front of the shop talking to the mechanics about ninjutsu. Rufus and Leigh sip sodas and smoke a joint Gear has drummed up.

"Tell me about the horse," Leigh asks Rufus.

"The horse?"

"Yeah. The one Laser killed with his . . ."

"Mind?"

"Right," Leigh giggles. "His mind."

"I saw it on the tape. Cody was there at the field."

"And the horse just falls over?"

"Yeah. Just died on the spot."

"And Laser?"

"He was messed up good. He fell over too. Cody said it looked like he'd had an aneurism or something. It was the freakiest thing he'd ever seen. Really, that whole horse thing is what committed Cody to the cause. That horse thing is the reason the S.A.D. is as strong as it is, why we have all these Irregulars. The message just spread out."

"What was the message?"

"What happened, that there's this guru running the show who has this power . . ."

"Guru?"

"Sure."

"Like he's a religious figure or something."

"In a way."

"Rufus, you ever think that maybe Laser's just a really good salesman? That maybe he's a good talker and has some sleight-of-hand skills?"

"Like a charlatan?"

"Yeah. Someone that can convince you you've seen something or that maybe you know something only you didn't really see it, you don't really know it."

Rufus takes a long drag on the joint and caches it. He blows the smoke at Leigh and says, "I have never thought that way. Never."

"Maybe you need to. I mean, do you really know Laser?"

"Of course."

"Do you think he keeps secrets from you?"

"No."

Leigh shakes her head. "You guys are so busy questioning everything about the world around you, trying to pull back the skin of things and see the truth through the lies, that you miss the deception right before your eyes."

Rufus gets up. "You just need to get to know him better is all. You'll be just like us in no time, Leigh. You'll see."

Rufus leaves and Laser comes out of the back room and sits down next to Leigh. "You won't convince them of anything," he says. Then he takes a puff of his albuterol.

"Why is that?" Leigh asks.

"I've never lied to them. They don't ask questions."

"So you don't have to tell them, huh?"

"No. Besides, I don't think they'd care."

Leigh grabs Laser's albuterol inhaler and takes a puff from it. She holds her breath and then lets it out slowly. Laser says,

"Won't do anything for you unless you've got bronchoconstriction."

Leigh laughs. "Is that right, Mr. Big Words?"

"Right. Asthma."

"I know. So, what triggers it for you?"

"Colds. Strong chemical smells sometimes. Stress."

"And you can't just cure yourself? You know, with your magic powers?"

Laser laughs. "The horse?"

"Yeah. The horse."

"I killed it with my mind."

"That's what they tell me. There's even some horrible snuff video of it."

"Just an experiment. I never really meant to kill the horse. I mean, I tried to but I didn't think it would work. It goes against every law of physics. At least the way we understand physics. Why don't you believe I did it?"

"It doesn't make sense. And it's you . . ."

"You just don't like that I did it, right?"

Leigh shakes her head. "I didn't say that."

"It's okay. The whole thing is inexplicable, really. I've done some serious training over the past few years, stuff with very respected masters. I've learned techniques that Westerners are simply not taught; a few grandmasters went against tradition to open their secrets to me. I know it sounds like the plot of a bad action film."

"It does a bit. Have anything to do with your dad?"

"Me killing the horse?"

"No. You getting into kung fu and whatever."

"Martial arts."

"Yeah. Those."

"No. My dad, the stuff that went down, all happened long afterward."

"But it helps, right? Being a superhero helps."

Laser kind of curls into himself, brings his knees up under

his chin. This is the most destructible Leigh has seen him and it looks sincere. Laser says, "My dad's failure didn't start my interest but it certainly strengthened it. I basically shut off from everything, including my mom. Being a sixth dan shidoshi certainly helps."

"Can you teach me anything?"

"Let's see . . ." Laser unfolds, turns to Leigh. "Your breathing is actually quite good. Have you taken yoga?"

"No. I mean, a few classes here and there."

"Well, you've got it down nicely."

Laser leans over and puts a hand on Leigh's shoulder and another on her knee. He says, "You need to be able to feel your chi. To find it inside you. Shiatsu massage can help to discipline your body, ensure that you are relaxed and open to receiving enlightenment."

"Will I be a ninja?"

Laser laughs. "We'll work on it."

"I hope you're not one of those sleazy sensei."

"Oh, yeah?"

"Yeah. I've heard stories."

"Like what?"

"Like the wise master who gets the cute young student into his bed to teach her some of the hidden arts. Oh, I've certainly heard all sorts of stories about that."

"I wouldn't worry."

"The worst thing about them, from what I've heard, is that once they've imparted their ancient wisdom, they find a new student. Can you imagine?"

"Not at all." He moves his hands slowly, positioning her.

Leigh stops him. "I'll bet you can't."

"You're my first and best *deshi*."

"*Deshi?*"

"Student."

Leigh smiles. "I'm your only *deshi*." She pulls Laser to her lips.

"I thought I was an asshole."

"I like being fascinated," Leigh replies.

They join Rufus and Cody in the back room with a board game. "It's the only thing he has," Cody says, dropping the box for Car Wars on the floor. "Sounds fitting, actually."

Leigh looks at the box and says, "This is like D&D or something."

Rufus says, "Cool."

Laser groans.

They end up playing, making up the rules of the game as they go along, and laughing so loudly that Gear comes back several times to chastise them. Leigh says, "Laser, shouldn't you be the one berating us?"

Cody agrees. "Yeah, old man Laser."

When they finally crash it's in a pile. Leigh's left foot is wedged against Laser's thigh and he can't sleep because he's too busy thinking about it. Having her warmth on him, even if it's just the sole of her foot, has him breathing slowly, cautiously. He doesn't want her to wake up and move it. He wants to have her foot there the entire rest of the night. Laser even moves himself closer, to get even more of her foot to rest against his leg. At one point he thinks of slowly rolling up his pant leg to have her skin flush against his but decides it's too risky.

He eventually falls asleep staring at her big toe.

With Gear behind the wheel, and Leigh, Rufus, and Cody squeezed into the backseat, it take them nine hours to drive to Boulder, Colorado.

Gear insists it would have been six but they had to make a dozen route changes to avoid various roadblocks and stop and fill up the tank at out-of-the-way stations.

Gear talks almost the whole drive. He talks about his daughter, who is eight years old and already knows the lyrics to nearly every Insane Clown Posse song—she delights in shouting "Fuckin' zombies for rocks!" during "Basehead Attack." Hearing this, Laser cringes. He looks over at Leigh and she's got her pointer finger at the side of her head like a gun, thumb raised. She mouths, "Please. Shoot. Me."

Laser stifles his laughter. Mouths, "I. Didn't. Pick. Him."

Leigh: "Thank. God."

In Boulder they bunk with an Irregular couple, Waylon and Ron, who live in a rented house just north of the University of Colorado campus. It's quaint, half hidden behind fir trees and reeking of paint. The front lawn is littered with sculptures. Most of them figures. Some appear half-formed, as though they are crawling from the ground. And in the long patches of grass are old potting wheels and shattered urns. In a thousand years this place will be mistaken for an archeological dig site.

Waylon is tall, with a potbelly and a goatee. His partner, Ron, has a similar shape though he's balding and wears thick glasses. There is also a woman living with them. Her name is Katja and she's an artist from Norway.

Laser walks into their place. "You have the screen?"

Waylon looks to Ron. "Charming as ever."

Leigh grabs Laser's hand. "Laser says hello."

Laser says, "Hello."

Waylon hugs him. Leigh then introduces Cody and Rufus. Ron claps and smiles and says to Leigh, "It's an honor to have you here. We never read the paper but . . . Well, you've kind of been in the news lately."

Leigh says, "You don't know the half of it."

Waylon shows them to their room. It's small. A bunk bed and a cot on the floor.

"Hope you weren't expecting five star," Waylon jokes.

"Do you have the screen?" Laser asks again.

"Of course," Waylon says. "You can actually relax for a few minutes."

"Thanks."

At dinner they sit around four tables that have been pushed together to make one large one, though it doesn't really. Waylon and Ron use three card tables and smash them up against their small dining room table. Each table differs in height and Cody and Rufus, sitting at the smallest of the card tables, have trouble getting their legs under. Waylon jokes that they've been "relegated to the kids' table."

Dinner is falafel and seitan with leftover panang curry. Ron apologizes for the paucity of the meal but once the wine is served, no one seems to mind. The first bottle is gone within minutes and then Katja busts out a bong and suddenly the whole room is high. After dinner there are truffles and some upside-down pineapple cake that Waylon picked up two days ago. It's overly sweet but no one seems to mind. Laser sits in a chair and fiddles with a cell phone while the rest of the party lazes about the small bungalow, moving from chair to couch to floor, playing cards and talking. When the laughter has subsided for more than fifteen minutes and everyone is looking around the room, their eyes still dancing with wine, Laser says, "Let's talk logistics."

There is a collective groan.

"Unfortunately," Laser says, "we're not here to party. We've got a lot of fucking work to do if this is going to work tomorrow. And don't even get me started on how stressed out I am about Vegas."

Ron says, "The green screen is set up to broadcast. It's in the basement."

Waylon adds, "Stratovision is up and running as well. Been running five-minute test signals all week. Works perfect."

"Can I ask what we're talking about?" Leigh butts in.

Laser smiles. "You're going to dig this."

"You going to broadcast the horse tape?"

Cody cracks up.

"No. Better," Laser says. "We're going to broadcast a video to everyone in the United States tomorrow. It will be on nearly every local station for approximately eight minutes. We're talking everyplace that has a television on—from homes to laundry mats to hotels to sports bars. Everywhere."

Gear says, "Bitchin'."

Leigh nods. "Cool but how?"

"Stratovision. It was developed during World War II. Waylon's the expert."

Waylon leans forward, clears his throat. "It is technically highly illegal but we'll be using eight outfitted Hercules turboprops—all old military, all unbelievably expensive and hard to get—to transmit a prerecorded message to all stations on the UHF band."

"Simply put, it's pirate television," Cody says.

Waylon adds, "It has never been done on this scale. Ever since Lucky 7 got hold of the Syracuse station in seventy-seven, pirate TV people have been dreaming of this. When I worked for the networks we used to sit around the break room and try and come up with practical applications for new technologies, ways to make this actually happen. But now, Laser, he's done it."

Leigh looks to Laser and Laser raises an eyebrow.

"So, what's the tape?" Leigh asks.

"Well," Laser says, "we've produced a little something that Cody actually put together. It's a bit of chaotic montage and it's quite daring. But the tape isn't finished. We still need the intro."

"Hence the green screen," Leigh says.

Laser says, "Hence the green screen."

"Who's doing it?" Leigh asks.

"We'd like you to."

"You were so good in Cincinnati," Ron adds.

"What would I be saying?" Leigh asks.

"Oh, we've got a script," Laser says.

"I'd like to see it."

"Of course."

Laser reaches into his back pocket and produces a folded, single page that he unfolds and hands to Leigh. Leigh reads it over, her face scrunched up. She turns to Laser and says, "This is pretty strong."

"It is."

"If you're willing," Ron says. "We can record it now."

Leigh pauses for a second, reads over the paper again, then says, "Fuck it. Let's do this."

Later, Laser and Leigh sit outside on the back porch and look at the stars. Leigh smokes and Laser nurses a beer. "You did a great job," he tells her.

"Thanks."

After a moment, Leigh asks, "Why did you want to save me?"

"You know."

"But why me?"

"You came to me, Leigh. You were looking for an out or an in, I guess."

Leigh shrugs. "Why did you agree? If it wasn't about money?"

"Fame. Art. The media firestorm. I planned all of this around it."

"Right."

"And," Laser adds, looking up at the sky, "I wanted to show you something."

"Show me what?"

"Life. Your ability."

"How's that?"

"I hate saying this because it comes off all stalkerish but I've always been fascinated by you. The way you carry yourself in public, the events you turn up at, your appreciation of the arts. When I heard a rumor that you were looking for an 'out,' something dramatic, I knew it was my chance to meet you and to liberate you."

"Liberate me? From what?"

"Yourself. Your situation. This whole thing," Laser says, spreading his arms wide. "*This* is about you. *This* is about you becoming the woman you've always wanted to be."

"How do you know what I want, Laser?"

"Your eyes, I can see it. They are brilliant."

"Is that a welcome to this fucked-up family?"

"Sure."

With that he kisses her full on the lips and passionately, strongly. She pulls him in and they tumble off the porch and onto the dry earth. Leigh pulls at Laser's clothing and digs her nails into the skin on the back of his neck. Laser takes Leigh's shirt off and runs his tongue between her breasts to her navel. She sighs, arches her back. "Don't hurt me."

He pulls her jeans down and moves his face between her legs. Leigh looks up into the night sky and the stars double and then triple. Supernovae explode and then collapse into darkness. The world spins furiously and the specks of light rain down upon her in droplets of millennia-old light. Leigh tugs at Laser's hair and pulls him to her lips. She groans. "I need you inside me."

There is a tightening feeling. A rush of warmth. Leigh closes her eyes. The ground beneath her sways in rhythm with her panting. Her fingers become fists and then waves and finally wings.

When she opens her eyes she is surprised to find herself crying.

Laser's face hovers over hers. "I love you."

The video plays continuously for six hours.

It unrolls on eighteen million television screens across the country and it opens with Leigh Tiller, standing against a CGI flag that undulates slowly and says S.A.D., looking directly into the camera lens that is slowly zooming in on her face: "Father, I am leaving you. I am leaving the life you created for me and I am going to destroy you. Not physically but financially. Not morally but mentally. Soon, the world will know just how corrupt and sad you really are. The world's going to find out just how corrupt all of this is—how corrupt all of us are. I'm sorry, Dad, but it's over."

The camera zooms in so her face fills the whole of the frame. "You, out there watching this, you aren't off the hook either. You have neglected your children. You have neglected yourself. Now is the time to shake off the disease of cheap modern living. Don't be dull anymore. There are thousands of people who work very hard every day to make you believe in what they want you to believe, to sell you what they want you to buy, to make you think that you're too fat or too thin or too dumb or too slutty or too smart or too ugly or too cheap. It is up to you to break their stranglehold on all of us."

Leigh pauses. Her eyes narrow. "Do not believe anything you've heard. Do not trust what you've been told. My kidnapping. My rescue. My father. Go with your gut and join us in revolution."

Leigh's face fades and is replaced with a white screen. Static ripples across its surface. Images move there. Then the static fades to black and in the black there is a white box. A white box that gets bigger and bigger. Or maybe it's just that the camera is zooming in closer and closer until the box nearly fills the screen. Two eyes open inside the box. The eyes of a woman with heavy eyeliner and super long lashes. The eyes hover transcendent for a minute and then ruby red lips appear below them. The lips move as the woman speaks, "We are Strategic Art Defense and we have come to free your minds."

A final message, white font, reads: "Join the Wave. One point five days. Vegas Strip. Bring your mom."

Leigh can't sleep.

Laser buzzes at her side, his mouth open and nostrils flaring. Even in sleep he seems ferocious, the way a tiger looks at rest.

Leigh gets up and sneaks out of the room, past Rufus sprawled out on the couch. She goes out to the back porch. The moon hovers above the tree line, flat like it is pasted there.

It is warm and the night smells of wildflowers.

Leigh holds herself tight and glows inside. She is so very proud of herself. Two weeks ago she could never have imagined herself like she is now. Telling the nation how horrible her father is. Telling her father to go to hell. She has demolished her name in only a few seconds. The feeling is elation.

This whole thing has been like a very aggressive game. Something like touch football where everyone involved is playing their very hardest. Everyone is sweating their asses off trying to make the touchdowns, trying desperately, almost rabidly, to connect the passes. Leigh has had competitive games where by the end the winner was clear and everyone was exhausted. She's had lacrosse games in high school that were like wars. After these games she had to run slow laps around the field to bring her adrenaline back down. This whole ridiculous adventure has been the same way. Only it's not a game. There are guns and killers and cops and an avalanche of upheaval.

Her world has been swept out from under her feet and she cannot imagine what it will look like when the pieces fall back into place. If they ever do. She does not worry about dying. After so many brushes with death—mostly brutal and strange and terrifying—Leigh's almost immune to the sting of despair. She does not worry about what tomorrow will bring because tomorrow is like another year. It is a decade away. It is unknowable. The elation she feels surges through every moment when her eyes are open. And now, now that she's officially, publicly, become one of "them," the elation rises like carbonation with every hammer of her heart.

Laser.

Leigh has not felt this way about a boy in so many, many

years. There were those who passed through her compass in college. Some that she even fell in love with but it was fleeting love, love that counted its breaths in semesters and days. Sometimes hours. The love was as real as the friendships she'd made. As real feeling as the drugs she was indulging in. Being young and rich and beautiful meant getting anything she wanted. It meant showing up at the dining hall and having heads swivel and for the first two years of college that was spectacular. By senior year it had worn off and Leigh was addled. Maybe it was that the drugs were becoming rote. The ragged evening parties that bled into afternoons, no longer intoxicating. The thrill, so to speak, was gone.

It was hard to tap back into that energizing vein. Being wildly upset about her father usually did it for a day or so. After college the drugs vanished and so did the friends. Leigh fell into what she'd call a "showy" rut. Life was merely the time between one walkway or premier to another. Everything routine and planned out, mapped and plugged in by Marchesa. She began feeling as flat and lifeless as she looked on screen. And then the kidnapping scheme popped into her head. Planning it—all the shadowy encounters and whispered directions—had given her a boost. Something to look forward to that didn't sparkle with a clean sheen. Waiting for the actual abduction was like waiting for Christmas morning. Then a blur. And now, Laser. Laser the asshole wizard behind the curtains of her life.

Leigh is herself again.

No. She is more than herself. She is the Leigh Tiller she was meant to be.

Leigh goes back inside and climbs into bed beside Laser. She watches the steady rise and fall of his chest and then lies down with her hand over his heart. She counts out the beats until she is fast asleep.

2.

The Serologist picks up a prostitute in Salina, Kansas.

She is blond, has stick legs and an underbite. She is hanging out by an overpass and says her name is Karen. When she gets in the car and sees the Serologist's face she holds her breath and turns away.

"I'm sure you've seen more attractive men," he says.

Karen shrugs. Says, "I haven't been doing this long. Most men are ugly."

The Serologist laughs. "Ugly, huh?"

"Yeah. Most of them."

"How old are you Karen?"

"Nineteen."

"Sure."

"Look, are we just going to talk? Either way it'll cost."

"How much?"

Karen pulls down the visor mirror and puts some lipstick on. She says, "Twenty for a blow job. Fifty for straight and an extra ten for anal."

"I'll give you a hundred if I can just hold you."

"Seriously?"

"And you tell me how old you really are."

Karen looks at the Serologist and smiles. She's missing two bottom front teeth but her smile is charming. The smile doesn't last long. She thinks for a second and says, "You promise you're not going to try something sick with me?"

"I promise."

They pull into a field and the Serologist turns off the headlights. The car shudders to silence and begins to cool. Karen sits with her shoes off and her feet on the dash. She smokes a cigarette and offers the Serologist a drag. He shakes his head. When she's done with the cigarette she throws the butt out of the window and then curls up next to the Serologist.

Her body is rigid. Her head on his chest.

He strokes her hair and says, "How old?"

"Fifteen," Karen squeaks.

"Wow."

"I haven't been out here that long. I'm not going to be either. I just need some money to get a car and get the fuck out of here."

"Boyfriend?"

"Rob. Beats the hell out of me always. Look at my thigh here."

Karen pulls up her already short skirt. There is a welt the size of a shoe on her inner thigh. "At least he didn't use the cigarettes."

"What about your parents?"

"They are good people. God-loving people. They go to church every Sunday and pray for my everlasting soul. Swear to Christ they do. All I tell them, every time, is that I was just born a bit wrong. Nothing that they did. I think I was just cursed."

"Drugs?"

"Yeah."

"What's your real name?"

Karen rolls over and looks up at the Serologist's barely human face and says, "Karen. Why do you care so much? My tits don't interest you?"

"They do," the Serologist says. "But I'm tired. I just want . . . I don't know."

"Fine," Karen says. She rolls back over. "Can I ask you what happened to your face? That okay?"

The Serologist says, "A car accident. My wife and my daughter were killed."

"Sorry."

"It was a long time ago. So long."

"How old was she?"

"My daughter?"

"Yeah."

"Your age."

Karen sighs. "I get it now."

"She was beautiful. Had everything going for her."

"That's sad," Karen says. "Let's talk about something else. What do you do?"

"I was a serologist. A doctor."

"Not anymore, though?"

"You know what's funny? Maybe two years ago this wouldn't be happening." The Serologist's eyes dance beneath the hoods of his mismatched eyelids. He says, "Two years ago, you'd probably be seeing me for a consultation. How funny is that?" The Serologist chuckles, his narrow shoulders shake.

"Not funny," Karen says.

"You're right." The Serologist nods. "It's not funny at all. It's sad really. Two years ago, before the accident, I wasn't the person you're sitting with. I guess the best word for it is 'uncanny.' How a person can change so dramatically, you'd think that it had something to do with evil or maybe possession. That's uncanny. Shocking, even. The fact of the matter is, what happened to me is proof that God just doesn't exist."

Karen says, "God does."

The Serologist shakes his head. He says, "No. Chemicals. We're big, floppy bags of chemicals. That's what I'd been taught in school. It's the science of the human body. But you don't really realize it. You don't know it down deep until something happens to you. You mess up the chemicals and you get a new person. Electroshock, medication, brain tumor, catastrophic accident. Those are the building blocks of making a new person. Me, it was a car accident. I go into the accident the me I was before, someone with high moral standards, a clear distinction of right and wrong. You could say I was even God-fearing. I come out the new me, someone who couldn't give a rat's ass about other people—someone as nihilistic as you get. I was reborn a sociopath. It was the chemicals that did that. There was no otherworldly intervention that made me evil. No hand of fate. Twist of shadows. Nah, we're just simple machines and I was rewired for bad."

Karen sits up and looks at the Serologist. "You're not going to hurt me, right? You promised."

The Serologist nods. "I won't."

Karen asks, "Can I go now?"

"Yes. Here." He pulls out his wallet and gives Karen two fifties. They drive back to the overpass in silence and as she opens the door to get out, Karen says, "You're a good person no matter what you say and God is looking out for you."

She gets out and closes the door. The Serologist says, "Wait."

Karen waits beside the idling car.

The Serologist gets out and grabs something from a bag on the backseat. It's a handgun. He gives it to Karen and she takes it from him, her hands shaking with the weight of it. The Serologist dips back into the bag and pulls out a box of ammunition. He hands this to Karen as well.

Before driving off he says, "Your boyfriend . . ."

"Rob."

"Right, Rob," he says. "You shoot him in the gut. Twice. You get him in the gut and he will never hit you again. He'll die slow. Suffer."

Then the Serologist leaves and Karen, putting the gun and bullets in her purse, waves after the car as it vanishes. Two red eyes in a sea of black.

3.

The Bisons, Don and Stevie, are kicking the shit out of Manu Coulibaly on the patio of their apartment when their friend Marie runs over screaming and knocks Don down.

He falls hard and hits his chin on the concrete. Blood everywhere.

Marie stands over him shouting, "You got a fucking phone call!"

Stevie continues to kick Manu, a slight nineteen-year-old from Mali, all over the patio. Marie tries to pull him off but she's sweaty and her hands slick and Stevie is strong. He kicks Manu over to the railing and smashes him in there. When Manu stops squealing and jerking around, Stevie kneels down and takes his wallet. There are two hundred dollars inside. Marie stands over his shoulder and looks at the cash. She smiles.

"Score," Stevie says. He turns to Don and his bloody gash of a chin and says, "We didn't even need to use the gun on this fucker."

Don, sitting, smiles, blood in his teeth. "How much?"

Marie says, "I just told you, you got a fucking phone call and it's super—"

Stevie punches her hard in her left breast and Marie wheezes and falls backward. "It's only two hundred bucks, bitch," he says. He turns to Don and says, "Check that nigger for shit."

Don crawls over to Manu and searches his clothes. "This dude is still alive," he says. "He's breathing all ragged like he got knifed but he's alive."

"What's he have?" Stevie asks.

Marie is crying. She says, "Why the fuck did you have to hit me like that?"

Don holds up a bag of white powder and says, "Bingo!"

Stevie asks, "What is it?"

Don opens the bag and sticks a bloody finger in and then puts it in his mouth and then says, "Tina."

"Let's smoke that shit!" Stevie shouts.

Marie has trouble getting up but she does and she stops crying and says, "Can I please have some?"

Stevie smiles, hugs her, grabs her ass and says, "'Course, baby."

They stumble inside and leave Manu bleeding on the patio. There are six other people crowded into the studio apartment and Brotha Lynch Hung blares from a cheap boom box. The place is a wreck. The television is on the floor, on its side, and scrolling distorted porn between bursts of static. There are two futon mattresses in the middle of the room and three patio chairs. The room is thick with smoke and ash and there is a naked girl passed out in the kitchen.

Stevie and Don kick people off two of the patio chairs and then sit down to smoke the meth. Marie sits on the floor by Stevie's feet. She sits and caresses his thigh, her hands shaking. Don hands Stevie a glass pipe and Stevie gets the pipe packed and then lights it. The meth burns red. He's the first to take a long drag, then he hands it to Don. He says, "Cut with cough medicine. Not great."

Don shrugs, takes a couple of drags and then hands the pipe to Marie.

Marie says, "Phone call."

Stevie asks, "Why the fuck didn't you tell us, bitch?"

Marie almost cries. Her voice tiny, she says, "I tried."

"Who?" Don asks.

"Some guy named Marcus. Said he was calling for another guy named Tiller."

"Holy shit!" Don bolts up. "What's the number?"

Marie looks on her hand. It's scrawled there in marker.

Don says, "Gimme your cell." Marie does. He heads out to the patio and dials standing over Manu's prostrate form.

Inside, Stevie stands up and starts to dance. Spins with his eyes closed. Marie heads to the kitchen and brings back three liters of Dr Pepper and a bulk bag of Smarties. A thin guy with a flaky goatee gets up and dances next to Stevie, the two of them throwing fists at each other. Stevie howls with laughter and the two of them start slamming into each other. The goatee guy falls on the television and the set smashes under him, glass crunching out into the carpet and acrid smoke spiraling up to join the thick cloud of smoke already making the edges of the apartment fuzzy.

Outside, Don says, "Tell Tiller sorry for the delay."

Manu groans and Don thinks to kick him but doesn't because Kip Tiller comes barreling onto the other end of the line something heavy. "What the fuck, Don? I don't know why I even bother with you assholes. If it weren't for the fact that you shit-for-brains were capable of massacres, I'd fucking have your scalps above the fireplace at my lodge in Aspen."

Don says, "We haven't had a gig in a while. Not that we're rusty or—"

"Look, I'm not calling to chat. I told your dad ten years ago that I'd keep you assholes employed and I stick by my word. I'm willing to pay you a shitload for some serious murders."

"Okay."

"You have heard about my daughter, I assume."

"Yeah. Of course. Sorry, man."

"Don't be. Here's the deal—I need you to kill my daughter and whomever she is with. Got it? I don't care if it's five nuns or a busload of preschoolers. All of them go down. That's number one."

"That's heavy, Mr. Tiller."

"Not as heavy as the fact that I had my best man sent out to do it and apparently he's either changed his mind or lost his mojo because he hasn't done shit but kill other people I didn't send him out to kill."

"Wicked."

"Indeed. And it gets better. I already hired a whole slew of motherfuckers to do this job, only so far none of them has been able to do it. I'm going to need you and your brother and whatever ruffians you can hire to not only get my daughter and who she's with but to also kill all the other fuckers I hired."

"Seriously? How many people are we talking? Is this like a coast-to-coast gig?"

"They are all headed in one direction—to me."

"Where are you?"

"Vegas."

"Heard that's almost all locked down."

"You can guess why."

"Uh-huh. I guess we need some names, some photos, some vehicle descriptions, last sightings, the usual shit."

"And for me to get you that I guess you're going to need to get your ass to a fax or a computer. I want this done pronto, fucker. I want it done slick and I want it done fucking right. If you fuck this up, Don . . . if you fuck this shit up you can't even imagine what unspeakable things I will do to you and your brother."

"Got it, Mr. Tiller. How much?"

"Marcus didn't give you a number?"

"Nah. At least not that I heard."

"How much do you want?"

"Fuck. I dunno. How about two million?"

"Done."

"That's after costs."

"What costs do you have? You need something special this time?"

"Had my eye on this one bazooka."

"Fine. Buy the bazooka, put a bow on it, and call it a gift."

Don busts inside the apartment shouting. Screaming. "We're fucking millionaires, brother!" He stops Stevie's mad dancing and whispers in his ear. Stevie's eyes go wide. Marie says, "I wanna know! I wanna know!"

Don kisses her full on the lips. "We're fucking rich!"

More meth. More coke. More cough syrup. Stevie dances for the next five hours. He's covered in sweat, naked and eyes crossed when he finally falls to the floor in the kitchen. He loses two teeth on the fridge door handle on the way down. Don masturbates on the naked girl passed out in the kitchen before falling asleep on one of the futons.

4.

Leigh and Laser are sitting on a rock overlooking a dam near Nederland and watching the sunset turn the sky and mountains and water orange.

Cody is updating them from a picnic table where he sits with Rufus and Gear. Cody says, "Five simultaneous actions in Lexington, Seattle, Oakland, Cheyenne, and Pensacola."

"How'd the Pensacola one go?" Laser asks.

"Great. Converted a full rig into a bio-fuel system overnight. Whole fleet is considering doing it based on the tech. News down there is buzzing with it."

"And Cheyenne?"

"New subdivision greened. All the grass replanted, solar panels installed, even windmills. The place looks a bit like Disneyland but the investors are digging it 'cause the media is creaming over it. Check that box."

"What's on the main line?"

Cody thumbs through some printouts. "All the majors are tied up in some Homeland Security Announcement about us being considered terrorists. They're linking us up with the ecoterror folks, even listed some black militant groups. Your picture was on the tube late last night. They've got you as Lester."

"How about Vegas?"

"Lockdown. Roadblocks. Whole nine yards. Tiller's expecting Armageddon."

The surface of the rock they're sitting on is warm and they

flatten themselves against it, soaking in the warmth, staring up at the pink cauliflower-head clouds and down into the reflections in the calm surface of the reservoir.

Leigh whispers to Laser, "I used to spend the summers with my aunt and uncle in Ohio and we would go out every night to the shore and watch the sun set over Salt Fork Reservoir. My uncle loved to tell me these urban legends. He believed them though, so I guess in his mind they weren't legends. His favorites were always about animals. You know, alligators in the sewers and stuff. He had this one story about giant catfish. Freaked me out as a kid and I would avoid the reservoir after he told me. For days I wouldn't go in and then, right before I was supposed to go back to New York, I'd make one big dash into the water to prove to myself that I wasn't afraid."

"What was the story?"

"He told me that catfish can get really, really huge. That fish will keep growing as long as they live. Especially catfish. He told me that around the world there are stories about giant catfish that eat dogs and children, just suck them down under the water in one gulp. The one story I remember most vividly was one about some construction divers working on an electric dam. They would dive deep enough that it was pitch black, work by lamps alone, hundreds of feet down. My uncle says that some of these men came up one day and refused to go back. Said that they saw giant catfish, as big as boats, swimming slowly along the bottom, creeping in and out of the lamplight. Gives me goose bumps still."

Laser says, "I like this uncle."

"He was awesome. Died of a heart attack when I was in high school. This whole thing we're in, it's kind of like that. I feel like the future is something lurking at the bottom of a real dark lake. Something just waiting to swallow us up."

Leigh sits up and puts her arms around her knees. The sun has dipped behind the mountains and now there is just a deep orange haze as the shadows lengthen and absorb everything and the lights of nearby homes flicker on. Leigh looks over at Laser, still lying flat on his belly, his arms propping up his head, and asks, "In your best dreams, what do you see happening?"

"I have a good feeling it'll be pretty dramatic."

"In a good way?"

"The best way."

"And us? Where do you see us going after this?"

Laser sits up and says, "Somewhere different—"

"I can't go back to the way things were," Leigh interrupts. "You know, the night I was kidnapped I was working on a movie. It was going to be my first role, this indie thing that, now that I think about it, was just trash. Maybe that was the point but it was ironic."

"What do you want?"

"This." Leigh spreads her arms wide, taking in the land-scape. "I want to be where it's quiet and people don't know who I am or who my family is. I can get a job somewhere, maybe not a small town, but a city I haven't lived in. Make new friends, start a new life."

"Sounds nice. I hope it happens."

"You're not confident though, right?"

"Right."

"Why?"

"I worry that no one is really ready for this. We're all so com-fortable. Even me. I'm comfortable doing this. No one really likes change if it involves too much work. For what we want to do, people will need to break their backs. And chances are they won't even live to see the results. We're planting trees here. I think it's much more likely that we will be jailed or worse. I'm ready for that, but still."

"But you're trying."

"Yeah. I have no other option. There is no off button with me."

"So visions of you as a farmer dad are out of the question, right?"

"Right."

"Guess I'll just have to settle for a revolutionary."

"If we live."

"Way to look on the bright side."

Laser sighs. "When this all first started, after our first few S.A.D. missions, I would lie awake at night just running off the adrenaline. My heart pounding and my brain electrified. I used to imagine that one day, if we tried hard enough, I would have enough money and manpower at my disposal to construct this doomsday device. I never figured out exactly what it would entail but it'd be big and bad and it would instantly slam the brakes on progress and we'd all have to start over fresh. Just erase everything. Like a restart button. It's a ridiculous thought, I know, but I suppose all of us have it from time to time."

"Can't say that I have."

"I saw it like this gleaming cube and I'd yell 'Banzai!' and hit the one button on the front of it, everyone cheering me on, and then . . . just white light. It would be beautiful."

"To be honest, it sounds freaky. Hope you don't ever get that wish."

Laser nods. "Kind of totalitarian of me, huh?"

"Totally."

"I'm a bit of a control freak even in my fantasies."

Leigh rubs Laser's thigh. She whispers, "We're working on it."

They sit in Gear's modified BMW with the engine humming outside Waylon and Ron's.

Laser, in the passenger seat, has shaved his head. Cody has as well. Rufus's hair is dyed black. Leigh's is dyed red. Gear looks the same. No one speaks; everyone sits there frozen as though they are listening to the engine, trying to pinpoint some minute rattle or hidden ting.

A cell phone rings. It's Gear's.

He answers. Says, "Sure." Hands the phone to Laser. Adds, "It's encrypted."

Laser gets on and immediately asks, "How many?" Then, "Excellent." And finally, "We'll be there later."

He hands the phone back to Gear and turns to Cody, Leigh and Rufus. "We're on. They've got five hundred decoys already lined up and probably more to come."

Cody whoops.

Gear asks, "Decoys of who?"

"Us," Laser says. "The five of us as we looked yesterday. Five hundred odd Irregulars and friends are driving to Vegas right now and all of them look like us."

"Think that will get us in?" Leigh looks concerned.

Laser says, "It will."

"And what then? I mean it's going to be pretty hard to do whatever you're going to do at my dad's casino without being noticed. He's paranoid. I'm sure the place is pretty much sealed up."

"Best part is," Laser says, "we already did what we needed at the casino. Our goal is just to show up there and raise the flag."

Cody motions with his thumb to the trunk. "Flag."

Gear says, "It's about a ten-hour drive normally. If we're able to avoid speed traps and can get up to ninety something, it might take six. When we get into town, we'll switch the Beamer for something a bit more exciting."

Laser's eyebrows go up. "Exciting?"

Gear says, "Just trust me on this."

5.

The Serologist has breakfast at a diner in southern Colorado. This place has been on the same tiny street corner for three decades. All around it are subdivisions and box stores. The Serologist has eggs over easy and sausage. He eats white toast with butter and strawberry preserves.

There is a small boy, maybe five years old, watching him from an adjacent table. The boy makes a face every time the Serologist chews. It's as though the kid is trying to read something in the scars. As though he's confused by the patterns he's trying to make out.

After breakfast, the Serologist has a third cup of coffee and sips it slowly, deliberately, watching the light traffic move outside. His phone rings just as he finishes his cup. It's Kip. "Cops found something you left behind."

"What's that?"

"What was left of that shrink you cut to bits. I thought you did things clean."

The Serologist pauses. He says, "I do. Must have floated back up."

"Must have."

"I'm not too concerned about it."

"I know you don't watch television but do you read a paper?"

"From time to time. Mostly just the comics."

"The shit has hit the fan major. The cops, the FBI, the fucking army, everyone is in on this now. Vegas is a fortress. There's no way they will get in and there's no way you will either. I suggest meeting them somewhere outside the city and finishing the job I hired you for."

"I appreciate your concern—"

"I'm not concerned about you, you fucking clown. I'm just getting all my remaining ducks in a fucking row and you're the last. If you want to work for me again, you'll get this job done and you'll save me some money."

"How's that?"

"As you already know, I've got some guns out for the same

target as you. They've been promised big bucks to take Leigh and you down. I'll admit to being a bit panicky at this point."

"Momma Gash. Black Sultans."

"Maybe others. Your one chance of getting back in my good graces is to finish my daughter and kill the rest of them. We're talking taking on an army here, but frankly I'd rather pay you than any of those fucked-up bastards."

"Sounds like a war of attrition."

"Don't give me that bullshit. All war is attrition. The only question here is who outlasts whom. The only pleasure is knowing that you won before you die."

"Fine."

The phone goes dead. The Serologist pays his bill and walks to his car.

Kip Tiller's helicopter lands on top of the Tiller Casino, just off the south end of the Vegas Strip.

He is wearing a double-breasted Armani suit and has Aviators on. He waves to a crowd that has assembled on the rooftop, the intense sun beaming off his forehead. Kip makes his way to a podium with an American flag.

Kip begins with a nod to the journalists assembled on the rooftop.

He says, "I'm happy to take a few questions."

A reporter in a baseball cap and vest asks, "How are you holding up?"

"I'm doing okay. I have faith—that lets me sleep a few hours a night. I just hope that this is all over in the next few days and that Leigh is back safely. I really just want to see her smiling again."

A woman with her hair in a bun asks, "People are comparing this to the Hearst kidnapping. What is your reaction to the pirate-video broadcast?"

"I've been answering phone calls for the past twelve hours straight, ma'am. Everyone that calls says the same thing—they imply that my daughter has for whatever reason joined up with these degenerates. My only answer, and what I'll say here, is that there are two options. First, she's being forced. Second, look up Stockholm Syndrome."

A woman with a nose ring asks, "Do you think the authorities are doing as much as they can? This has become a national-security issue now. These people are being classified as terrorists."

"Well, they are. That's not even in doubt. They were the moment they took her. Anyone who inflicts and delights in terror is a fucking . . . excuse me, a lousy terrorist. I'm a bit emotional as you can imagine and lack of sleep doesn't help. The truth is, I'll agree to whatever helps get my baby back."

A large man in a polo shirt asks, "What do you think they're hoping to do in Las Vegas? Do you think it has anything to do with the new casino?"

Kip Tiller laughs. "I bet so. But I think they'll have difficulty doing anything they planned considering we've got every security guard and off-duty cop in the city patrolling the halls of the hotel. If they're looking for a standoff, they've found one here."

A woman in a tiger-print vest asks, "Can you tell us about the Tiller? The building was recently denounced in a prominent architectural digest as the ugliest building on the Strip and environmental groups have been chastising you for—"

"Let them blather," Kip interrupts. "We've built it because the American people want it. It has all the luxury that Americans want. Think of it in terms of the SUV. If you can afford to drive a car that requires a lot of gas, then drive it. So what if it's not the most popular thing in the world to a bunch of liberals? They don't speak for the bulk of Americans who want comfort and are willing to pay for it. As far as the look of the casino, well, this wasn't built for liberal arts grads. This was built for mainstream America. That will be all, thanks."

With a wave that's more middle finger than thanks, he leaves.

6.

The drive over the mountains is slower than expected.

Laser has prescheduled stops to pick up cell phones from Irregulars along the way. Most of the time it involves pulling over to meet someone at the side of the road. Someone who comes running up to the car with the phone and shoots Leigh a thumbs-up and a smile. The phone calls Laser makes are short, just him nodding and saying, "Okay."

After the fifth such stop and the fifth phone call, Leigh asks, "What's up?"

Laser says, "We're good. The Irregulars are in place."

"What's the final tally?" Cody asks.

"Fifteen hundred."

Rufus says, "Sweet Jesus."

"I thought the place is all blocked off," Leigh says. "How would they all get in? I mean we're going to have a hard enough time as it is."

"Most of them have been there for weeks," Laser says. "A few hundred drove or flew in a few days ago, right before your rescue. Others? Who knows? But the good news is they are there. Good news is we're ready to rumble."

Near two in the morning they slip into Las Vegas from the east. It takes them longer to reach the city center than it did to cross over the Rocky Mountains. Each block, they stop while Gear listens in on the police scanner. When everything is clear he pulls forward to the next block and so on until it feels like they've traversed the whole city crab-walking.

"Danja's," Gear says when they pull into an alley. From there he leads them to a massive hangar-sized garage behind a Kmart. A woman, mid-thirties, with a crew cut and suspenders meets them at the door. She says, "I'm Danja."

"Hi, Danja," Laser says. "We hear you have a vehicle."

"Oh, I do," she says. "Check it out."

She turns around theatrically; there's something like a tank behind her. It's long, submarine-like and has twelve wheels. The wheels are stacked on each other in the shape of a triangle. The front of this thing looks like an airplane.

"What the fuck is that?" Cody says.

Laser walks up to the vehicle and runs his hand along its metal siding. "The Landmaster. It's a prop from a flick from the seventies called *Damnation Alley*."

Danja is psyched. "Yes! That's it."

"No. Wait, did you just say it was a prop?" Rufus asks.

"Yeah. But it's fully functioning," Danja says.

Rufus says, "But it's a prop."

"No. Yeah, but not now. It was used in the movie as a special effect but the vehicle is real. I mean, this baby can actually get up to eighty—at least that's as far as I've gone—on the open highway and it doesn't need as much gas as you'd expect. Maybe as much as a big RV."

Laser says, "It'll get the job done."

"Sorry, boss, but weren't you the level-headed one that hated my silver pistols? You should be totally against this. I mean, this is a serious antique," Cody says.

Laser says, "Things are different now. We need something strong."

Leigh adds, "This looks plenty strong."

Danja opens one of the doors on the side and everyone climbs up the short ladder to get a look inside. It's big and empty. Bunk beds. A shower. A gun rack mounted on one wall. Shotguns. Rifles. A submachine gun. Two handguns. Knives. A

samurai sword. There are two side doors, a hatch on the ceiling
to the roof and a big rear door. The cockpit has two seats, four
closed-circuit television screens, a mess of switches and gears,
and a big wheel like on a sailing ship. Danja says, "Thirty-five
feet long. Eleven tons. This baby has a three-hundred-ninety-
one-cubic-inch engine. It's aquatic. Can go over any terrain.
Those thirty-eight-inch tires out there rotate around each
other. The Landmaster hits a boulder it'll just roll over it. Cars
too."

"What movie did you say this was from?" Cody asks.

"*Damnation Alley.*"

Rufus says, " That was the one with the giant scorpions, right?
That is totally going to happen. Read about it in *Fate.*"

Danja laughs. "This is one of the finest vehicles ever created.
Sat for years in a back lot and fell apart. Until one of the engineers who built it bought it back and kept it on his used-car lot
as a sideshow attraction. I was on vacation with my parents and
saw it and just kept thinking about it. Dreaming about it. Guy
who owned it finally sold it to me five years ago."

Cody steps up into the cockpit and looks out the front wind-
shields. "I'm sold. If it can really go as fast as you say, I don't
think we'll have any problem with what we've got planned. Actually, what do we have planned?"

Laser says, "Oh, just something spectacular." He turns to
Danja. "You'll drive this thing for us?"

She says. "Yeah. It'll cost you, though. City of Las Vegas doesn't
exactly let me take this thing out on Sunday joyrides. It's wide.
Too wide for the small city streets. If I take this out, and go as
fast as we're talking, I'm going to be slamming into things. Lots
of property damage. Shitloads. And I need all my costs covered
for damage to the Landmaster. This baby is my life."

"How much?"

"At least enough to cover the court costs. The repairs. We're
talking hundreds of thousands, boys. I haven't gotten pussy in

two weeks because I've been prepping this for you," Danja says. "I'd hate to have wasted all that time."

Gear says, aside, "She's something of a grinder."

"Can't we just rent a Humvee?" Rufus asks.

"No," Laser says. "This is the perfect machine. This is the ending we're looking for."

"The ending?" Danja grinds her teeth.

Laser says, "Figure of speech."

They head back out to the BMW to get their stuff. Rufus pulls the seed gun out and says, "Wait until Vegas sees this shit. We'll have to reload on some desert seeds, though, don't think I brought enough—" He stops short when three kids carrying automatic weapons jump onto the hood of the car. One of them, thin and short with big ears and lazy eyes, says, "You motherfuckahs think you could drive aroun' with all dis shit on your ride and not have no one notice?"

Gear, chest puffed out, says, "Get off my car, assholes."

The kid with the lazy eyes says, "Ain't no way to talk to some niggas that got guns. Besides, your shit ain't driveable no mo'." He points to the front right tire and the bright orange boot on it.

"What do you want?" Laser asks.

The kid jumps off the hood. Standing, he's even shorter. "Oh, shit, my man, we don't want nothin' from you but your lives."

Laser raises his hands. "Everyone wants something. Who's paying you?"

"Don't matter that." The kid raises his gun, holds it sideways like he's a gangster in a movie. "Ain't no amount of money you could come up wit' could make this go away. Sultans gots pride."

"Tell 'em, Rail," the kid on the hood says. "Let's waste these crackers."

Rufus flips the seed gun up and aims it at them. Cody says, "Don't think that's gonna work—"

But Rufus fires before he can finish and two seed packets fly high and then plop down on the hood of the car, spilling seeds and soil. The kids bust out laughing.

One of them says, "You gonna get us dirty or somethin'?"

Another: "Wack vegetarian killers or some shit."

Furious, Cody says, "You just fucked up major, Rufus."

He braces for the gunshot but before it comes there's the sound of an airplane taking off just behind them and then a horn blasts and it sounds just the way Cody imagines the horn on a cruise ship would. The garage doors behind them explode open, sending shards of wood the size of coffins spinning off into the alleyway. Cody dives to the left, tackling Rufus. Laser grabs Leigh and pushes her to the right and prays it's far enough.

The Landmaster barrels out of the garage and smashes into the front of the Beamer and one of the kids sitting on the hood goes flying backward through the windshield into the backseat where he slumps forward, his teeth dropping out of his open mouth like golden pebbles.

Danja, in the cockpit of the Landmaster, with a leather helmet and goggles on, grinds the gears to get the vehicle in reverse but it doesn't budge.

Rail has spun free of the car and runs toward Laser and Leigh, firing his gun. His shots go wide and wild, pinging off the Landmaster and a light post. Somewhere half a block away a window shatters.

Rail is almost on top of them, his gun pointed level, when half his face vanishes as though a mirror has passed over it. His body goes flying sideways and smacks into the back end of the Landmaster.

Laser looks to Leigh, her lower lip cut and oozing. "You alright?"

Leigh nods. "I think so. What just happened?"

"Shit's hit the fan."

"Who shot him?"

"I don't know."

There is a second shot and Laser looks up to see the third kid, this one looking manic, standing above Gear. Gear has a hole the size of a nickel in his forehead. The kid shouts over, "One motherfucker down! Four to go. Yo, Rail! Where you at?"

The kid sees Rail's blasted corpse and looks stunned.

"You fucker's shoot him?" he asks Laser and Leigh.

Laser shakes his head.

"Who the fuck shot him?"

Laser stands up, fists clenched. He walks slowly toward the kid. "What's your name?"

The kid says, "That don't matter."

"How old are you?" Laser asks, stepping closer.

The kid shakes. "Ain't no matter."

Laser says, "You can't be more than thirteen."

"I'm fifteen, motherfucker."

"No. You're not."

"Am too!"

"Put that gun down and tell me your name."

The kid struggles to hold the gun up. He says, faintly, "Fly."

"Fly?"

"Yea."

"How old are you, Fly?"

"I'm twelve."

"Fly, you should put the gun down. You saw what happened to your friends. You don't want that, do you? Put the gun down and you can walk away no problems."

Fly drops his gun to his side. "I just want to leave."

"You can," Laser says. "You can just turn around and go."

For the first time, with his gun down, his face slackened, Fly looks like the kid he is. He cracks a smile and turns to go but falls to the pavement. Laser and Leigh hear the thunderclap after he's fallen, after the blood has already started to pool.

Laser looks up the alleyway and sees a figure standing there with a rifle. It is the man he met at the diner in Ohio, the man who killed Tyrell outside the Abako Apartments. This man raises the weapon and trains it toward them.

Laser shouts, "You didn't have to kill him!"

The man says, "It's what I do."

"He was just a kid."

"I'm not a good person. I've always known that."

"This isn't about you."

The man laughs. As he gets closer, Laser can feel Leigh trembling. He says, "Your father is like me, Leigh. He's evil. I'm here to kill you, just like those poor black bastards were. I'll let you know that I don't think I'm going to take pleasure in this. Not this time. For me, the thrill is gone."

Laser says, "You don't have to. This can end right here for you."

"That kid right there," the man says. "I think I saw his soul rise up to heaven."

Then he levels his rifle, eye to the scope.

Laser turns to Leigh. "Run!" Leigh jumps up and bolts, Laser running just behind her. Pushing her forward. There is a crack and something in Laser's left leg breaks. His shoe floods with warmth as though he's stepped into a hot tub. There is no pain, just the squishy sensation of running with wet socks.

They jump in front of the Landmaster. Danja slides open the side door and Cody and Rufus drag Laser and Leigh inside. They collapse. Cody asks, "Where is he?" Laser doesn't need to answer because a slug hits the rear of the Landmaster and the hull reverberates. Laser checks his foot and finds no wound but there is blood gushing from his calf. "I've been hit," he says.

Rufus asks, "Gear?"

Laser shakes his head.

Danja punches the Landmaster forward, rolling the massive vehicle up and over the Beamer. The car crunches under the weight of the vehicle and a cloud of dust and glass plumes out.

Another round smashes against the back of the Landmaster and Danja raises a finger. "That fucking asshole is killing the paint job!"

"What time is it?" Laser asks.

Cody says, "It's nearly four."

"We might as well do this now," Laser says.

Rufus says, "Seed gun's still in the car. Pretty unpsyched about leaving it."

The Landmaster plows out onto a side street lined with strip malls and run-down apartments. The vehicle is so wide it's crashing into parked cars. Cars rock, windows shattered. So many car alarms are going off it sounds like an army of metal crickets has invaded the city. Inside the Landmaster Cody is tending to Laser's leg wound. He's got his pants hiked down and Cody is probing the wound with a pair of tweezers he found in a first-aid kit Danja had stashed in the cab.

Laser grimaces as Cody prods.

"Bullet went clean through. Missed the bone but got the muscle here pretty bad. Walking is going to be a serious chore."

"Can you stitch it?" Laser asks.

Cody nods. "Sure, but you're going to need some pain meds."

"No. No meds."

Rufus says, "Harness that chi, Laser."

"Right."

Leigh holds Laser's had as Cody stitches up both sides of the wound. It is difficult as the Landmaster rocks and rumbles around corners. Danja is going fast but she hasn't opened it up. She curses every time she hits a car. "Fucking paint will be shot to hell," she says. Her goggles are fogged.

7.

Marcus awakens Kip Tiller around five.

He is in his penthouse atop the Tiller Casino, lying in a bed with two naked showgirls, their legs so intertwined it's nearly impossible to tell where they meet up. Marcus shakes Kip gently. Whispers, "Mr. Tiller. Mr. Tiller."

Kip jolts upright. Eyes blink furiously. "What the fuck, Marcus?"

"Outside."

"What are you saying?"

"There's an army outside the casino."

"What?"

"An army."

"What fucking army? The U.S. Army?"

"No. Some other army. Outside right now."

Kip gets up and walks to the windows in the living room overlooking the Strip. He pulls back the thick curtains to reveal a heaving mass of humanity surrounding the base of the casino and choking the end of the Strip. Kip was at Woodstock and at one point he had run up on stage and raised his arms high and taken in the enormity of the crowd that surged just a few feet below him. This looks the same. But from the penthouse the faces are all just pink blurs; it is a mosaic of people, like a painting in a museum diorama that suggests distance but gives no particulars. The people below, men and women, are all wearing the same color.

Kip turns to Marcus. "Who the fuck are these people?"

Marcus says, "The police are saying they're wearing uniforms. Police say they are an army."

"Whose?"

"Strategic Art Defense."

Kip turns to Marcus, furious. "This is America, Marcus. Did I just wake up in the Twilight Zone or something? People can't just go around and make their own armies, can they? I fucking pay a shitload of taxes for these degenerates to go around playing soldier and fucking with my business?"

"I'm told they aren't armed, Mr. Tiller."

"They singing campfire songs?"

"I'm not sure, Mr. Tiller."

"Get the police on the phone and that asshole at the FBI. Tell them I want these people cleared out of here. Let them know that as a business owner with a very large investment in this city, I consider this an affront. I consider this an act of terrorism on par with the kidnapping and rekidnapping of my daughter. I want fighter jets called in here. I want tanks. I want—" Kip goes slack-jawed. He walks over to the window, his face pressed up against the glass.

"What is it, Mr. Tiller?"

Kip points. "That . . ."

Marcus walks over to the window. Squints. He sees the crowd parting just up the street near the Tropicana. Moving slowly through the crowd is a tank or what looks like a tank. From their vantage point in the penthouse, it's almost like the long, high vehicle is a battering ram headed slowly but effortlessly toward the casino.

"What is that?" Marcus asks.

"It's fucking war is what it is."

A phone rings. Marcus rushes to pick it up. He answers and his face goes pale, the blood just rushing away. He holds the phone up and says, "It's for you, Mr. Tiller."

Kip grabs the phone and pushes Marcus out of the way. "Who is this?"

"Dad?"

"Who is this?"

"It's Leigh, Dad. Don't you recognize my voice?"

"Leigh?"

"Yeah."

"What is going on? Do you have anything to do with these people out here?"

There is a pause. "Why, Dad?"

"Why what?"

"Why do you want me dead?"

"I don't, baby. Don't believe anything they've told you. It's all lies. Lies."

"But the scarred man. The hit man. He told us everything. Those kids—"

"Fucking bastards! Don't listen to them, Leigh. I'm your father. I love you."

"No, Dad. I don't . . ."

Kip panics. "Leigh, listen to me. Where are you?"

"I'm outside, Dad. About to come in."

"Come in? Come in where? Not here, Leigh. It's too dangerous here. We've got armed guards on every floor. We've got a battalion of soldiers standing out front. It's not safe here, Leigh. Make them turn around."

Kip runs to the window and presses his face against the glass. Craning his neck he can see the security guards at the entrance standing linked like a fence against the uniformed tide. The tank has made its way to the base of the stairs leading into the building. Kip looks closely and can see a hatch on top of the tank open. There, he sees a face and a hand waving.

Leigh says, "You're going to want to brace yourself, Dad."

8.

The Serologist is sitting in an unfinished room on the twenty-fifth floor of the Tiller Casino, watching the Landmaster make its way up the steps of the building, when there's an earthquake.

The entire building begins to shake.

The Serologist breaks out in a toothy grin. "What have you done now?"

He crouches in a doorway, a knife at his own throat.

The walls fall in around him.

* * *

In the penthouse, Kip drops the phone and backs away from the window.

The shaking is abrupt.

Clouds of white dust come charging out of the air vents.

Marcus goes tumbling to the floor and the showgirls come running out of the bedroom naked, screaming. They run out into the hallway and disappear down the stairwell.

Kip sits down on a leather couch that twists and buckles under him. He rolls a joint on the galloping coffee table but his hands are shaking and the weed goes everywhere.

He gives up and leans back and closes his eyes.

"Bring it," he says.

Then the shaking stops. Kip opens his eyes, and the room, Marcus, his own hands are coated with a thin layer of white dust. It is as if it has suddenly, inexplicably snowed.

The guards outside lay down their weapons when the crowd comes pushing in.

Television helicopters circle the building like vultures, and on the ground, mixed in with the uniforms, are news crews and reporters snapping off pictures furiously and shouting into microphones and cassette recorders.

The hundreds swell inside, following the Landmaster as it rumbles into the casino's grand foyer. The vehicle stops in front of an empty fountain and the side door opens. Leigh, Laser, Cody and Rufus all step out into the winter wonderland of the place. Laser is handed a megaphone by a uniformed woman. He turns it up as loud as it will go. "We have one hour to clean it up. Let's go!"

The people in uniform pull trash bags from their pockets. Some of them with backpacks pull out cleaning supplies. Some brushes. Others have walkie-talkies and notepads. Even more have cameras and laptops. Cody takes a big white flag with the S.A.D.

logo and runs it up to the roof. He's as giddy as a schoolkid prepping for a food fight.

"You want a tour?" Laser asks Leigh.

"Is my dad still here?"

"He's in the penthouse."

"Is he staying?"

"He's stuck. We've got remote locks. Don't worry, take a breather and look around. Then, if you want, we can go see him."

Laser leads Leigh over to the atrium, leaning on her for support. Leigh remembers that in the models the atrium was an enormous empty place with a single spiral staircase. The drawings tacked to her dad's office walls showed potted plants, leather couches, a bar, and a grand piano. The walls were faux Venetian—made to look like they were cracked stones. None of that is here. Instead, the walls are covered in graffiti and wheat-paste posters. The place vibrates with color and life.

"We had people do all this over nights during the past two months. Each and every inch of the casino is an exhibit. The entire structure is a museum, a monument of sorts. We paid off construction teams. We brought in our own engineers. We've had a hand in every step of the construction for the past seven months. The artwork—every room is different—is by the hundreds of Irregulars you see here now. Street kids. Taggers. Even professional artists from as far away as China."

"How'd you hide it?"

"We hung drywall over it. Room by room. The way we worked, it had to be done very slowly and secretively. You'd never believe how difficult the timing on this was."

Laser leads Leigh to the second floor, where there is a balcony overlooking the atrium. The walls here are done in mirror fragments. The mirrors catch the light, drift and flicker with different colors. They stop by several rooms. One has walls made of grass. "It's all alive," Laser says. "We have a hidden water system worked in with the plumbing. This was a real bitch and there are twenty-two rooms like this." Another room the walls are clear Plexiglas. The adjacent rooms are visible. "This is for the more daring clientele," Laser says. "Or just exhibitionists."

In a bridal suite there is a bank of solar panels facing south. "We want the building to be green. A lot of the work still needs to be done but I think it'll be as close to sustainable as a building this size can be."

"Isn't this illegal?"

"Of course, but once people see it, they'll drop charges. Happens every time."

"Not my dad."

"Maybe not. But it won't matter."

"Why's that?"

"Check out the television."

They stop in the bar on the third floor. The whole of the room is covered in what looks like fur. "Fake," Laser says. There is a bank of television screens on one wall. All of the screens have the same image—a video of Kip Tiller on the telephone. "We bugged the penthouse," Laser says. "Recorded it all."

On the video screens Kip says, "As you already know, I've got some guns out for the same target as you. They've been promised big bucks to take Leigh and you down. I'll admit to being a bit panicky at this point . . . Momma Gash. Black Sultans . . . Maybe others. Your one chance of getting back in my good graces is to finish my daughter and kill the rest of them. We're talking taking on an army here, but frankly, I'd rather pay you than any of those fucked-up bastards."

Leigh starts to cry and Laser holds her tight to his chest. She pounds her fists on him and says through her tears, "I want to see him."

Laser says, "Okay."

They walk to a bank of elevators and get in the first to arrive. Inside there is a uniformed Irregular; she smiles and nods to

Laser. He says, "Hey there." The woman grins, says, "I can't believe this worked."

Laser hits the penthouse button and the elevator begins its
smooth climb upward. When they pass the fifteenth floor is when
Laser realizes he's seen the woman in the elevator with them
before. She's wearing a ball cap but her face is too familiar. The
tattoos on her neck. Laser turns around to get another look at
the woman and that's when she drops a butterfly knife from
her sleeve into her palm and flicks it open.

"Not going to be that easy," Momma Gash says.

She slashes with the knife and catches Laser on the side, the
knife running just under his shirt and nicking each rib as it
stutters up. Leigh pushes herself back against the elevator
doors and kicks out at Momma Gash but misses.

Momma Gash lunges again at Laser, this time burying the
knife in his right thigh. She pulls it out fast and goes to stab
again, Laser sinking to the floor of the elevator, his face con-
torted, when Leigh catches her around the waist and throws
her back against the wall of the elevator.

They fall to the floor, wrestling each other for the knife.

At floor thirty, the elevator doors open and Laser spills out
into the hallway. A young Hispanic Irregular waiting there
kneels down beside him. Laser actually recognizes him as a tag-
ger from the Bronx. "Push me back in!" Laser yells. The guy
does and then the elevator doors close again.

Leigh is pulling Momma Gash's pompadour off or at least
trying to.

The knife under them, Momma Gash arching her back so as
not to stick herself. She spits in Leigh's face and claws at her eyes.

Laser pulls himself up and stumbles over to the two entan-
gled women. He waits a few beats, a few rolls and shouts, before
kicking Momma Gash in the left ear with his right foot. There is
a crunching sound and Momma Gash screeches, letting go of
Leigh. Leigh pulls herself up and Momma Gash rolls suddenly

to the right, her body quivering as though she's having an epileptic fit. Leigh sees the knife. She grabs it and throws it to Laser. He catches it, picking it out of the air, turns it around, and buries it to the hilt in Momma Gash's neck.

When the elevator doors open on the top floor, Laser tumbles out covered in blood. Leigh falls out as well, panting and shaking. They sit there for a few moments, the elevator doors trying to close on their legs but bouncing back.

Close and bounce.

Close and bounce.

9.

Kip Tiller inspects the penthouse walls and frowns.

They're covered in posters for old porn films from the seventies. Literally layer upon layer of them. And each and every one, on every wall, has a photocopy of Kip's face where the faces of the performers should be. "Absurd," Kip says, surveying the walls. "Who the fuck does this?"

There is a noise at the front door. A key. A lock tumbling.

Kip turns to see Laser and Leigh stumble into the room.

Laser is holding the butterfly knife.

Kip says, "Bravo, fucker. Bravo."

"Can you give me an answer, Dad?" Leigh asks.

Laser sits down on one of the couches and Marcus takes the opportunity to bolt, disappearing out the front door with not so much as a glance back. Leigh says, "Dad, can you?"

Kip sighs and sits in a leather chair across from Laser. He pulls a cigarette from his pajamas, lights it, and then inhales deeply. He offers one to Laser. Laser accepts and reaches across the table for it and then Kip lights it for him. Kip says, "You are one tenacious motherfucker, I'll give you that."

"Dad?" Leigh demands.

"I don't know what to tell you, Leigh. I can't make excuses for my behavior. I can tell you that it's really nothing personal."

"How can you say that?"

"I'm a businessman, baby. I say things like that all the time."

"Was it money?"

"Sure. That and the need to look in control."

"That's pathetic. I just want you to know that I did it for you. The whole kidnapping thing was so that you'd love me again. So that you'd respect me. So that you'd bring me back and let me be your daughter."

Kip shakes his head. "Guess this just goes to show that I'm not worth it."

"Did you ever even love me?"

"Of course. Until I set you free and then—"

Kip stops there. He stares at the open door behind Leigh and Laser and then chuckles. "Well, isn't this a big, happy reunion."

The Serologist steps into the room. He holds a gun out in front of him as though he's being led by it. Like it's a divining rod. He takes a seat next to Laser, facing Kip. He says, "I like what you've done with the place. It's funny, but the room I was in, when the walls came down, underneath were these graffiti angels. Hundreds of them. And cherubim as well. I'm taking that as a sign. Sure as anything."

Kip scowls. "Why the change of heart now?"

"I suppose you can only do something like this for so long."

"Bored?"

The Serologist smiles. "No. Just humbled."

Kip says, "I'll double it."

The Serologist looks to Laser. "What do you think?"

"You already shot me once. I think you've done enough."

Kip says, "Shoot him again and I'll triple it. Aim for the head this time."

The Serologist turns to Leigh and says, "Sorry." Then he stands, walks over to Kip, puts the barrel of the gun against his temple, and shoots. Kip slumps forward and crashes into the coffee table. He is not dead but lies there, mouth gulping like a goldfish freed from its bowl. He says, sputtering with blood, "Who's . . . going . . . to . . . to . . . feed . . . the dogs?"

Leigh screams and falls to her knees.

Kip's eyes roll back and his frame softens.

The Serologist, wiping blood splatter from his hands, says, "You know, before Cain killed Abel he spoke to him. In the original Hebrew it's vague. It only says something to the effect of 'Cain said to his brother' and then he kills him.

"The text seems pretty clear, and there have been all sorts of commentaries on it, that Cain isn't an evil person necessarily. Maybe they got in a quarrel as brothers do? Maybe it was an accident? Maybe he was jealous? Whatever the case he killed him and the reasons were never recorded. It's as if the act only erases any justification for it. You ever think about that?"

Laser shakes his head. Leigh sobs, "No."

The Serologist says, "I don't think it's about the act of murder. What's important is that murder erases life and erases meaning. It's like a text that is wiped clean at the end of a sentence. You can't recall what it was about but you remember that you had read it at one point and now it's gone."

With that the Serologist gets up. He hands Laser his gun and says, "You might need this still."

"I'm not going to kill you," Laser says. "I'm done."

The Serologist says, "I know." And then he walks out the front door.

Outside, the sound of sirens fills the air. Laser stands up, weak from blood loss and gritting his teeth against pain. He puts a hand on Leigh's shoulder and squeezes it. Leigh looks up at him. "Did it have to end this way?"

CHAPTER EIGHT
Smash up

1.

They pile back into the Landmaster and Danja starts it up, reversing out fast.

"The route clear?" Laser asks Cody.

Cody says, "All clear. You're bloody as hell."

Leigh says, "We had some problems."

"Jesus," Rufus says, looking at Laser's bloody shirt. "Stitches again?"

"We had a run-in with that scooter bitch," Laser says. "Done now."

"And your dad?" Cody asks Leigh.

"Done now," Leigh replies. "Done."

Danja yells back to everyone, "You need to buckle up now!"

They do and Danja kicks the Landmaster into high gear, plowing out behind the casino toward the airport. At the helm of the Landmaster she's a mad scientist flipping switches and pulling levers and spinning the wheel wildly. Her bare arms glisten with sweat, red from the cockpit lights. The Landmaster growls louder the faster it goes. And it shakes. It rattles like it's coming apart. Laser thinks of a wooden roller coaster he rode with his grandfather in Maryland when he was twelve. Of how it shook and seemed like it was going to rattle to pieces at every turn. His grandfather saw the worry in his eyes. "Don't worry," he told Laser on one of the achingly long climbs, "these wooden coasters are designed to be forgiving. They bend with the bends. Turn with the turns." Laser hopes the Landmaster is as forgiving as Danja takes it up to seventy miles an hour.

The road ahead of them is clear. There are no cars on the street, just lining it. Blocking it off. And in the street are people. One every few yards along the edges.

Laser points them out to Leigh. "Irregulars clearing the way."

The sound of sirens comes wailing in. Danja has a police-radio scanner skittering and spitting up in the cockpit and she turns it up. They can all hear the dispatcher going nuts, sending patrol cars up and down the Strip. She says, "Behind us."

There is no rearview but cameras mounted on the rear bumper. Small television screens in the cockpit show a fish-eye view of the road behind them and the cascade of cop cars following fast and furious. In the distance they can see the Tiller Casino and the S.A.D. flag whipping.

Laser tells Cody, "Give the signal."

Cody produces a cell phone and yells into it. "Now!"

Every third Irregular on the road pulls a strip of spikes from a canvas bag and tosses it out into the street as the Landmaster whizzes past. In the rearview screens there is what looks like a sandstorm, cop cars spinning wildly out of control. They hear sirens burp and bleep and the cars collide.

A mile ahead there is a blockade. Cop cars lined three deep that have managed to circumvent the Irregulars. The police stand out in front with megaphones and guns raised high. This looks like a scene from a film. Cody says, "I used to love this part in the movies."

The Landmaster's guts squeal as Danja kicks it up another

gear and the speedometer hovers somewhere around eighty. She starts laying down the horn and the cops in front of the patrol cars begin to fire. The sound is like children popping plastic-wrapping bubbles and the bullets bounce off the exterior like pebbles. Danja complains again about the paint job, then yells for everyone to "Brace it!"

The cops scatter a few seconds before the Landmaster plows into and over the cars. It's like a monster-truck rally and Rufus starts cheering when the cockpit goes vertical, the sky and light rushing in, as the Landmaster careens over the second row of patrol cars and crunches the last row in a squall of broken glass and splinters of metal.

Hitting pavement again, the Landmaster is greeted with a rush of bullets striking the back of the vehicle and then they're off and running, nothing ahead by empty desert.

"We're clear!" Cody shouts. "Holy shit."

Danja says, "Not completely."

She points up into the sky where a handful of helicopters hover ominously.

"How are we going to lose them?" Rufus asks.

"Going to be hard," Danja says. "Nothing but scorch out here."

"We going to run out of gas?" Cody asks.

"Not likely," Danja says. "But these birds will be on us the whole way unless we find cover. I'm sure the cars are only a few miles back. This is a death race we're locked in now."

The police scanner burbles. "*Headed north on . . . In pursuit . . . Dispatch . . .*"

Laser borrows Cody's cell and makes a few calls. He says nothing, just nods. When he tosses the cell back to Cody he says, "There is a chopper waiting for us at Lake Mead. We should head for the abandoned railway tunnels there."

Danja says, "That's not the way we're headed."

"Can you turn us that way?"

Danja unfolds a tattered map on her lap. "Yeah. A few miles up. Bound to run into someone though. Fairly heavy traffic."

"I'll see who we can get out there."

The road ahead is straight and the Landmaster picks up even more speed as it races toward a series of low, red mountains in the scrubby distance. Laser unbuckles his belt and asks Cody to take a look at his ribcage. The gore has soaked through his shirt but the wound is not particularly deep. Cody sprays some antibiotic on and then wraps gauze over the seeping wounds.

"Anyone else need attention?" Cody asks.

Leigh rolls her head on her shoulders and closes her eyes. "I could really use a massage right now. I don't like the idea of just hurtling off into the desert to eventually be arrested."

"We won't," Laser says. "Stay positive."

The police scanner barks. "*Keep on, keep on . . . News feed . . . Copter . . .*"

Danja turns the Landmaster toward the east at a dusty, unmarked intersection. She has to slow the vehicle down significantly to do it and spins the wheel as though she's steering a sailboat over the rusted desert. That's when the shockwave hits; the Landmaster heaves and shakes.

"I think we were just hit by something!" Danja shouts.

The two rearview screens are out. Just shouting static.

Cody sticks his head into the cockpit and pushes his face to the angled glass to see to their right. "It's a bus," he says. "Some hippie bus."

Laser bolts forward. "What bus? Let me see."

He takes Cody's place and the bus pulls up.

It's a beat-up school bus painted black with two massive metal horns soldered to the front just above the grill. Inside Laser can see four people, all men. One driving, all of them waving.

"The Bisons," Laser says.

"What!?" Danja yells.

Laser says, "I know these guys. We're in trouble."

The bus pulls out onto the road in front of the Landmaster and a hatch on its roof opens. One of the men inside pops up smiling and waving. Danja instinctively waves back but immediately feels stupid. "What do they want?" she asks Laser.

"Us," he says. "They're kind of like mercenaries."

"Kind of?"

"Well, pretty much just like, only these guys are nuts."

"Should we slow down?"

"No. We need to ram them."

Danja stomps on the gas and the Landmaster jerks forward into the back of the bus. It lurches. The man in the hatch disappears, rocked back inside. The Landmaster falls back as the bus sidewinds. The bus slows and comes up alongside the Landmaster. There is a clang of metal and Danja shouts, "They're trying to board us!"

"How?"

"Take a fucking look."

On one closed-circuit television screen Laser can see a grappling hook lodged in the railing along the top of the Landmaster. A rope extends out to the bus and one of the bus's occupants is scrambling across.

"Jesus!" Laser darts to the back of the bus and readies himself to climb up on the roof.

He is stopped by Leigh. She's holding a rifle. "Let me."

"What? No. This isn't—"

"A game. Right, I know. Let me. We don't have time to argue."

"I'm going up with you."

They climb the ladder to the roof and then Laser carefully pops the lid and pokes his head out. He is there a quarter of a second, just long enough to see a man in leather pants standing with a sawed-off shotgun pull the gun's trigger. There is a shriek of metal as the shotgun pellets ricochet off the roof. Laser turns to Leigh. "Head for the back."

Cody and Rufus grab guns from the wall rack. Laser tells

them to hang tight, watch the front. Then he tells Danja to open the rear door.

She balks. "Yeah, right. You'll tumble out. Can't do James Bond shit in here."

"Just open the fucking rear door!" Laser shouts.

Danja flicks a switch and the hydraulics kick into gear. The rear door lowers slowly. Behind them is a swirl of dust against the blinding blue of the sky. Laser turns to Leigh, his eyes half-closed in the churn of sand infiltrating the back of the Land-master. "Use the rifle to prod the lid open when I give the signal. I'm going to climb up behind him."

Leigh positions herself on the ladder and Cody stands in the clouds of dust at the rear door as Laser climbs up and out. They are going faster than Laser has anticipated and the wind howls around his ears something fierce. He climbs up to the roof and peeks over. The man in leather pants stands with his back to Laser by the lid, shotgun lowered and ready. Laser climbs back and gives Cody a thumbs-up.

Cody turns to Leigh. "What's that mean?"

Leigh says, "I'm supposed to hit the lid."

"But what if the dude is standing right there?"

"I think that's the point."

Laser clambers back up the ladder and then out onto the roof. He crawls along slowly; leather man stands in place like a statue. Laser is about ten feet from him when someone on the bus, head sticking out of the hatch on top, yells, "Gristle! Yo, there's some motherfucker sneaking up on you!"

Leather pants looks up. "What?!"

The man at the hatch yells, "Look behind you, fuck wad!"

Leather spins around, raises the shotgun. Laser's eyes widen and he bites down hard on the inside of his cheek. Can feel his mouth flooding with the penny-metal taste of blood. He steels himself for the shot and his heartbeat slows to nothing. Then he sees Leigh pop up with the rifle raised, finger wrapped around the trigger.

The man sticking up out of the top of the bus shouts, "Shit, Gristle, shoot that motherfucker and turn around! The bitch is coming up out—"

A crack of gunfire shakes the air. Laser watches as the man yelling from the bus falls backward, a red ribbon of blood falling apart in the air around his head. Below, Laser hears Cody shout, "That's how it's done Jersey-style, asshole!"

The man in the leather pants seems confused. He stands facing Laser but the shotgun is lowered. As he begins to turn towards Leigh, Laser stands and pounces. He has seen this done in movies several thousand times. The bad guy is tackled atop moving trains, buses, even airplanes. It is nothing like it is portrayed in film. Laser misses by at least three feet but he gives leather pants enough of a scare that the man jumps out of the way, misses his landing, topples off the side of the Landmaster and is crushed beneath the wheels. Before climbing inside, Leigh throws the grappling hook off the roof. The bus veers away.

"Two down, two to go," Laser says, climbing back inside the Landmaster.

Leigh hugs him.

"Thanks, Cody." Laser gives Cody a strong shoulder squeeze.

Cody says, "What's freaky is I'm getting used to this."

Danja shouts from the front. "Bond later. We need to lose these assholes now. One of you get up there and start shooting or something."

Cody volunteers to head up to the roof with the submachine gun.

"Wait," Danja says. "They're coming back fast."

The bus swerves back toward the Landmaster and Danja speeds up again, ready to collide. Just before impact another man pops up out of the bus's hatch like one of those carnival groundhogs. This guy's got something metal with him. Something cylindrical and gleaming. A rocket launcher.

"Fuck me!" Danja shouts and cranks the wheel to the left. The Landmaster almost comes to a complete stop and everyone in the cab with the exception of Danja goes flying against the hull, the sound of the impact reverberating inside their skulls.

Before Laser slams into the windshield he sees the missile launch, its white nose cone speeding forward, pushed ahead of a sterling cloud.

Then everything goes to hell.

The rocket hits the left front wheels of the Landmaster and the entire stack of them explodes, sending bits of rubber and metal as high as the rotor blades of the circling helicopters. The vehicle stutters into a gully and buries its nose in the orange dirt. A pitter-patter of kitten feet falls over the Landmaster as a ton of earth rains down on the hood, covering the vehicle in a thin, fine dusting of topsoil.

Danja is the first one up and about the cockpit.

She shakes Laser to make sure he's alive and he mumbles something about his head. He has a large gash just above his right eye that he can add to his growing collection of wounds. Laser tries to stretch away the pain and says, "Everyone okay?"

Danja looks back. She sees Rufus and Cody brushing themselves off, Leigh rubbing her wrist. "You all okay?" she asks.

"I think my wrist is broken," Leigh says. "It's black."

Rufus says, "My head is spinning. Cotton in my ears."

Danja turns to Laser. "They'll be alright."

Laser stands. "We need to get out of here."

Cody pulls himself over to the gun rack and grabs a shotgun.

"There's ammo in the tool box," Danja tells him.

Cody takes the shotgun and loads it. Then he loads two handguns and gives one to Rufus and one to Leigh. Danja asks for the three knives and Laser takes the samurai sword. Leigh jokes. "Ninja time, huh?"

There is a moment of silence before they open the top hatch on the Landmaster. Each of them listening intently for the sounds of someone on the vehicle, of someone trying to clamber in. "Chances are," Laser says, breaking the reverie, "they're just waiting for us to pop out of the top and then they'll cut us down. I'll go first, up top. You all see if you can get out through the side door."

"That's suicide," Cody says. "Why don't we all just bust out blasting? I can pop the top with the shotgun and just spray the area."

"Let me handle it," Laser says. "This is my battle."

"What's he mean?" Danja asks.

Cody shrugs.

Laser kisses Leigh full on the lips. She says, "You're being stupid."

"Maybe." Laser cracks his knuckles. Tightens his grip on the sword.

"Did you really kill that horse with your mind?"

"No."

Laser takes three huffs of albuterol and then opens the lid and climbs out.

2.

Stevie and Don are standing on the road, looking down at the Landmaster smoking in the gully below.

"I think this fucking thing was in a movie I saw once," Stevie says.

"Looks familiar."

"To you too?"

"Yeah."

"I think it was some sci-fi flick that Dad used to watch. Think he had it on laser disc or something. You remember that?"

"Yeah."

The Bisons are holding submachine guns. Their palms are sweaty and they keep looking up into the sun to see the helicopters rotating around them.

"Like flies," Stevie says. "Cops will be here in less than five."

"Should we go in there and just cap them?"

"No. Wait. They'll come out. He will for sure."

There is a grinding sound and the top of the Landmaster swings open the way the brothers imagine a submarine door would. A man steps out with a samurai sword, the blade sparkling in the pale sunlight.

"Hey there, Laser!" Stevie shouts. "Long time no see."

Laser nods to the brothers. "Bisons."

"When we got the fax from Tiller our mouths just dropped," Don says. "I mean, what are the chances that you'd be mixed up in this shit too? Nah, what are the chances that you'd be in charge of this shit?"

"Pretty good, we figure," Stevie adds.

"This is my gig," Laser says. "It's what I do. When did you boys start running for Tiller? I always assumed you'd wind up somewhere in Cuba or Gaza."

"We got back on the meds. Had some rough spots," Don says. "Meds?"

"Our own devising," Stevie answers. "We don't recognize the other people you're with, Laser. Other than the Tiller bitch. What's this crew? What's this S.A.F. shit?"

"S.A.D. This is my team. I've been very successful."

"And those animal-costume freaks?"

"Not me."

Don asks, "How's the brain fungus?"

"Fine," Laser says. "Under control."

Stevie shakes his head. "Dr. Rollin loved you the most. We were just scraps."

"What's the plan?" Laser asks. "Cops'll be here in only seconds."

Don says, "Plan is we drop you."

"Tiller's dead, though. Money's gone."

"Who says?" Stevie's voice grinds. Gets louder.

"I say. Saw him killed. You can ask Leigh. The scarred man shot him dead."

"Bullshit," Stevie says. "His man Marcus called us just an hour ago."

"Marcus is a body without a head now."

They can hear the sirens. On the horizon a column of crimson dust.

"What's the plan?" Laser asks again. "You're not getting her."

Firecrackers sound and Cody and Rufus come gunning out from behind the crippled Landmaster. Stevie and Don dive to the road and bullets ricochet around them, sending sparks into the mirages that hover above the asphalt. Laser jumps down from the Landmaster and runs up the gully wall shouting at the top of his lungs. He's not saying words. It's more a mantra. A primal scream.

Stevie stands again to meet him, gun raised, but before he can fire, the samurai sword in Laser's hand moves like light and Stevie's head spins like a top, a spiral of blood circling off of the blade. Don's eyes go wide. He is able to squeeze the trigger and sends a spray of metal between Laser's legs. Nothing hits.

Laser takes a deep breath and then howls again.

The sword sings and falls and cleaves Don's forehead in half. Laser leaves it there and turns back to face Leigh, who is walking around the side of the Landmaster with a hand to her mouth as though she's just seen the end of the world.

"I'm sorry," Laser says.

CHAPTER NINE

Two days later

1.

This is the first time Leigh's been able to see Laser.

The past forty-eight hours they've been cooped up individually in cells or in small hotel rooms or on airplanes. It's hard to tell. Feels as though they've traveled cross-country. They've been shuffled about with black canvas bags on their heads and prodded into rooms where the lights are too bright and Muzak is piped in. They don't know where Cody or Rufus or anyone is. Whether they're a mile above the ground or under it. Now, they're finally able to see each other. Now, there is no armed guard in the room. There is a one-way mirror, a bland table, and two crooked chairs. Now, they are alone.

Leigh hugs Laser as soon as she sees him. She sits down on his lap and wraps her arms around his head and kisses him hard and takes in the smell of him. Makes a hurt face when she notices his black eye.

"You holding up?" she whispers.

Laser says, "I'm okay. You?"

"They're letting me out this afternoon."

"Not a chance here."

"What are they telling you?"

"The list is very long. A ton of acronyms. My lawyer seems to think it could either mean a life sentence or a slap on the wrist. Guess there's no middle ground unless I go with the insanity defense."

"I wanted to ask you about that."

Laser says, "Yeah. I know."

"Who are you?"

Laser pulls Leigh back. Looks her dead in the eye. "I am the person you know. The one who set all this up, the one who rescued you. I just never told you about some of my history. My illness . . ."

"Those people who kidnapped me. You knew them?"

"Yes."

"But we killed them. Killed the two out in Vegas as well. These people, were you in an asylum with them?"

"I was."

"And the doctor?"

"His name was Dr. Rollin. He had this really crazy idea about where schizophrenia really came from. The root cause of it. The way it worked at the Institute, he kind of ran wild. Administration just slapped his hand but let him do what he needed and what he needed was to train us to bring down capitalism."

"What?"

"That's the cause of schizophrenia. He trained us as cultural warriors. Me, my background with martial arts, I was his golden child. Dr. Rollin trained us for war."

"Terrorists?"

"Cultural warriors."

Leigh hugs Laser again. Gets close. Her face on his. "Laser, why were you there?"

Laser shakes his head. He nuzzles her.

"Why, Laser?"

"I was twenty. Just back from Japan. Attacked my landlord because he was stealing from me. He was following me. He had a machine, a loom, he used to control me from anywhere in the world. Doctors said it was paranoid schizophrenia. . . ." A tear rolls down Laser's cheek but his face shows no emotion. Leigh wipes the tear away and kisses the eye it fell from.

Laser collects himself. "After the trial I was institutionalized. There for twenty-seven months, lost in a fog, before Dr. Rollin came in and everything changed. He took me off my meds. Helped me to utilize my training . . . to focus my strength on my illness. Dr. Rollin taught me to free myself and recognize the reality of . . . He started the group his third year at the Institute. At first it was just a support group, rap sessions. But he let us know his personal take a few months in and then, well, we really got rolling. He faked a bunch of papers, paid off some people and got me out two years ago. More than me, there were three of us. . . ."

"Cody and Rufus?"

"No. I met Cody after all this. I was teaching then, stable."

"But Rufus seems so . . ."

"No."

"And the horse?"

"Veterinarian said it was freak luck. Horse had an aneurysm. I found a different vet who would give it a clean bill of health. Just a chance coincidence. Synchronicity. We were in that field three days straight staring down that horse. Probably would give any animal an aneurysm."

"Anyone else know this?"

"No."

"All the actions. All your ideas . . ."

"I'm insane. But they worked, they still work."

"They do, Laser."

"I did this all for you, Leigh. This whole thing, you're the greatest art of it all. I swept you from your life on stage and I opened you up to my world. At first, I had this vision that I would make you a revolutionary but I didn't need to. You were already there."

Leigh closes her eyes. Kisses Laser along the eyebrows before moving down to his lips and then following his jaw line and neck. His rough hands along her spine. He grabs her so tightly his hands shake.

"Everything will be fine," she whispers. "I know it."

Before they can kiss again a bright light comes on in the room and a young man with a shaved head and thick glasses walks in and says, to Laser, "You're being transferred."

Laser asks where.

The man says, "I can't tell you that."

Laser squeezes Leigh's hand. Says, "I have loved you for weeks now."

"Weeks?"

"Since I first saw you at the window. I didn't want to love you then. But I couldn't help myself. I . . . just couldn't."

Leigh smiles and then men rush in and separate them. Blindfolds are put on. Laser's irons latch down and he is shuffled out of the room and into darkness.

Months pass.

He remembers only the movement. Sounds of machinery. He suspects an airplane based on the noises and movement but he could be wrong. Time passes in a fuzzy stupor. He did not feel the shot go in but he's certain he has drugs on board. Senses are stilted. There is a bag over his head most of the time. When the bag is not over his head he is blindfolded. No one speaks to him. No one speaks around him. He only hears distant chat like a television a few rooms over. He contemplates the idea that maybe he hasn't moved at all.

He is sitting in a stiff chair when the bag and blindfold are removed.

It takes several seconds for his eyes to adjust to the light. They water excessively and he wants desperately to wipe them. He blinks instead. Eventually, with enough eye rolling, he can see clearly. Laser is sitting in a prison cafeteria. The place is empty save for one man in a burgundy suit and sunglasses. The man has red hair and a blonder goatee. "Howdy," he says cheerfully. "Welcome to hell."

Laser has to work up some saliva, clear his throat before he can speak. "Hell?"

"Yeah. Helena, Washington. My name is Ronald and you are in one of the country's newest and, might I add, finest correctional facilities. Our facility is a private one. We run it at a profit. And we have a contractual agreement with the federal government that we will be quote unquote holding your ass for the foreseeable future. As an enemy of the state, you, my dear conscript, don't exist outside of this place any longer. You have effectively slipped down the rabbit hole. Wanna go for a tour?"

Laser nods. "My legs."

"We'll leave the irons on for now, Mr. Mechanic."

Laser stands and his entire body aches. He's sure it's the drugs. "What did you guys give me?"

"Not us. Feds probably loaded you up with all sorts of great shit."

Laser groans. "I'd like to get to my cot."

"No worries, bud. Follow me."

Ronald leads the way and Laser does the Frankenstein shuffle after him. The prison is massive and most of it is painted light pink. "Keeps them calm," Ronald says. "Studies have shown that mild colors, like our branded pink here, soothe. Like watching the fish tank at the dentist's."

The walk is long and Laser's head is swimming. He does not hear the details, just flitting bits of information about the "processing of prisoners" and something about "the hole." He finds it odd that he sees no inmates and comments on it. Ronald smiles. "This facility, you won't see them. Everyone has their own little room with no view. Solitary, friend."

Farther they go the more Laser wonders about Leigh. About where she is and how she's holding up. He assumes considering her role in things and her background that she got a slap on the wrist and was sent home. Cody? Rufus? He can only guess. Perhaps he'll see their faces pressed up against the reinforced plastic windows one day. Though it has never been in his nature to regret, Laser feels bad for the way things have turned out. As they walk along polished, featureless pink halls, Ronald gesticulating wildly, Laser wishes he'd told Cody and Rufus to bail after the rescue. He wishes he'd never met Tyrell. Each passing window contains a windswept tableau. The perspective may change but the landscape doesn't. In each Laser only sees the face of an Irregular he's doomed to solitary confinement or worse. The skyline is not black with smoke, tanks and helicopters aren't patrolling the grounds, there are no civilian armies at the perimeters shouting for change, demanding to bring the walls down. He knows, just by looking at the sky, by looking at Ronald's glowing face, that the revolution has been extinguished.

Laser stops and watches a crow settle on the top branches of a spruce tree standing in the open and says, "We were so close."

Ronald walks over, puts a hand on Laser's shoulder. "You stirred up quite a mess. They'll be cleaning up after you and your crew for months to come. Years maybe. You proud of that?"

"I think I am."

Ronald leans in. "I would be. Come on."

They take an elevator to a sub-basement and while it's underground it looks the same as the floors above it. Same unremarkable pink and shiny with long crisscrossing hallways to everywhere and nowhere. Ronald leads Laser to a door with no window, just a thick handle like you'd see on a door inside a submarine and a key-punch pad. Ronald enters a code on the pad and something heavy clanks inside the door. He nods to Laser. "Go on in."

The door swings open easily despite its massiveness. Laser steps inside and the door clangs shut behind him. He is standing in a room ten times the size of the one he'd imagined he'd be stuffed in. If anything it most resembles an office. There are leather couches and chairs, shelves lining the walls, desks, computers, and even artwork on the walls. On a couch in the middle of the room sits Leigh. Standing behind her: Cody and Rufus.

They wave.

Laser falls to his knees. The sigh that escapes his lips is as long as the corridors it echoes down. He laughs, tears collecting in the corners of his eyes, and asks, "What the fuck?"

Leigh walks to Laser, kneels down beside him and kisses him on the forehead. "You're safe. We're together. Tiller Inc. owns this prison, and I'm taking control of my father's affairs and, well, I've decided to make it your new headquarters."

"I thought I'd never see you ag—"

Leigh kisses Laser again. Hard. They embrace and Laser asks, "How?"

"Best lawyers money can buy. I am a Tiller. It was easy to get me off the hook. You know, Stockholm Syndrome and all. You can find a psychiatrist who'll tell you anything. You, Cody, and Ru will have to do some time but I figure it'll be easier doing it here."

"Where is here?"

"Have a look."

Leigh helps Laser up. She walks him to a window behind the couch. Sliding back the blinds, she reveals a courtyard where hundreds of people stand at attention. They are all wearing orange band uniforms. "These are your Irregulars," Leigh says. "This facility is a kind of two-fer. On top we have the 'prisoners' and below, here, we have your training camps. You want a revolution, let the Tiller Family Foundation pay for it."

"Are you fucking kidding me?" The grin on Laser's face nearly cracks.

"No."

"But . . . everything I told you? I mean, everything about me."

"That you're bug-fucking nuts?"

Laser looks away. "Yeah."

"Maybe lasting change only comes from someone who sees things from an angle that no one has ever even imagined. They say that great thinkers think outside the box, but baby, you don't even think near the box. You're in a tetrahedron or something. With my billions and your alien intellect we can rebuild the world."

"They will try and shut this down. We can't keep it a secret."

Leigh shrugs. "Yeah, so?"

Cody and Rufus walk over to the window. Cody says, "I haven't been able to sleep for like two days imagining all the crazy shit we can do."

Laser takes a deep breath and holds it for a count of ten before he turns to Leigh and says, "We ready for this?"

"As I'll ever be."

Laser smiles. He kisses Leigh and then whispers, "Banzai."